"Where is it?" she shouted. "I need it so no man can get within three feet of me. No man. Including you!"

He took a step closer.

"Don't!" she shouted, backing up. "Don't come any nearer."

Being filled with fear was more dangerous than being filled with anger. That went for people as well as animals. Black Horse held his arms out to his sides as he would while approaching a cornered horse. "No one will hurt you, Poeso," he said quietly.

"I know they won't," she shouted. "I won't let them! I won't let anyone hurt me ever again!"

The way she shook entered his heart, made it pound with an unknown anger. She had been mistreated, badly, at some time, someplace. "I won't let them, either," he whispered.

"I won't let you hurt me."

"I will not hurt you," he said. "I will protect you. I will stop all others."

Author Note

Black Horse and Lorna's story came to me as an image of a young woman stripped down to her underclothes and standing in the middle of a river surrounded by Cheyenne warriors. At the time, I was in the midst of writing *Saving Marina* and didn't have the time to fully embrace a new story.

Most writers—I'm assuming—are also avid readers, so I found a few novels about the Cheyenne.

Years ago, I formed the habit of reading every night. Sometimes it's just a chapter or two; other times, I'll stay up half the night to finish a book that I just can't put down. Therefore, even after spending hours writing about the Salem witch trials, when I went to bed, I'd read about the peaceful Northern Cheyenne.

I must say, those two cultures merging as I fell to sleep produced some peculiar dreams.

Such is the inner world of a writer. Our imaginations just don't know how to rest.

I sincerely hope you enjoy spending some time in Wyoming as Lorna discovers Black Horse is indeed *Her Cheyenne Warrior*.

LAURI ROBINSON

HER CHEYENNE WARRIOR

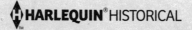
HARLEQUIN® HISTORICAL

Recycling programs
for this product may
not exist in your area.

ISBN-13: 978-0-373-29883-9

Her Cheyenne Warrior

Copyright © 2016 by Lauri Robinson

Printed in U.S.A.

A lover of fairy tales and cowboy boots, **Lauri Robinson** can't imagine a better profession than penning happily-ever-after stories about men (and women) who pull on a pair of boots before riding off into the sunset—or kick them off for other reasons. Lauri and her husband raised three sons in their rural Minnesota home and are now getting their just rewards by spoiling their grandchildren.

Visit laurirobinson.blogspot.com, Facebook.com/lauri.robinson1 and Twitter.com/laurir.

Visit the Author Profile page at Harlequin.com for more titles.

To my brother Jeff.
Finally.
Love you.

Prologue

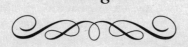

January 1864, Land of the Northern Cheyenne

The gathering brought leaders from bands near and far, despite the snow-covered grounds and days of short light. For some the journey had been long and difficult, but the attacks against many tribes on land to the south and east had required the tribal council to join together. The harmony and peace that the Tsitsistas—The People—sought and held in high regard was once again being challenged. Not just by the white men, but by younger members of the bands.

Black Horse listened with intent as both the elder and the younger chiefs spoke of conflicts with the white men, of sweeping illnesses and attacks that affected not only the Cheyenne, but threatened bands of all the Nations. Chosen by members of this council eight years ago to be the leader of The Horse Band, Black Horse was known for his slow-to-rise temper. He did not rile easy, but when he did, he was a fierce warrior whom few dared oppose, which meant that his opinions were respected and sought after. But on this day he could not deny the shift in attitudes of many of the leaders. Several Great Chiefs, those of the older generation, were absent; they had departed this earth, some killed in attacks, others dead from the white man's illnesses. The younger generation that had replaced them were not following the traditional path of advocating for peace.

Several of the these leaders wore war shirts made of deerskin and decorated with hammered silver coins taken from white men, and they demanded revenge with a ferocity more in line with the Southern Cheyenne than the northern bands. Black Horse was of the younger generation but he was not a new leader, and his values had been learned from those who had come before him. His heart and soul and his vision had been challenged by the white man, and at times still weighed heavy inside him, despite his commitment to peace.

While the smoking pipe was passed around the circle, he listened through the long hours of arguments and suggestions. Although he could understand the anger and frustration of those demanding more direct action, his overall view remained unaltered. Believing that the best plan for prosperity was to remain steadfast to the way of life The People had always known, Black Horse chose his words wisely.

"Tsitsistas," he started slowly, while nodding to include each leader sitting around the large circle, "are of small number because we know that Mother Earth can only host so many of her children. Just as the grass can only feed a specific number of buffalo, elk and deer. If there are too many of any one kind, some will starve, die, until Mother Earth can rebalance the numbers again. We do not know this number, only Mother Earth has this knowledge, but Tsitsistas should remain small in number so all can eat rather than see some starve."

"Too many Tsitsistas have died," Otter Hair argued.

"The white man's sickness and the battles they rage have made our number even smaller. Soon we will disappear. This is the white man's wish, and we must stop them before none are left."

There were times when looking another directly in the eye was considered bad manners, but not when disciplining. Black Horse leveled a glare upon Otter Hair—named for the strips of otter fur braided into his hair—until the other leader dipped his chin, acknowledging that Black Horse had not given permission for another to speak. He would not rise to anger during a tribal council, but neither would he tolerate misbehavior. To interrupt another was always bad manners and never allowed.

He held silent long enough for all to understand his displeasure with Otter Hair before saying, "The death of every Cheyenne, of every brother, every sister, is felt across our land, but we cannot let the pain cloud our vision. It is our duty, that of each chief in this council, to see Tsitsistas survive. To assure every member of our band is fed and taken care of, and to assure the next generation has much land with plentiful food. This cannot happen when all we discuss is battles with the white man. We must talk of the hunting season and health of our people. The white man is not our concern."

He paused in order to draw on the pipe that had once again reached him and let others consider the truth behind his words. He also used the time to attempt to settle the stirring inside him. It was difficult to strive for peace while a sense of injustice infiltrated Cheyenne land. Inside, where he tried not to look, he saw changes and knew that more were coming. He also knew that Maheo—The Great Creator—would show him what must be done when the time was right.

Passing the pipe to Silver Bear, Black Horse added,

"The white men continue to fight each other where the sun rises. They do not care about future generations and will kill many of their own kind without help from Tsitsistas. When their war is over, the Apache, the Comanche and our southern brothers who decorate their clothes and horses with the scalps of white men will attack the survivors. We will council again then, if our help is needed."

Chapter One

July 1864, Nebraska Territory

If a year ago someone had told her she'd be a part of a misfit band of women, wearing the same ugly black dress every day, and have calluses—yes, calluses—on her hands, she'd have laughed in their face. Then again, a year ago she'd had no reason to believe her birthday would be any different than the nineteen previous ones had been, complete with a party where friends plied her with frivolous gifts of stationery, silly doodads and fans made of colorful ostrich feathers.

Lorna Bradford lifted her stubby pencil off the page of her tattered diary where she'd written *Tomorrow is my birthday,* and questioned scribbling out the words. It wasn't as if there would be a celebration, and she certainly didn't need a reminder of what had happened last year. That night was the catalyst that had brought her here, to a land and a way of life that was entirely foreign to her. But somehow, though she had once been a stranger to it, she had begun to grow used to this life, this land, and to feel at home, as amazing as that seemed.

Wearing the same dress day after day didn't faze her

as much as it once would have; and the calluses on her hands meant she no longer needed to doctor the blisters she'd suffered from during the first few weeks holding the reins of the mules.

Nibbling on the flat end of the pencil, Lorna scanned the campsite she and the others had created for the night. Stars were already starting to appear. Soon it would be too dark to write in her diary. Maybe that was just as well. She had nothing to add. It had been an uneventful day. God willing, tomorrow would be no different.

Lorna pulled the pencil away from her lips and twirled it between her thumb and fingers. She made a note of some sort every night, and felt compelled to do so again. Perhaps because it was habit or maybe because it marked that she'd lived through another day. Despite the past. Despite the odds. Despite the obstacles.

In fact, her notations were proof they were all still alive, and that in itself said something. The four of them might be misfits in some senses of the word, but they were resilient and determined.

Meg O'Brien was most definitely determined. She was over near the fire, brushing her long black hair. Something she did every night. The care she gave her hair seemed odd considering it was covered all day and night by the heavy nun's habit. Then again, the nun's outfits had been Meg's idea, and the disguises had worked for the most part. Soon Meg would plait her hair into a single braid and cover it with the black cloth, a sign her musing was over for the evening. Though boisterous and opinionated, Meg sat by herself for a spell each night. Lorna wondered what Meg thought about when she sat there, brushing her hair and staring into the fire, but never asked. Just as Meg never asked what Lorna wrote about in her diary each night.

Lorna figured Meg had a lot of secrets she didn't want

anyone to know about, and could accept that. After all, they all had secrets. Her own were the reason she was in the middle of Nebraska with this misfit band.

She and Meg had met in Missouri, when Meg had answered Lorna's advertisement seeking passage on a wagon train. The railroad didn't go all the way to California. A stagecoach had been her original plan, but the exorbitant cost of traveling on a stage all the way to California was well beyond her financial resources, thus joining a wagon train had become her only choice. When she'd answered the knock on her hotel room door, Meg had barreled into the room asking, "You trying to get yourself killed?"

Lorna had pulled her advertisement right after Meg had explained that wagon trains heading west had slowed considerably since the country was at war and that Lorna would not want to be associated with the ones who would respond to her advertisement. Meg had been right, and Lorna would be forever grateful to her. They'd formed a fast friendship that very first meeting, even though they had absolutely nothing in common.

The clink and clatter coming from inside the wagon, against which Lorna was leaning, said Betty Wren was still fluttering about, rearranging the pots and pans they'd used for the evening meal. Betty liked things neat and orderly and knew at any given moment precisely where every last item of their meager possessions and supplies was located. Too bad she hadn't known where that nest of ground bees had been. Perhaps then her husband, Christopher, wouldn't have stepped on it.

The wagon train had only been a week out of Missouri, and Christopher had been their first fatality. He'd died within an hour of stepping on that bee's nest. Others had been stung as well, but none like him. Lorna had never seen a body swell like Christopher's had. A truly unidentifiable corpse had been buried in that grave. She'd never seen a woman more brokenhearted than Betty, either, and was glad that Betty only cried occasionally these days.

Betty's heart was healing.

They eventually did. Hearts, that was. They healed. Whether a person wanted them to or not. Even hate faded. That was something she hadn't known a year ago. A tightening in Lorna's chest had her glancing back down at the notation in her diary. The desire for retribution, she had discovered, grew stronger with each day that passed.

"Can't think of anything to write about?"

That was the final member of their group speaking, Tillie Smith. She, too, had lost her husband shortly after the trip started, while crossing a river. The water wasn't deep, but Adam Smith had been trapped beneath the back wheel of his wagon, and it was too late by the time the others had got the wagon off him. Trapped on his back, he'd drowned in less than two feet of water. It had been a terrifying and tragic event.

"I guess not," Lorna answered, shifting to look at Tillie, who was under the wagon and wrapped in a blanket. More to keep the bugs from biting than for warmth. The heat of the days barely eased when the sun went down, but the bugs came out, and they were always hungry. How they managed to bite through the heavy black material of the nun outfits was astonishing.

"You could write that I say I'm sorry," Tillie said.

"I will not," Lorna insisted. "You have nothing to be sorry about."

Tillie wiggled her small frame from under the wagon, pulling the blanket behind her. Once sitting next to Lorna with her back against the same wheel, she wrapped the blanket around her shoulders. "Yes, I do. If not for me, the rest of you would still be with the wagon train. You should have left me behind."

Lorna set her pencil in her diary, and closed the book. After the death of her husband, pregnant Tillie had started to hemorrhage. The doctor traveling on the train—a disgusting little man who never washed his hands—said nothing could be done for her. In great disagreement, Lorna and Meg, as well as Betty, who'd latched on to her and Meg for protection as well as friendship by that time, had chosen to take matters into their own hands. The small town they'd found and the doctor there had tried, but Tillie had lost her baby a week later. It had taken another three weeks— since Tillie had almost died, too—before the doctor had declared she could travel again. The wagon train had long since left without them, so only the four women and their two wagons remained. That was also why she and Meg only had one dress each. They'd started the trip with two each, but had given the extra dresses and habits to Betty and Tillie. Four nuns traveling alone were safer than four single women. That was what Meg had said and they all believed she was right.

"Leaving you behind was never an option," Lorna said. "And we are all better off being separated from the train. They were nothing more than army deserters and leeches. There wasn't a man on that train I trusted, and very few women."

"You got that right," Meg said, joining her and Tillie on the ground.

"Furthermore," Betty said, sticking her head out the back of the wagon, "taking you to see Dr. Wayne was our chance to escape."

Lorna turned to Meg, and they read each other's minds. Neither of them would have guessed that little Betty, heartbroken and quieter than a rabbit, had known of the dangers staying with the wagon train would have brought. Lorna and Meg had, and had been seeking an excuse to leave the group before Tillie had lost her husband and become ill.

Betty climbed out of the wagon and sat down with the rest of them. "I wasn't able to sleep at night with the way Jacob Lerber leered at me during the day. Me! With Christopher barely cold in his grave."

The contempt in Betty's voice caused Lorna and Meg to share another knowing glance. Jacob Lerber had done more than leer. Both of them had stopped him from following Betty too closely on more than one occasion when she'd gone for water or firewood. Gratitude for the nun's outfits had begun long before then. Everyone had been a bit wary of her and Meg, and kept their distance, afraid of being sent to hell and damnation on the spot. When Tillie had become ill, no one had protested against two nuns taking her to find a doctor. In fact, most of the others on the train had appeared happy at the prospect.

"But," Tillie said softly, "because of me, we might not get to California before winter. It's midsummer and we aren't even to Wyoming yet." Glancing toward Meg, Tillie added, "Are we?"

Meg shook her head. "But I've been thinking about that. There are plenty of towns along the way. I say wherever we are come October, we find a town and spend the winter. It would be good if we made it as far as Fort Hall, but there are other places. Having pooled our supplies, we have more than enough to see us through and come spring, we can head out again."

Betty and Tillie readily agreed. Meg had become their wagon master, and they all trusted her judgment. None of them had anyone waiting at the other end, and whether they arrived this year or next made no difference.

To *them*. To Lorna it did. She needed to arrive in San Francisco as soon as possible. That was why she was on this trip, but she hadn't told anyone else that. Not her reasons for going to California nor what she would do once she arrived and found Elliot Chadwick. That was the first thing she'd do. Right after getting rid of the nun's habit. However, she also wanted to arrive in California alive. Others on their original train had told terrifying stories about being caught up in the mountains come winter, and claimed they couldn't wait for Tillie to get the doctoring she'd needed.

Meg's plan of wintering in a small town, although it made sense, wasn't what Lorna wanted to hear. She didn't want to pass the winter in any of the towns between here and California. The few they'd come across since leaving Missouri were not what she'd call towns. Then again, having lived in London most of her life, few cities in America were what she'd been used to, not even New York, despite having been born there.

"Lorna, you haven't said anything," Meg pointed out. "Do you agree?"

Meg might have become their wagon master, but for some unknown reason, they all acted as if Lorna was the leader of their small troupe. "Yes," Lorna answered, figuring she'd hold her real opinion until there was something she could do about it. "Wherever we are come October, that's where we stay." She turned to Tillie. "And no more talk of being sorry. We are all here by choice." Holding one hand out, palm down, she asked, "Right?"

One by one they slapped their hands atop hers. "Right!" Together they all said, "One for all and all for one."

As their hands separated, Lorna reached for the diary that had tumbled off her lap. Too late she realized the others had read the brief entry she'd written for the day.

The women looked at one another and the silence thickened as Lorna closed the book.

Tillie picked up the pencil and while handing it back said, "How old will you be tomorrow?"

Lorna took the pencil and set it and the book on the ground. "Twenty."

"I'm eighteen," Betty said. "Had my birthday last March, right before we left Missouri."

"Me, too," Tillie said. "I'm eighteen. My birthday is in January."

The others looked at Meg. She sighed and spit out a stem of grass she'd been chewing on. "Twenty. December."

Betty turned to Lorna, her big eyes sparkling. "I have all the fixings. If we stop early enough tomorrow, I could bake a cake in my Dutch oven."

Lorna shook her head. "No reason to waste supplies on a cake...or the time."

Silence settled again, until Tillie asked, "Did you have cake back in England? Or birthday parties?"

Lorna considered not answering, but, ultimately, these were her friends, the only ones she had now. Meg didn't, but Betty and Tillie, the way their eyes sparkled, acted as if living in England made her some kind of special person. No country did that.

"Yes," she said. "My mother loved big, lavish parties, with all sorts of food and desserts, and fancy dresses."

"What was your dress like last year?" Betty asked, folding her hands beneath her chin. Surrounded by the black nun's habit, the excited glow of her face was prominent.

Lorna held in a sigh. She'd rather not remember that night, but couldn't help but give the others a hint of the society they longed to hear about. "It was made of lovely dark blue velvet and took the seamstress a month to sew."

"A month?"

She nodded. "My mother insisted it be covered with white lace, rows and rows of it."

"You didn't like the lace," Meg said, as intuitive as ever.

Lorna shrugged. "I thought it was prettier without it."

"I bet it was beautiful," Betty said wistfully. "How many guests were there?"

"Over a hundred."

Tillie gasped. "A hundred! Goodness."

Lorna leaned back against the wagon wheel and took a moment to look at each woman. In the short time she'd known them, they had become better friends than anyone she'd known most of her life. Perhaps it was time for her to share a bit of her story. "It was also my engagement party. I was to marry Andrew Wainwright. The announcement was to be made that night."

While the other two gasped, Meg asked, "What happened?"

"Andrew never arrived," Lorna answered as bitterness coated her tongue. "Unbeknownst to me, he'd been sent to Scotland that morning."

"Sent to Scotland? By whom?" Betty asked.

"His father," Lorna said, trying to hold back the animosity. It was impossible, and before she could stop herself, she added, "And my stepfather."

"Why?"

Night was settling in around them, and inside, Lorna was turning dark and cold. She hated that feeling. Her fingernails dug into her palm as she said, "Because my stepfather, Viscount Douglas Vermeer..." Simply saying his name made her wish she was already in California. "Didn't want me marrying Andrew." Or anyone else, apparently. Since he'd made certain later that night that it would never happen.

"Why not?" Tillie asked.

At the same time, Betty asked, "Oh, how sad. Did you love Andrew dearly?"

As astute as ever, Meg jumped to her feet. "Lorna will have to finish her tale another night. It's late, and morning comes early." She then started giving out orders as to what needed to be done before they crawled beneath the wagons.

No one argued, and a short time later, Lorna and Meg were under one wagon, Betty and Tillie under the other. Meg didn't utter another word, and neither did Lorna. There was nothing to say. She'd never told Meg what had happened that night back in London. She didn't have to; her friend seemed to know it was something she didn't want to remember. To talk about. Just like a hundred other things Meg seemed to know.

Lorna shut her mind off, something she'd learned how to do years ago, and closed her eyes, knowing her body was tired enough she'd fall asleep. That was one good thing about this trip. It was exhausting.

The next morning, when the early-dawn sunlight awoke them, they all crawled out from beneath the wagons. No one complained of being tired or of sore muscles as they began their work of the day. Breakfast consisted of tea and the biscuits Betty had made the night before along with tough pieces of bacon. Betty insisted they have meat— bacon that was—once a day. She'd save the grease and make gravy out of it tonight, as she did every day. A year ago, Lorna would have quivered at such meals. Now she simply accepted them, and was thankful she didn't have to depend upon herself to do the cooking.

Another good thing about these women was that they were affable without any of the falseness of those she'd known all her life. Each one wished her a happy birthday with sincerity and no expectations of learning more. That was the good thing about mornings. It was a new day. A new start. The conversation of last night was as dead to her as everything else she'd left behind.

Once the meal was over, she and Meg gathered the mules they'd staked nearby and hitched them to the wagons while the other two cleaned up their campsite. Lorna appreciated that Betty and Tillie didn't mind doing those chores. Kitchen duties had never appealed to her, not like the stables. That was one thing she missed, the fine horseflesh that had lived in the barns back home. Her father had taught her to ride when she was very little, and the memories of riding alongside him were the only ones she cherished and refused to allow to become sullied.

Once set, all four of them climbed aboard the wagons.

The lead wagon was Meg's and she drove it; the second one was Betty's. Tillie's had been lost in the river accident that took her husband's life. This morning, Lorna sat in the driver's seat of the second wagon. She and Betty, as well as Tillie, took turns driving it. Another chore she didn't mind. Each step the animals took led her farther and farther away from England, and closer to California.

Tillie was on the seat beside her and Betty beside Meg. The trail they followed was little more than curved indents in the ground. Summer grass had grown up tall and thick, and Lorna wondered how Meg deciphered where the trail went and where it didn't.

"Meg says we might cross into Wyoming today," Tillie said.

"We very well may," Lorna answered. They'd passed the strange formation of Chimney Rock a few days ago, and ever since then, Meg had been saying they'd be crossing into Wyoming soon. Truth was, as far as any of them knew, they might already have entered Wyoming. It wasn't as if there was a big sign saying Welcome to Wyoming or any such thing. The area was neither a state nor territory, just a large plot of land the government hadn't figured out what they wanted to do with yet. That was how Meg described it.

Lorna, like the others, had long ago put their trust in Meg's knowledge. Although she had no idea how Meg had acquired such knowledge, it was admirable.

"Do you ever wish you hadn't left England?" Tillie asked.

"No," Lorna answered. She'd have to be dense to believe what she'd revealed last night wouldn't eventually bring about questions, but she didn't need to elaborate on them. Leaving England had been her decision, and she'd never questioned it. Nor would she. She was glad to be gone from there, and far from everyone who still lived there.

"Will you ever go back?"

"No."

"You don't like talking about it, do you?"

"No," Lorna said. "That part of my life is over. No need to talk or think about it." That, of course, was easier said than done. And a lie. Some days the memories just wouldn't stop. More so today, an exact year since her stepfather had stolen the one thing that had been truly hers, and only hers. She'd win in the end, though; once she arrived in San Francisco, Douglas would get his due.

"Adam and I lived in Ohio," Tillie said. "I've told you that before, but I didn't mention that Adam's father said he either had to join the army or go west."

"I know," Lorna said.

"How would you know? I never mentioned it."

"Because most every man on that wagon train had made that same choice."

"He chose west because of me," Tillie said. "I was afraid he'd die being a soldier."

Lorna held her breath to brace for what was to come. Tears most likely, and more blame. Tillie was a fan of both. The girl had had a hard time, Lorna would admit that, but at some point, enough becomes enough, as she herself had learned.

"Can I tell you something?" Tillie asked.

"Yes." The answer hadn't been needed. Tillie would go on either way.

"I'm glad we went west. I'm sorry Adam died, and that I lost the baby, but if he'd gone to the army, I'd be living with his parents now and would never have met you, or Meg or Betty. I would never have known how strong I am. How much I can do."

Lorna glanced sideways just to make sure those words had come from Tillie. It wasn't likely a stranger had appeared out of nowhere and jumped up on the seat beside her, but hearing Tillie saying such things was about as unexpected. After assuring herself that it was Tillie's big brown eyes looking back at her—her curly red-brown hair was well covered by the black habit—Lorna grinned. "I'm glad you came west, too." She was sorry for Tillie's losses, but had said that plenty of times before. "And I'm glad you're on this trip with me," she added instead.

They conversed of minor things then, just to lighten the monotony of the trail. Tall grass went on as far as they could see in this wide-open country. There were a few small hills here and there, and a large line of trees along the river that ran just south of them. They'd camp near the river again tonight, like every night. Meg said farther into Wyoming, they wouldn't have the water they did here in Nebraska. Lorna hoped they wouldn't have the high temperatures, either. It was unrelenting. The yards of black material covering her from head to toe intensified the heat, making the sun twice as hot as it ever had been in England.

By the time they stopped for the noon meal, Lorna questioned if she'd ever been so sweaty and miserable in her life. She wasted no time in unhitching the mules and leading them down to the river for water. The poor animals had to be beyond parched.

"Sure is a hot one," Meg said, dropping the lead rope as her mules stepped into the water and started slurping.

"Miserably so." Lorna pushed the tight habit off her head and lifted the heavy braid of her hair off the back of her neck to catch the breeze. The relief wasn't nearly enough. "I feel like jumping in that river and swimming clear to the other side."

Meg looked up and down the river, and then over her shoulder where Betty and Tillie were busy seeing to the noon meal. It wouldn't be much, just more tea and biscuits, and maybe some dried apple chips.

"Why don't we?"

Lorna pulled her gaze off the other women to glance at Meg. She was smiling, which in itself was a bit rare. "I don't know," Lorna said, trying to conceal how her heart leaped inside her chest. "Why don't we?"

"No reason I can think of," Meg said. "You?"

Lorna shook her head. "Not a one."

Meg glanced up and down the river one more time. "I gotta say, a swim sounds like a better way to celebrate a birthday than any stupid party with fancy dresses covered in lace."

Lorna laughed. "I agree. And getting out of these heavy dresses for a moment would be heavenly, Sister Meg."

Meg laughed. "Then, stake down your mules, Sister Lorna."

Grinning, and with her heart skipping with excitement, Lorna didn't waste a minute in staking the animals and then unbraiding her hair. She hadn't been swimming in years, but it wasn't something a person forgot. Hopefully! Then again, submerging herself in that cool river water would be worth almost drowning.

Meg shouted for Betty and Tillie to join them. In no time, all four of them were stripped down to their underclothes and running for the water, giggling like girls half their age. The water was as refreshing as Lorna imagined and not nearly as deep as it looked. She was halfway across the river before the water reached her waist, at which point she pinched her nose and fell onto her back. Sinking beneath the water was trivial, yet the most spectacular event she'd had in months. When she resurfaced, she stretched out and slowly kicked her feet to propel her around as she floated on her back. The water was like taking a bath, except that it smelled earthy and pure instead of cloying and sweet from the various flower oils her maid, Anna, had drizzled in the brass tub before she'd proclaim the bath was ready.

Of all the people she'd thought of over the past year, Anna hadn't been in her memories at all. Yet the woman should have been. She'd been the one mainstay in her life, clicking her tongue and waggling a finger at the slightest misstep. Maybe that was why. As Tillie had pointed out, learning to take care of oneself was liberating. Lorna liked that. Taking responsibility suited her.

Stretching her arms out at her sides, she smiled up at the bright blue sky. Not answering to anyone was liberating, too. So was not being committed to doing anything or being anywhere she didn't want to be or do.

This was how her life would be from now on. Free to do as she pleased.

"Well, well, well, what do we have here?"

The chill that encompassed her had nothing to do with the water. Lorna dropped her feet. As they sank into the soft sand, she turned to where the familiar male voice had come from.

Jacob Lerber stood on the riverbank, along with three other men who looked just as uncouth. They reminded her of the stories she'd heard about wolves, complete with evil eyes and yellow teeth.

All four of them had guns hanging off their waists. She'd learned since coming to America that only those who didn't mind killing broadly displayed their weapons. Which was why she kept hers hidden, and would have had it on her right now if she hadn't decided to go swimming. As it was, her little gun was still in a deep pocket in her dress...which was on the shore not five feet from Lerber. The man who'd sold her the tiny pistol had said it wouldn't do any harm at a distance, but if a man got within three feet of her it would stop him dead in his tracks. The very reason she'd bought it. No man would ever get that close to her again.

"What do you want, Lerber?" Meg shouted.

"Hush," Lorna hissed, inching her way to where the others stood in the waist-deep water. What Lerber wanted was obvious—making sure he didn't get it needed to be the focus.

"Well, now, I was just worried about the four of you out here all alone," Jacob drawled. "Thought I best backtrack and check how you fine ladies were getting along."

"More likely you got kicked off the wagon train," Meg yelled.

Lorna agreed, but hushed Meg again. "We're getting along just fine," Lorna said. "Thanks for stopping."

"Thanks for stopping?" Betty hissed under her breath.

"Shush," Lorna insisted.

"You can shush us all you want," Meg snapped. "They ain't leaving. Mark my word."

"I know that," Lorna replied. "I'm just trying to come up with a plan."

"What you ladies whispering about out there?" Jacob shouted. "How happy you are to see us?"

The others beside him chortled, and one slapped him on the back as if Jacob was full of wit.

Intelligence was not what Jacob was known for. "Delighted for sure," Lorna answered while gradually twisting her neck to see how far the opposite bank was. The men hadn't yet stepped in the water. From the looks of Jacob's greasy hair, he was either afraid of or opposed to water. If she and the others swam—

Her brain stopped midthought. What she saw on the other side of the river sent a shiver rippling her spine all the way to the top of her head. Lorna shifted her feet to solidify her stance in the wet sand and get a better view, just to make sure she wasn't seeing things. The way her throat plugged said she wasn't imagining anything.

"Indians," Meg whispered.

That was exactly what they were. Indians. Too many to count. And they weren't afraid of water. Especially the one on the large black horse who was front and center. He was huge and so formidable the lump in Lorna's throat silenced her scream as his horse leaped into the water like a beast arising from the caverns of hell. The very image of her worst nightmare.

Water splashed as other horses lunged to follow him, and the Indians on their backs started making high-pitched yipping noises.

Frozen by a form of fear she'd never known existed, Lorna couldn't move, didn't move until the screeches of the women penetrated her senses. She spun to tell them to hush, but her attention landed on the other riverbank, where Jacob and his cronies ran beside their horses, attempting to leap into their saddles before the animals left them afoot. All four managed to mount, and watching them gallop away would have been a relief if the riverbed beneath her hadn't been vibrating.

Waves swirled as the Indians rode past. Their stocky horses were swift and surefooted, and leaped out of the water to take after Jacob and his men. Their crazy yipping noises echoed off the water, the air, and vibrated deep inside her.

"What are we going to do?" Betty was asking. "What are we going to do?" Lorna spun back around, toward the bank still lined with huge horses and bare chests. One by one, the horses stepped into the water, and her fear returned ten times over. As her gaze once again landed on the great black horse hurdling the opposite bank, she muttered, "Hell if I know."

Chapter Two

Black Horse slowed his mount while signaling four warriors to pursue the white men. It would take no more than that. He then spun his horse around to return to the riverbank and the women. Moments ago the four of them had been frolicking in the water like a family of otters in the spring. The sight of it, how their white clothes had puffed up around them, had made his braves laugh. He did not laugh.

One of his hunting parties had reported the women—four of them in two wagons—traveling alongside the river two days ago. At one time, many wagon trains traveled this route, but since the white men started fighting each other, the trains had almost disappeared. He had liked that, had welcomed the idea of fewer white people on Cheyenne land. The peace his people had known while his grandfather had been leading their band was his greatest desire. Inside, though, he knew peace would only happen when the white man and the bands learned to settle disagreements without bloodshed. He had left the last tribal council knowing that would not happen any time soon. Although many had agreed with him, some had not.

If not for the white men reported to be trailing these

women, he would have let the women pass through Cheyenne land without notice, but he could not allow Tsitsistas to be blamed for what could happen to them.

Stopping at the water's edge, Black Horse drew in a breath of warm summer air and held it. Bringing white women into his village would upset the serenity, but so would the army soldiers if something happened to the women. This was Cheyenne land, and his band would be blamed.

The tallest woman, the one with long brown hair that curled in spirals like wood peeled thin with a sharp knife, was not crying like the others, or running for the bank. She stared at him with eyes the same blue as the living water that falls from the mountains when the snow leaves. There was bravery in her eyes. A rarity. All the white women he had met acted like the other three. Other than Ayashe—Little One—but she had been living with Tsitsistas for many seasons.

Keeping his eyes locked on the woman's, he motioned for braves to gather the others and hitch the mules to the wagons, and then nudged his horse toward the water. The woman did not move. Or blink. She stood there like a *mahpe he'e*, a water woman, who had emerged from the waves during a great storm, daring to defy a leader of the people. He had to focus to keep his lips from curling into a smile. Only a white woman would believe such was possible.

She held up one hand. "We come in peace."

No white person comes in peace. Not letting anything show, especially that he understood her language, Black Horse lifted his chin and nodded toward the wagons. *"Tosa'e nehestahe?"*

The frown tugging her brows together said she did not understand his question of where she came from. He had not expected her to know the language of his people, but

had wanted to be sure. Others like her had come before.
Dressed in their black robes that covered everything but
their faces, they tried to teach people about a god written
on the pages of a book. Each Indian Nation had their own
god and no need to believe in others, or books.

Faint victory shouts indicated his warriors had caught
up with the men that had disappeared over a small knoll,
and Black Horse waved a hand toward the wagons, indicating the woman should join the others.

Her cold glare glanced at the other women putting their
black dresses over their wet clothes. Only white people
would do that. Their ways made little sense.

Turning back to him, her eyes narrowed as she asked,
"What do you want with us?"

There were many advantages to knowing the white
man's language, and more advantages in not letting that
knowledge be known. He waved toward the wagon again.

Her sneer increased. "What? You grunt and wave a
hand, and expect me to know what you want and to obey?
Let me assure you that will not happen."

She was not like the other holy women he had encoun-
tered. They had all been quiet and timid. She was neither.

Earlier she had skimmed across the water with the ease
of an otter, and catching the sense she was about to do so
again, Black Horse urged Horse into the water.

The woman looked one way and then the other, and
then, just as he expected, she shot under the water.

The water was not deep enough to conceal her or her
white clothes, and he tapped his heels against Horse's sides.
He caught up with her just as she lifted her head out of
the water, and the look of shock on her face made him
hide a smile.

"Get away from me, you filthy beast," she shouted.
"Get away!"

As one would a snake, Black Horse shot out a hand and grabbed her behind the head. Grasping the material between her shoulders, he lifted her out of the water. She was as slippery as a fish and her fingernails scratched at his arm while she continued shouting and kicking her feet. Despite her fighting, he draped her across the front shoulders of Horse. Keeping her there took both hands, but Horse needed nothing more than a touch of heels to spin around and return to the bank. He and the animal had been together since Horse had been a colt. Shortly after acquiring Horse, others had started calling him He Who Rides a Black Horse, and though many events had occurred that offered to provide him with a different name, he did not take one. He liked being known as Black Horse.

Her kicking and squirming almost caused her to slip from his hold when Horse stopped on the bank to shake the water from his hide. In that one quiet moment, Black Horse could feel her heart racing against his thigh. It startled him briefly, the contact of another person. It had been a long time.

Once Horse started walking again, she started her kicking, squirming and screaming all over and Black Horse renewed the pressure on her back. When Horse stopped near the wagon, Black Horse balled the material across her back into his hand. Just as he started to lift her, a sharp sting shot across his leg.

Before her teeth could sink deeper, he wrenched her off his lap and dropped her to the ground. *"Poeso,"* he hissed. She had the claws and teeth of a *poeso*—a wild cat. There was no blood, because the hide leggings had protected his skin. They had protected him against far worse, but he still had to rub the sting from the area.

His braves as well as the other women were watching, waiting to see what would happen next. If he had been only a warrior, the braves would have laughed at what the white woman had done, but because he was the leader of their people they stood in silence, waiting to follow his next move, whatever he chose it to be.

The woman continued to hiss and snarl like a cat, having no idea she had just offended a leader of the Cheyenne Nation, and Black Horse accepted her ignorance. He prided himself on being a highly respected leader, one who did not make decisions based on spite, but on thoughtful deliberations. He ignored her screeching while gesturing for the men to finish hitching up the mules—until one word she said caught his attention.

Black Horse jumped off Horse and wrenched the bundle of clothes out of her hands, searching until he found what she was after. Holding up the little gun, he laughed. It was smaller than his fingers.

"Laugh all you want, you beast!" she shouted. "It can still kill you. It's called a gun."

Why did all white people think only they knew what guns were? The fur trade wars over a century ago had brought guns to all the people, back before Tsitsistas had started following the buffalo. But guns wore out and could not be repaired, and were much less accurate when it came to hunting than bows and arrows. Their thundering noise scared more buffalo than their bullets killed.

He tucked the gun in the pouch hanging on his side and tossed the clothes at the woman, along with the pair of stiff boots that were lying on the bank. Shrill calls from his returning warriors filled the air and he grinned. Just as he had known, each brave led a horse behind him.

"They killed them that fast?" the woman asked, eyes wide.

"Hova'ahane," he answered, knowing she had no idea he had just told her no. Tsitsistas were not conquerors.

Not the northern bands. His warriors rarely killed unless threatened. It was his goal to make sure it remained that way.

"Tahee'evonehnestse," he said, once again waving toward the wagon, telling her to get on with the others, who had obeyed his braves while this *poeso* battled him. There was always one. Always a *he'e*—a woman—who refused to listen; for a moment he wondered if saving her, if being a fair and just leader, was worth the trouble.

Lorna knew the brown beast of a man, with black hair hanging way past his shoulders and wearing a scowl as fierce as the rest of him, wanted her to get on the wagon with the others, but she wasn't about to. Men, no matter what nationality, thought that because of their strength they could order women about, make them grovel and beg and plea. She'd lived that way once, and never would again. Furthermore, this man was worse than all the others she'd known. Stronger. The strength of his hold could have easily broken her spine, and his thighs had been harder than logs. The fact he hadn't killed her said one thing. He was saving her for worse. Much worse.

That wouldn't happen again.

Turning toward Meg, Tillie and Betty, who were peeking out of the canvas opening in the back of Meg's wagon, Lorna shouted, "Get out of there! We can't go with them!"

"We don't have a choice," Meg answered. "We only have one gun, and if you haven't noticed, there are twenty of them."

"I don't care how many there are!"

"You may want to be killed," Meg said, "but I'd like to see tomorrow."

"Which we won't if we go with them," Lorna insisted. "These are Cheyenne Indians. They're peaceful."

Just then the beast grabbed her by the back of her camisole again, and the back her bloomers. "You call this peaceful?" she shouted at Meg between screaming at him to let her go.

Lorna kicked and continued to scream, but the black-haired heathen carried her to the wagon and tossed her inside as if she weighed no more than a feather pillow. Unable to catch hold of anything, she hit the other women and they all tumbled among the crates and chests. Before they managed to get up, a brave jumped in the back.

His presence had Tillie and Betty whimpering, and Meg pulling Lorna's hair.

"Stay down," Meg hissed. "The Cheyenne are peaceful Indians, but I'm sure they'll only take so much from a white woman."

"I'll only take so much from them." Lorna wrenched her hair away from Meg. The wagon lurched and she planted a hand on top of a trunk to spin around. Another brave was driving. "Did you hitch up the mules?"

"No," Meg said. "The braves did while you were arguing with their chief in the middle of the river."

"How do you know so much about Indians?" Lorna asked.

"I told you, I made the trip to California before."

Meg had told her that, but Lorna hadn't believed it. Whether she acted like it or not, Meg wasn't old enough to have gone all the way to California and back to Missouri. At least that was what Lorna had believed up until now. Meg did seem to know a lot about a variety of things they'd needed to know along the way, including Indians, it appeared, but she had figured Meg had learned most of it from reading about it. Just as she had. She'd also hoped they wouldn't encounter any Indians. None.

Flustered, Lorna said, "He's not a chief. He doesn't have

a single feather in his hair." Or clothes on his body, other than a pair of hide britches and moccasins. She chose not to mention that. The others had to have noticed.

"They don't wear war bonnets all the time," Meg said. "White people portray that in paintings and books because it makes the Indians look fiercer."

Lorna glanced at the brave sitting on the back of the wagon. "No, it doesn't." If you asked her, a few white feathers among all that black hair might make them look more human. Not that humans had feathers, but wearing nothing other than hide breeches and moccasins, these men looked more like animals than humans. Especially the beast who'd plucked her out of the water. The one who'd stolen her gun. She would get that back. Soon.

She was where she was because of a man, and another, no matter what color his skin might happen to be, was not going to be the reason her life changed again. Was not! She'd fight to the death this time. To the very death.

"Give me those," she snapped while snatching her clothes from beneath the feet of the brave who sat on the tailgate. It was difficult with the wagon rambling along at a speed it had never gone before, and with the others crowded around her, but Lorna managed to get dressed—minus the habit—and put on her boots.

She then scrambled past Meg and over the trunks until she stuck her head out of the front opening. The brave was too busy trying to control the mules to do much else. Lorna climbed over the back of the seat—despite how Meg tugged on her skirt—and sat down next to him. The other wagon was following them at the same speed. The braves surrounding them had their horses at a gallop, too. The mules would give out long before their horses would; even she could see that.

Whether he was a chief or not, the man on the black

horse was a fool to force the animals to continue at this speed. She needed these mules to get her to California.

"What's his name?" she asked, pointing toward the leader of the band. The one atop the finest horseflesh she'd seen since coming to America. If she had an animal like that, she could have ridden all the way to California, and been there long before now.

The brave hadn't even glanced her way.

"What do you call him? That one on the black horse?"

The brave didn't respond.

"Him," she repeated, "on that black horse, what is his name?"

The brave grunted and slapped the reins across the backs of the mules again.

Lorna let out a grunt, too, before she cupped her hands around her mouth. "Hey, you on the black horse!" When he glanced over one shoulder, she added, "You better slow down! Mules can't run like horses!"

He turned back, his long hair flying in the wind just like his horse's mane. The two of them, man and horse, appeared to be one, their movements were so in tune.

"Did you hear me?" she asked.

"Everyone heard you," Meg said from inside the wagon. "Hush up before you irritate him."

"I don't care if I irritate him," Lorna answered. "He's already irritated me."

"He saved us from Lerber." That was Betty. "They all did. Shouldn't we be thankful for that? Show a little appreciation?"

Lorna spun around to let the other woman know her thoughts on that. Words weren't needed. Betty cowered and scooted farther back in the wagon.

"My guess," Meg said, "is that is Black Horse. He's the leader of a band of Northern Cheyenne."

Lorna shot her gaze to Meg. "How do you know that?" The name certainly fit the man.

"I'm just guessing," Meg said. "They'll slow down after we cross the river. They are putting distance between us and Lerber."

"Distance? Why?" Lorna asked. "They killed Lerber."

"No, they didn't. I told you they are Cheyenne. They just stole their horses."

"You can't be sure of that." Lorna certainly wasn't.

"They are the reason I said we had to take the northern route," Meg said. "The Indians are friendlier. Southern Indians, even bands of Cheyenne, are the ones that kill and kidnap people off wagon trains. They use them as slaves."

Lorna had assumed Indians were all the same, no matter what band they were. "How can you possibly know that?"

Meg chewed on her bottom lip as if contemplating. After closing her eyes, she sighed. "My father was a wagon master. He led a total of eight trains to California. Two of them, I was with him."

Lorna hadn't pressed to know about a family Meg never mentioned. "Where is he now?"

"Dead."

The word was said with such finality Lorna wouldn't have pushed further, even if she hadn't seen the tears Meg swiped at as she sat down and looked the other way.

Lorna swiveled and grabbed the edge of the wagon seat. The horses and riders ahead of them veered left and the wagons followed, slowing their speed as they grew nearer to the trees lining the river. A pathway she'd never have believed wide enough for the wagon, let alone even have noticed, widened and led them down to the river. The brave handled the mules with far more skill than she'd have imagined, or than she had herself. As long as she was being honest with herself she might as well admit it.

With little more than a tug on the reins and a high-pitched yelp, he had the mules entering the river. The water was shallow. Even in the middle, the deepest point, it didn't pass the wheel hubs.

In no time they'd crossed the river and traveled into the trees lining the bank on the other side. Just as Meg had suggested, their pace slowed and remained so as they made their way through a considerable expanse of trees and brush. The trail was only as wide as the wagon, and once again, Lorna sensed that you had to know this trail existed in order to find it. She did have to admit the shade was a substantial relief from the blazing sun they'd traveled under for the past several weeks. She'd take it back though, the heat of the sun that was, to regain her freedom from this heathen as big as the black horse he rode upon.

He hadn't turned around, not once, to check to see if they'd made it across the river or not, but she'd rarely taken her eyes off him.

"Where are you taking us?" she asked the brave beside her.

A frown wrinkled his forehead, which didn't surprise her. English was as foreign to him as their language was to her. Turning toward Meg, she asked, "Where are they taking us?"

"Their village would be my guess," Meg said.

"Why?"

"I haven't figured that out yet."

"I have," Lorna said. "To kill us, right after they rape us."

"No, they won't," Meg insisted. "But that is what Lerber would have done."

Lorna didn't doubt Meg was right about Lerber, nor did she doubt that this band of heathens would do the same. Despite Meg's claims. She'd read about the American Indians, in periodicals from both England and New York.

Anger rose inside her. If only the railroad went all the way to the West Coast she would have been riding in a comfortable railcar, like the one she'd traveled in from New York to Missouri. There had been heavy velvet curtains to block out the sun and a real bed. Tension stiffened her neck. Getting to California was worth sleeping on the hard ground, and no one, not even a band of killer Indians was going to stop her from getting there.

"Look at that."

Lorna turned at Tillie's hushed exclamation. As the wagon rolled out of the trees, a valley of green grass spread out before them, with a winding stream running through the center of it. Teepees that looked exactly like ones in the books she'd read were set up on both sides of the stream, hundreds of them. The scent of wood smoke filled the air and a group was running out to meet them on the trail. It wasn't until they grew closer that she realized the group was mainly children and dogs. Some of the dogs were as tall as the children they ran beside, others tiny enough to run through the children's legs, and many of them were decorated with feathers and paint. She'd read about Indians doing such things to their horses, but not their dogs.

What strange creatures they were, these Indians, and for a brief moment, she wondered what her mother would think of this peculiar sight. Mother hated America, which was partially why Lorna had chosen to return here. Maybe these creatures were part of the reason her mother hated her father's homeland so severely.

Lorna had told herself she'd love America, if for no other reason than to spite her mother, but painted dogs were hard to ignore. As hard to ignore as the man on the black horse.

Most of the children now ran a circle around him, yipping and clapping. The last trek of their journey he'd led them at a pace the mules were much more accustomed to—slow, miserably slow. As their train rumbled forward, the smaller children and their dogs headed back toward the camp, whooping and yelling in their language. It sounded ugly and harsh, especially when shouted at such a volume. A few of the group, older boys it appeared, ventured all the way to the wagons, where they chattered among themselves and pointed at her sitting on the seat as if she were a circus attraction.

Usually, children and their innocent tactics humored her, but these, as scantily dressed as the big man on the black horse, were alarming. She waved a hand to shoo them away, but they laughed and continued walking alongside the wagon. Shouting, telling them to be gone did little more than make them laugh harder, and mimic her.

"Aren't they adorable," Tillie whispered.

It hadn't been a question, but Lorna answered as if it had been. "Hell, no!"

"Sister Lorna!" Tillie reprimanded. "You shouldn't curse."

Being scolded wasn't necessary. She'd rarely said a curse word before in her life, but today, they were jumping out of her mouth like frogs. Justly so. "I'm no more of a sister than you are, and I doubt the disguise will do us any good here."

"Nonetheless, you shouldn't curse. Especially not in front of children."

"These are Indians," she answered. "Heathens. The children are just like their parents. Their leader," she added with renewed scorn. "Besides, they can't understand a word we say." Then lifting a hand, she pointed to the others now rushing out to greet them. "None of them."

"Oh, my," Tillie whispered.

"Oh, yes," Lorna mocked. "Oh, my."

There was now a great amount of shouting, and barking dogs, and those whooping sounds that made the hair on the back of her neck stand straight. The entire village, or at least half of it, now approached the wagon. Old and young lined the trail, babbling strange words and pointing as if watching a parade. The men were shirtless, other than a few who actually had on shirts or vests—stolen from white men they'd killed most likely—and the women had on hide dresses covered with beads and other trinkets. Most of the men wore ankle-high moccasins on their feet, but some men and almost all of the women wore fringe-topped boots made of hide that came up to their knees.

Their little wagon train, still led by the beast Black Horse, traveled all the way to the center of the encampment before stopping. The men on horseback, all except their leader, road several fast circles around the wagons, yipping loudly. The ones leading the horses they'd stolen from Lerber were the loudest, and in turn, received the loudest cheers from the crowd that had gathered.

Their screeches and chants were enough to make a person's blood run cold. Lorna's did, and she turned to Meg. "Friendly, you say."

The astonishment, which was a combination of fear and shock, on Meg's face sent Lorna's heart into her throat.

Chapter Three

The white women in the wagon cowered together, holding on to each other as fear filled their eyes. Except for the water woman. She had not covered her mass of curls with the black material like the others, and her stare was not full of fear. It was cold and directed at him. Returning her stare, Black Horse lifted his chin, and allowed the celebration to continue. Acquiring horses, no matter how small the number, was a great accomplishment for any warrior. Because all bands were preparing for the hunting season, raids on Crow or Shoshone for horses had not happened since Tsitsistas had started to move north, and his warriors were enjoying the reception as much as if they had brought home dozens of ponies.

Four other bands had joined his to follow the great herds of buffalo, which was the way their fathers and their fathers' fathers had done it. Displaying the rewards of the day before other warriors caused great excitement for his entire band.

The bands would separate again after the hunt, each leader taking his people to where they would continue to hunt for deer and elk and then reside until the snow once again melted. As long as the white soldiers continued fighting each other far away, where the sun rose each morning, his people would have another peaceful winter.

A shiver tickled his spine and he hardened his stare at the white woman. More than one tribe had been led into a trap set by the white man. The massacre in Nebraska had been a trap, and the white man's want of the yellow rocks had caused many other battles. Two winters ago in the land the whites called Minnesota a large number of Sioux had been killed and the survivors had been forced to move west, into Cheyenne land. This spring, after the tribal council, messengers had said the white man found more yellow rock north of Cheyenne land. There would be more battles. More tricks. More traps.

Black Horse lifted a hand. The reception had lasted long enough. *"Nehetaa'e!"*

His command was instantly obeyed. The warriors slowed their ponies and those gathered near quieted. He then commanded four braves who were married to each take a white woman to their lodges and have their wives look after them. Then he commanded others to take the wagons outside the last circle of lodges and search them thoroughly.

Mahpe he'e, water woman, as he'd aptly named her in his mind, was again the only one to protest, biting and scratching Rising Sun as he attempted to lift her out of the wagon. Black Horse turned away, knowing the warrior was much stronger. After dismounting, he handed Horse over to the young boy waiting for the duty.

"Hotoa'e?" the boy asked.

"Hova'ahane," Black Horse answered, shaking his head. They had not found buffalo on this day, but soon would. Sweet Medicine promised a successful hunt. Not just to his band, but the others camped with them.

The boy, Rising Sun's child, nodded and started to lead

Horse away, but stopped at the sound of his father's howl. Black Horse spun around to spy the woman launching herself into the air, claws out.

He caught her by both arms and held her in the air. She would have landed on his back and dug those claws deep into his skin if he had not turned around. Like a mountain cat. *Poeso* was a much better name for her. She was as wild and most likely as devious as a cat.

Her feet struck his shins as she shouted into his face, "Give me my gun, you ugly heathen!"

He spun her around, but that just made her kick backward. The heels of her boots made his shins smart. Grasping both of her arms in one hand, he wrapped his other arm around her waist to hold her close to his side where her feet could no longer meet with his legs. He lifted his head to shout for Rising Sun to come get her, but the warrior had dread in his eyes. His wife, Little Dove, who was wiping at the blood trickling down her husband's arm, did not look at him. Did not need to. Black Horse recognized that she did not want the responsibility of the white woman any more than her husband, but they would take her if he told them to.

The white woman was still shouting, and squirming. Black Horse had had enough, and told her so. *"Nehetaa'e!"*

"Don't shout at me in that wretched language!" she yelled in return.

Black Horse tightened his hold and glanced around, looking for someone to take the woman. Not a single warrior met his gaze. They all stood stock still, waiting to hear who he would command to take her. Except Sleeps All Day, who scurried away as if suddenly remembering an imminent task. The celebration must have awoken him. Sleeps All Day, along with those he oversaw, stood guard through the moon hours while others slept, and took great pride in his post. He was also unmarried, and therefore not one who could take the woman.

A just leader does not request others to do things he would not do himself, and Black Horse stood by that. Always had. It was part of the reason his band was so strong.

Turning slowly, Black Horse caught the gaze of the only person looking at him. She Who Smiles. His mother-in-law was a gentle woman, not one he could turn this wild *poeso* over to, even though She Who Smiles stepped closer, nodding.

It was a moment before the white woman stopped shouting long enough to hear She Who Smiles's soft voice.

Poeso twisted and after giving his mother-in-law a cold glare, turned it on him. "What does she want?"

Black Horse had to bite his tongue to keep from answering in her language. There had been no fear in her eyes before, but it was there now. For no reason. She Who Smiles never raised a hand at anyone. Not even him. Not even after he'd killed her daughter. She Who Smiles did not blame him for Hopping Rabbit's death. No one did. Except him. He had fallen for one of the white man's traps, and it had stolen his family from him. If he had been a mere brave, he would have revenged the death of his wife and his son, but a leader had to think of what was best for all, not just for himself.

"What does she want?" the white woman repeated, this time with excruciatingly slow pronunciation.

Burying his thoughts in that dark and hollow grave inside him, he nodded. *"Epeva'e,"* he said, telling her it was all right for her to go with She Who Smiles.

Lorna shook her head. She had no idea what he'd just said, but understood she was to go with this woman. Not likely. She wasn't about to go anywhere without her gun. As Black Horse's hold lessened, she spun. During her fight to get away from the other Indian in order to retrieve her gun from him, she'd lost sight of Meg, Tillie and Betty.

The area that had been as crowded as a marketplace was now empty, and eerily quiet. Even the wagons were gone. She spun back around. Black Horse had completely released her, but there was no sense in attempting to attack him again. His strength was beyond her. Her ribs could very well be bruised from the hold he'd had on her a moment ago.

Softly, the tiny woman whispered something in their language. Coming from her, the words didn't sound nearly as harsh or ugly as when he spoke. The woman had kind eyes and her long black hair was streaked with gray, which made her look soft and pretty rather than old as one would think.

"I don't know what you are saying," Lorna said, frustrated. "I don't know what anyone is saying, or doing, or…" She pinched at the bridge of her nose in an attempt to hold back the tears. Crying would not accomplish anything, nor would it change anything. She'd promised herself she'd never be in this predicament again. Never be at the mercy of someone else. Ever. She'd crossed the ocean alone, and traveled from New York to Missouri alone.

Lorna lifted her chin. She could do this, too. Glancing between Black Horse and the tiny woman, she chose the woman. Escaping her would be easy. Then she'd find Meg, Tillie and Betty, and the wagons. By nightfall, they'd be well away from these heathens.

Squaring her shoulders, she stepped away from the man and closer to the woman.

They said a few words to each other, things she couldn't understand, but Lorna didn't let that bother her. She'd find a way to get her gun back. It was still in the pouch hanging off his waist. Considering his strength, getting it back would not be easy, but not a whole lot had been easy the past year, and that hadn't stopped her.

He gave her a nod before turning and walking away. Lorna watched to make note of which tent, or teepee as she had read they were called, he entered. As she'd informed Meg, she'd read about the American Indians while on the train from New York and wasn't completely ignorant of their ways. However, the teepee he ducked down to enter looked no different from the dozens surrounding it. She tried counting from the end of the row, so she'd know which one was his, but there wasn't a row. Instead, the teepees made a complete circle. Several circles actually. One large one with several smaller ones inside it.

The woman said something softly and gestured for Lorna to follow. She did, all the while trying to make sense of the layout and how to get back to the teepee Black Horse had entered. The farther they walked, the more confusing it became. The circles of teepees were not full circles, but half circles that formed another circle, and then another one. The entire area was a full circle of teepees. The layout was as symmetric as it was perplexing.

Other women and children, as well as a few men, went about their business, never glancing their way as she followed the older woman. The chatter that had once gone silent was about them again, but this time it wasn't frightening, it just was. Like the noise at the market square or in a neighborhood full of children and good cheer. So were the colors. The teepees were brightly decorated, and Lorna couldn't imagine where the Indians got the paint from, for it surely wasn't something people on wagon trains hauled, and she assumed that was how the Indians got most everything they needed. They stole it.

Unless, of course, there was an army post nearby. Most of those had been abandoned, from what Meg said. The soldiers were needed back east to fight against one another. The thrill of having an army post nearby quickly dissolved. From what Meg had said, the few army men left in the west could not be trusted. Then again, she hadn't been right about the Cheyenne Indians being friendly, so maybe there was a lot she wasn't right about.

Friendly Indians would have chased away Lerber and his cronies and left them alone. Not have stolen their wagons and brought them here.

The Indian woman had stopped before a teepee and nodded slightly. Lorna glanced around a final time. While walking, she'd kept an eye out for her friends, but hadn't seen a glimpse of any of them. She wasn't a fool. Attempting to run away in the maze of tents would get her nowhere.

With a nod of her own, Lorna bent down and entered through an opening the Indian woman held apart. The interior was primitive. As had been her home the past few months, but while sleeping beneath a wagon, she'd been surrounded by familiar things. Here, she didn't recognize much of anything. The teepee was circular, with tall logs that allowed her to stand once she'd entered. The narrow poles, at least twice as tall as she, were rather remarkable. They appeared to be identical in length and circumference and neatly fit together at the top, leaving a hole that allowed the sunlight to brighten what might otherwise have been a dark and confining space. Despite the sunlight, it was surprisingly cool inside, and much larger than she'd imagined.

"Nehaeanaha?"

Lorna turned to the other woman and shook her head while shrugging. "I don't know what you are saying."

The woman put her fingers to her lips. *"Nehaeanaha?"*

"Eat?" Lorna mimicked the action. *"Nehaeanaha* means eat?"

Repeating the action again, the woman nodded. *"Ne-haeanaha."*

"Why would it need so many syllables?" Lorna asked.

The woman frowned.

Shaking her head, Lorna said, "Never mind."

"Nehaeanaha?"

Considering their lunch had been interrupted, food didn't sound too bad. It would give her time to create a plan. "Sure," Lorna said. "Why not?" Then, trying her best to copy the other woman's word, she added, *"Nehaeanaha."*

The woman's smile never faded as she gestured for Lorna to sit on a pile of what looked like animal furs before she moved to where several things sat along the edge of the teepee—bowls and such. A few minutes later the woman handed Lorna a wooden bowl with chunks of jerky and a wooden tumbler full of water.

Once her thirst was quenched, Lorna took a bite of the jerky. It was hard and rather tasteless, but she ate it. That was one thing she'd learned since leaving home. Picky eaters went hungry, and hungry people had no energy. She needed all the energy she could get. There was a lot she had to do, and little time.

The woman refilled her bowl as soon as Lorna took out the last piece. Although her stomach could handle more, her jaw couldn't. "No, thank you," she said. "I've had enough."

Still smiling, the woman nodded and took away the bowl.

"What is your name?" Lorna asked.

The woman shook her head and shrugged.

Lorna pointed at her chest. "Lorna." Pointing at the woman, she asked, "Your name?"

The woman nodded and said a single word long enough it would have filled up an entire diary page.

"Uh?" Lorna asked. There was no way she could even attempt to pronounce what had been said.

Smiling brighter, the woman pointed at her lips.

"Happy?" Lorna asked. "You're happy?" Shaking her head, she added, "I'm glad someone is."

The woman pointed at her lips again, making her smile bigger.

"I see your smile." She pulled up a fake one. "See mine?"

The woman giggled.

Lorna giggled, too. These were some strange people. Whether it was her name or not, Smile was a fitting name for the woman. Lorna drank the last of her water and held out the cup. "Thank you."

Smile returned the cup to the edge of the teepee and then carried something else across the small area. To Lorna's surprise, it was a hairbrush, a primitive one, but it would do the job. Her hair was a mass of snarls after swimming, and she reached for the brush.

With another ten-syllable word, Smile refused to hand over the brush. Instead, she sat down beside Lorna and started to brush her hair. Anna used to do that, but she'd been merciless when it came to wrenching apart the curls that twisted among each other, whereas Smile was gentle, brushing small sections at a time.

Other memories of England floated through Lorna's mind. Of her mother. A memory she'd forgotten. Mother had never brushed her hair because once, when Lorna had been very little, Mother had cut it all off. Right to the nape of her neck. Her father had been furious and forbade her mother from ever touching her hair again. Mother hadn't. Even after her father died. Lorna had been only seven, and didn't remember a lot about him, considering he'd been absent more than not, but she did remember riding with him, and that hair-cutting incident. How mad he'd been over it.

Smile said something, and the memories disappeared as quickly as they'd formed. "I don't understand what you're saying," Lorna said again.

With her smile never faltering, the woman rose and crossed the small space again. This time toward a pile of things on the other side of the opening. When she turned around, she was holding a hide dress, much like the one she wore. She then pointed at how Lorna's dress was still wet in spots.

Lorna shook her head. "Oh, no," she said. "My hair needed to be brushed, but we aren't playing dress up. Wet or not, I'm not putting that on. I need to find my friends." It was clear Smile didn't understand. Lorna rose and crossed the room. Taking the dress from the other woman, she folded it and placed it on top of a pile of other things. "My friends," she repeated. "The other women with me. I must find them so we can leave." Waving a hand toward the teepee surrounding them, she said, "We can't stay here. We are going to California." Since the other woman didn't understand a word she said, Lorna added, "I need to check on an investment, one my father willed to me. I'll be a very rich woman then. I could pay you to help me escape."

Lorna sighed then, knowing the Indian woman had no idea what she'd said. "I've told you more than I've told the women I'm traveling with."

Still smiling, Smile nodded again.

Lorna shrugged but she smiled, too, and nodded. It felt good to tell someone else, even if they didn't understand. "When I find Elliot Chadwick—he was my father's partner, and I met his brother in New York—I'm going to see my stepfather pays for what he did to me."

Chapter Four

Black Horse circled the wagons one more time. They carried foodstuff and clothing, pots and pans, blankets and odd things he did not know the purpose of, but which held no value to him. There were no cases of books like the other holy men and women had tried passing out; nor were there guns or fire water.

He turned to Ayashe, who was gingerly picking through things.

"I no remember what some things are…are for, but no secrets. No traps," she said. Known as Little One to Tsitsistas, Ayashe had lived with their band for many seasons. A band of Southern Cheyenne had brought her north one hunting season. Before that, she had been on a wagon train that had been attacked. Too young to be a slave, she had been left with his band when the southerners returned to their land. Black Horse believed One Who Heals—a powerful and respected medicine woman—had been the reason the southerners had left Little One behind. They turned children of all ages into slaves, even those younger than Little One had been, but One Who Heals was firmly against such behavior.

He had asked Little One to search the wagon, to look

for things the white men might use as traps, or for things the other men could have been after.

"Men no want stuff," Ayashe said, dropping a blanket. "Bad men want the uh…uh…woman. Women."

There were times she could not remember the right words. One Who Heals had told him he must make her speak her language, so she did not forget it, and he abided by that, but insisted it was only with him that she used English. Others having such knowledge could be dangerous. The language was strange, and had been hard to learn, but he was thankful he had. It had been useful many times.

Already having come to the same conclusion about what the white men at the river had wanted, Black Horse nodded. He turned to scan the compound. Men like that would not remain without horses for long. They also carried trouble. After telling the warriors to put everything back in the wagon, he gestured toward Little One. "Come."

Near his lodge, he stopped a young boy and told him to have She Who Smiles bring the white woman to him. Four men were no threat against his warriors, but he wanted to know why they were on Cheyenne land.

He then seated himself in the center of his lodge. In colder times, there would be a fire smoldering in front of him, but during the long sun days, cooking was done outside, keeping the lodges a cool reprieve from the heat. Ayashe sat beside him, as requested. She had grown into a woman over the past winter. Warriors would soon start requesting her as their wife, and it would be up to him to determine whom she would marry. A task he would contemplate very seriously, as he did all the decisions he made for his band. This one would be difficult. He looked upon Ayashe as a sister, and cared much for her.

The flaps of the teepee opened and the white woman poked her head in as if not certain she would enter or not.

He almost grinned. The desire surprised him. He was not happy to see her again. Holding his lips tight, he gestured she should enter.

She pulled her head back out and whispered something he could not decipher, but heard She Who Smiles's soft voice responding.

A moment later, the woman entered. A strange sensation stirring inside him made him frown. Her hair had been combed, but otherwise she looked no different than before. There was still hate in her eyes.

"Tell her to sit down," he told Ayashe in Cheyenne. "And ask her name."

Used to translating, Little One said, "Black Horse says you sit, and tell your name."

"You speak English?" the woman asked, her eyes instantly bright and wide.

"You sit," Little One said.

The woman did so, without glancing his way. "What's your name?" she asked.

"Ayashe, Little One. What they call you?"

"Lorna, my name is Lorna Bradford. Where are my friends? Where are our wagons?"

Although not necessary, the routine was for Ayashe to translate everything said into Cheyenne, and she did so.

Black Horse pondered the woman's name for a moment, and wished he could say it aloud, for it sounded odd in his head. He responded by saying her friends and wagons were safe, and waited for that to be translated by Little One.

"Safe? Where? Where are they?"

Little One repeated what the woman had said, and then told the white woman that he had questions he wanted her to answer.

"I won't tell him anything until I'm told where my

friends are," the woman responded, giving him a solid glare.

Black Horse held his response until Little One repeated the command. He lifted a brow and shook his head. Once again in Cheyenne, he said, "Tell her she is in no position to demand things."

Upon hearing his words translated, the woman crossed her arms and glared harder.

He lifted his chin just as bold and defiant, silently telling her he could sit here as long as she could. Longer. They would not break camp to follow the buffalo until a scouting party returned with news that they had found the main herd. Only stragglers had been spotted so far, but the Sun Dance had been performed. The sacred buffalo skull, stuffed with grass to assure plenty of vegetation for the buffalo and therefore plenty of buffalo for the people, sat near the sun pole in the center of the village, rejuvenating its soul to call out to the great herds. The herds would soon arrive. Sweet Medicine never failed.

His thoughts returned to the white woman. The idea of her in his lodge when darkness arrived stirred his blood. Turning to Little One, he said, "Tell her once she answers my questions, you will take her to her friends."

Little One was still speaking when Lorna started shaking her head. "No, tell him to bring them here, to his tent, or teepee, or whatever you call it. Once I see they are unhurt, I'll answer his questions."

Black Horse bit the tip of his tongue. Unhurt? Who did she think they were? The Comanche? While Little One repeated what the woman had said, Black Horse kept his stare leveled on Poeso—a much more fitting name than Lorna. If he had called one of the other women into his lodge in the first place, he would already have his answers.

Never shifting his gaze, he told Little One to find a

camp crier to run and tell the warrior families to bring the other women to his lodge.

Without question, Little One rose.

Poeso grabbed Little One's arm. "Where are you going?" Fear once again clouded her blue eyes when she turned on him. "Where are you sending her?"

Although her fear did not please him, Black Horse offered no answer. Neither did Little One as she broke free and slipped out of the lodge. Poeso started to rise, but he grabbed her arm, forcing her to stay put.

"Let go of me, you brute," she whispered.

The fear flashing in her eyes turned his stomach cold. She tried to twist from his hold; and though he considered letting her go, he knew she would run if he did. For a brief second, he considered telling her—in her language—that she was in no danger, but chose against it. Little One would return soon.

"You are nothing but a beast, a heathen," she said between her teeth, hissing like a cat. "And I want my gun back."

The thought of her little gun made him grin.

"You think that's funny? You think it's funny to abuse a woman?"

He was far from abusing her. If she calmed her temper she would know that. He rather liked her hissing and snapping. It made her eyes sparkle and her cheeks turn red. Furthermore, few women dared speak to him so. None. Not in a very long time. Hopping Rabbit used to snap at him when they were married. He had given her the name Hopping Rabbit then, after she'd become his wife, because of how she used to hop about the lodge.

Holding his breath, he waited for the pain that appeared in his chest whenever he thought of his dead wife to build, and then let it go as he blew out the air. It had been two winters and two summers since she had died. Their baby, still inside her, had died, too. That was the way. Death was part of the continuation of life. Everything came from and went back to the earth to rebirth another time, but the end of one life had never hurt him like Hopping Rabbit's. He never blamed himself for the death of someone as he did his wife and child. Because he had killed them.

A white man at the fort, not a soldier, but one who trades many things, had said Hopping Rabbit would like the white material. It was tiny and soft and had flowers sewn on it. Little One had called it a handkerchief, and Hopping Rabbit had liked it. She held it to her nose, drawing in its smell and smiling. For two days. On the third she became ill. On the fifth, she died. One Who Heals said it was the white man's sickness. That her medicine could not stop the white man's poison.

"I know you can hear me. You might not understand my words, but you can hear me."

Black Horse sighed as his attention returned to the white woman. The Shoshone, miles and miles away, could probably hear her. He did not need that. Did not need his or any band believing he was befriending the white man.

"Where did you go?" she asked as Little One entered the lodge. "What did you do?"

Little One smiled as she sat down, but said nothing. Pride filled him. She was more Cheyenne than white.

"What? You can only speak when he tells you?" Poeso asked. "Speak only when spoken to? You can't live your life like that. You have to stand up for yourself. Speak your own mind. If you give a man an inch, they'll take a mile. Don't let this beast rule you. You—"

"My brother is not a beast," Little One said sharply.

Black Horse's stomach flipped. Little One could be as snippy as this white woman when the need occurred. A trait all white women must possess. He should have called One Who Heals into his lodge. Perhaps her great medicine would work on Poeso.

"And I speak whenever I want," Little One continued. "When I have something to say."

The white woman looked startled, and snapped her lips closed as noises sounded outside the tent. Her gaze shot to him. He told Little One to open the doorway so she could see her friends.

Little One nodded and rose, and then said, "You stay. Just look."

As soon as the flap was pulled back, Poeso shouted, "Meg, Betty, Tillie, are you all right?"

"We're fine, are you?"

"Yes, I'll be out in a minute."

Black Horse waved a hand, and Little One let the flap fall back into place and returned to sit beside him. It took a moment for him to remember what information he wanted from this woman. The wind that had entered his lodge had filled the air with Poeso's scent, and that had stirred a longing in him. "Ask her who those men were at the river."

Little One did so, and "Hoodlums" was Lorna's answer.

That much he knew, but waited for Little One to translate it into bad men. "What did they want?"

She sat quiet for a moment after Little One repeated his question, and glanced toward the flap covering the entrance of his lodge. "Ever since Betty's husband died, Jacob Lerber, the leader of that group of men, had been watching her, waiting to catch her alone. We were all part of the same wagon train, until Tillie became ill after her husband died. That's when Meg and Betty and I took her and left the wagon train. She needed a doctor. We found one, and as soon as she was better we continued on. We are on our way to California. We don't have anything of value. Just the supplies we need. There is no reason to keep us here. We won't tell anyone where your camp is, if that's what he's afraid of. In truth, we hope we don't see anyone along the way. Four women traveling alone might look like an easy target, but we aren't. We have weapons."

Black Horse found himself biting his lips together to keep from grinning at how she contradicted herself, and at her mention of weapons. A tiny pistol and old rifle were not weapons. He noted something else while she spoke. Her voice was like that of the people from across the great waters. His father called it England. Where many of the white men come from. Long ago they crossed the great water to take land away from various Indian tribes. They broke promises and angered many. Several tribes, including the Southern Cheyenne along with their Arapaho allies raided unprotected settlements and wagon trains. The retribution of that was still to come. Black Horse had envisioned that would happen when the white men stopped their war against each other. One Who Heals had confirmed it.

Little One told him, "I'm not repeating all that."

Black Horse nodded and gave himself time to settle his roaming thoughts. The white men fighting each other was good for the tribes. The more men killed, the fewer the Indians needed to battle. Peace and harmony had been the way of Tsitsistas for many generations, long before they had to start following the buffalo to feed their families. He strived for that kind of peace, the kind his father's father had told stories about. Such harmony could not be found with mistrust living between the bands and the white man. Too many tricks had been played by the white man's gifts and words. Just as the white trader had tricked him with the poison in the gift he had brought home to Hopping Rabbit, others had been tricked, and others had died. Their poison took many shapes and arrived in many ways. This did not make him hate all white men or seek to harm them. That would spoil his blood, and that of his tribe. A leader could not do that, but he listened carefully to his insides when it came to trusting anyone.

"Did you tell him what I said?" Poeso asked.

"Yes," Little One answered.

"It didn't sound like it."

"The Cheyenne language is different from yours," Little One explained. "It is easier."

"It doesn't sound easier," she answered.

In order to hide his grin, Black Horse told Little One, "Ask her if others are coming. Going to California. Like her. Holy women dressed in black."

"No," the woman answered when Little One translated his question. "We aren't real nuns. We bought the outfits in Missouri as disguises. It was Meg's idea. Said we'd be safer wearing them. We gave Betty and Tillie our extra ones after their husbands died and we left the wagon train."

Black Horse withheld another grin as Little One repeated portions of what had been said. For someone not set on speaking, Poeso said plenty. He turned to Little One. "Tell her they are welcome to spend the night in our camp and leave in the morning."

Little One frowned, but nodded and did as instructed.

"We don't want to spend the night," she said. "We'll leave now."

He waved a hand, signaling that was fine with him. He was done with this white woman. Their outfits would keep them safe from other tribes. Many thought those kind of holy white women had special powers. He knew better, but it made no difference, and he would tell his warriors to watch for the white men and steal their horses again if needed.

When Little One finished saying she could leave, Poeso turned to him. "I'll take my gun now."

He laughed. "Tell her she can have it after she rides away."

"After I ride away? That would be impossible," she said after Little One translated.

"My brother is done with you," Little One replied. "You leave lodge. See your friends."

"I'm not leaving without my gun," she insisted.

Little One looked at him. She was as frustrated with this woman as he. Which was not surprising. Little One was even more wary of whites than he. Black Horse shrugged his shoulder. He would not give this woman her pistol, no matter how tiny it was, until she was far away. "Tell her a brave will follow them as far as the river and give it to her then."

That seemed to satisfy both of them, and in unison, Little One and the white woman rose to their feet. Neither bid farewell. He did not expect them to, but did wonder what would become of this woman. This *poeso*. She had the spirit of a mountain lion, and he allowed a grin to form at that thought. If those men from the river were smart, they would forget about these women, especially this one. She was filled with trouble and sprouted it as she walked.

Lorna couldn't get out of the teepee fast enough. The chief didn't frighten her, but he did make her blood boil. He was so arrogant and haughty, she wanted to— Her train of thought stopped right there. Rushing forward, she hugged each of her friends.

"You are all right?" she asked. "No one hurt you?"

"Heavens, no," Tillie said. "They have been so kind. I had a delightful lunch."

"I did, too," Betty supplied. "With a wonderful couple who had three little boys, and…"

Lorna stopped listening to turn to Meg. Once again, the look on her friend's face almost stopped her heart. "Meg? Meg, what is it?"

Meg didn't turn her way, and Lorna spun to see what was holding her friend's interest so deeply that she'd all but turned to stone.

Little One was staring back at Meg, and frowning, as if confused.

Lorna bounced a glance between the two of them, wondering what each of them saw. Neither of them was frightening. In fact, other than that Little One had brown skin and Meg white, the two looked vaguely similar to one another.

Meg finally spoke, but it was to Little One. "Carolyn?"

"No," Lorna said, "her name is Little One. The Cheyenne call her Aleaha, or something like that."

"Carolyn." Meg pulled the habit off her head. "It's me, Margaret. Your sister."

Lorna was not expecting that. Neither was Betty or Tillie, considering how they gasped. She spun, only to spy Little One with one hand clasped across her mouth and tears trickling down her cheeks.

Turning back toward Meg, Lorna felt her shoulders slumping. Meg was crying, too, and the next moment, Meg and Little One were hugging.

A cold shiver rippled Lorna's spine, and she turned all the way around. Black Horse had left his tent, and the look on his face made her stomach clench. He wasn't impressed by what he saw, either.

Chapter Five

Once again, Lorna found herself seated in the chief's tent, but now her friends sat beside her. Little One, Black Horse, and an old woman called One Who Heals completed the circle. Unlike the one she'd called Smile, this older woman's long hair was completely gray and stringy, and deep wrinkles covered her face. And Lorna doubted this woman had smiled in years.

"Isn't it amazing?" Tillie whispered. "Meg finding her younger sister. They look so much alike."

"I know," Betty answered. "They have the same brown eyes and black hair. Oh, I'm so happy I could cry."

"Me, too," Tillie replied. "It's a miracle."

Stuck between the two of them, Lorna pulled her eyes off the old woman to whisper, "Miracle?"

They nodded. Lorna drew in a deep breath and counted to ten. Everyone in the camp had brown eyes and black hair, but that didn't matter. Her thoughts were on the situation and there wasn't a good outcome from this little family reunion. If the sisters wanted to stay together, that meant either Meg stayed here, leaving the rest of them with no one to guide them to California, or Little One—Carolyn— came with them, which wasn't about to happen by the look on Black Horse's face.

The man hadn't impressed her before, but now, the way he glared at Meg as if she had eight legs and multiple eyes, had Lorna's ire growing by the second.

Betty and Tillie were acting as if they were witnessing a *miracle*. She shushed them by saying, "It's not a miracle." When they glanced at her, one on each side, she nodded across the small circle. "They don't think so, either."

Black Horse and the old woman, One Who Heals, were arguing. At least that was what it sounded like. It was hard to determine considering their strange language sounded harsh no matter what was said. The two of them, Black Horse and the old woman that Little One had told Meg was a medicine woman, barely waited for the other one to stop talking before they started, making it impossible to follow. He kept repeating one word. *Hova'ahane*. She'd heard him use it before, back at the river, but hadn't known what it meant back then, and couldn't figure it out now, either.

The hide dress the old woman wore was decorated with a unique design that looked like four arrows crossing each other, which she kept pointing to while releasing long and complicated words that at times rhymed with one another, making it hard to know if she was repeating things or not.

Black Horse made no hand gestures or facial expressions, other than to glare at Meg as if she was a bug he'd like to squash. That alone increased Lorna's ire.

"What are they saying?" Tillie asked.

"I don't know," Lorna answered, looking toward Meg. Her friend didn't look her way, no matter how hard Lorna tried to get her attention. Instead, Meg kept her eyes on Black Horse, with her chin up. Lorna admired Meg right then, more so than before perhaps. Meg wasn't bowing to this man like she had back at the river. It was about time.

When Little One joined in the argument, he cut a hand through the air. *"Nehetaa'e. Ne'haatovestse."*

The two Indian women looked at each other, but it was Little One who spoke. *"Hova'ahane. Ne'haatovestse."*

Lorna wished she knew what they were saying. What they were repeating. It was so frustrating. She couldn't join in without knowing what they were arguing about. The subject was obvious. Meg and Little One being sisters, which was also very complex.

Little One rattled off several long and convoluted words, but Lorna recognized a beseeching tone in the young woman's voice, and no one could miss the pleading in her eyes. It was clear Black Horse saw it. He rubbed his forehead before he said something soft and almost gentle.

Both the older and young woman smiled, and Little One reached over and patted his knee. He sat cross-legged, and laid a hand on top of hers. The look the two of them shared made Lorna's stomach gurgle. One didn't need to be an Indian to read what passed between them. These two loved each other. Good heavens, were they married? Is that why he was arguing so fiercely? Fearing his wife might leave with her newfound sister?

Lorna pressed a hand to one of her temples. This whole situation was bad enough. Meg's sister didn't need to be married to the chief to make it worse.

"My brother, the Great Chief Black Horse..." Little One started.

Lorna snapped her head up. That was right. Little One had called him her brother earlier. A sigh of relief snagged in Lorna's throat. That was impossible. He couldn't be Little One's brother. That would make him Meg's brother, too.

"...has many questions."

Lorna's patience was wearing thin. They all had many questions, and this wasn't getting them answered. "What does *hova'ahane ne'haatovestse* mean?" she interrupted.

The way she said it didn't sound exactly as they had, so she explained, "You two kept saying that to one another."

Little One glanced at Black Horse and when he finally nodded, she said, "*Hova'ahane* means no, and *ne'haatovestse* means listen to me."

Lorna gave a slight nod while letting that settle. Seemed like a long word to mean no. "What's *nehetaa'e* mean?"

"Enough."

Lorna nodded again. It made sense. He'd used that word to stop the braves from circling the wagon upon their arrival.

"My brother make…" Little One paused and tapped her chin with one finger as if she was thinking about what to say next. "Request," she said. "He has request of you. All you."

There was no surprise in that. "What is it?" Lorna asked.

"Black Horse has a secret," Little One said softly. "Must keep guarded."

Lorna didn't move, but shifted her eyes between the woman and man sitting across from her. A guarded secret? That they were married and pretended to be siblings?

"Few in our band know that One Who Heals and Black Horse understand and speak the English language, and…"

"Can speak—" Lorna had to draw in a breath as anger exploded inside her, and her attention snapped to Black Horse. "You've understood every word I've said?"

The sly grin on his lips made her want to march out the door. She would if she had someplace to go. Without Meg's directional guidance, she'd never get all the way to California. She could get lost in Hyde Park. Had more than once. In all fairness, it was a large park.

"Yes," Black Horse said before he nodded to Little One.

"He wants your word you will not tell others," the Indian woman said.

"Our word?" Lorna spat. "He'll get no such—"

"Please?" Little One said softly. "I do not want to have to translate every word said."

"Of course he has our word," Meg said before turning to the rest of their misfit group. "Doesn't he?"

Twittering like little birds, Betty and Tillie agreed instantly. Lorna, looking at Meg, shook her head, until the pleading in her friend's eyes was more than she could take. Then she turned to him. "I won't make any promises."

He said something to Little One, and though Lorna didn't know the words, she understood the meaning. It was as close to *I told you* as if he'd spoken those exact words.

Little One and Black Horse started conversing again, but stopped quickly when the older woman made a hissing sound.

The top of Lorna's head started tingling as the woman's deep-set eyes glared her way.

"Speaking *Mo'ohta Mo'ehno'ha* knowledge will split tongue like snake," the old woman said.

Meg whispered, "*Mo'ohta Mo'ehno'ha* means Black Horse."

Lorna had figured that out by the way the old woman had pointed at him. Although One Who Heals reminded Lorna of an old crone in a nightmarish fairy tale, she wasn't falling for any such foolery, nor was she scared. She'd stopped believing in fairy tales—good and bad ones—years ago. "No, it won't."

Expecting a full argument, Lorna was taken aback when One Who Heals merely shrugged.

"Agree," Meg said coldly. "For once, Lorna, just agree."

"I've been agreeing with things—"

"This time your life depends on it," Meg interrupted. "All our lives depend on it."

All of their lives had been depending on things since they started this journey west, so that wasn't anything new.

"What if that was your sister?" Betty asked quietly, "Wouldn't you want—"

"No," Lorna snapped. There was no one in her family she ever wanted to see again. She had no siblings, but that wasn't the issue. Letting the air out of her lungs, as hard as it was, she had to admit, at this moment in time, conceding was her best choice. "Fine," she said. "I won't tell anyone." It wasn't as if any of the Indians would understand her anyway. Not unless they also knew English, like their leader. Some leader he was, keeping secrets from his people.

All eyes were on her, but no one spoke. When the silence grew thick, Lorna sighed again. "I said I won't tell anyone."

The glint in Black Horse's eyes said he didn't believe her, but he turned toward Meg. "Why you say Ayashe your sister?"

"Because she is," Meg answered. "She was captured when our wagon train was attacked ten years ago. By the Dog Men of a Southern Cheyenne band. She was six, and I was ten."

"Why not capture you?" he asked.

Lorna's teeth dug deeper into her bottom lip. She wanted to hear Meg's answer, but could see the tears glistening in her friend's eyes, and that made her angry with Black Horse for asking. If Meg had wanted to share that part, she already would have. When Meg closed her eyes briefly, Lorna said, "What does that matter?"

Black Horse gave her a cold glance before turning back to Meg.

Meg was twisting her hands together and her lips quivered.

"You don't have to tell him," Lorna said.

Meg let out a breath and nodded. "Yes, I do." Lifting her gaze to Black Horse, she answered, "Because I hid and they didn't find me. My father was the wagon master. When the scout returned saying the water hole we needed to reach had dried up, he and several other men rode ahead to search for another water hole. That's when the Indians attacked. While we were camped. I had wandered away from the wagons, not for any particular reason, just exploring as I often did. When I heard the commotion, I hid in the rocks." Tears trickled down her cheeks. "I stayed there until it was over, and…and until my father returned."

Sitting beside Meg, Little One reached over and squeezed Meg's hand. "I glad you did. I glad you hid and not captured."

"Pa never stopped looking for you," Meg said. "He died looking for you, and I promised him I'd find you."

Things started clicking in Lorna's mind. Before she could stop herself, she asked, "This was your plan all along, wasn't it? To find your sister. It wasn't to go to California at all."

There was anguish in Meg's eyes, but also honesty. "Yes. My father guided trains west every year, mainly to learn where Carolyn might be. Two years ago, when he finally admitted I was old enough, he let me join him. He'd discovered the tribe that had taken her had left her with a northern band years ago. He fell ill and died before we could head out again. No one would hire me to guide a train, and I didn't have enough money to go out on my own."

Lorna's stomach turned hard. She felt as betrayed now as she had back in England. "So you convinced me to outfit your wagon and insisted we take the northern route just so you could find her. That's why you wanted to separate from the rest of the train, and why you said we should go swimming today, and…"

"I said we could go swimming because we were all hot," Meg said. "I didn't know we were near Black Horse's camp."

"But you hoped," Lorna said. Meg's duplicity was eating at her insides. "You were hoping and didn't care what happened to the rest of us." It shouldn't surprise her. No one had ever cared what happened to her.

"That's not true," Meg said softly. "I've cared what's happened to all of you. I've—"

"No arguing, now," Betty piped in, although it was in a whisper. "Not in front of our hosts."

"Betty's right," Tillie said. "Besides, one for all and all for one."

Lorna wanted to scream, but bit her lips together.

Meg turned to Black Horse. "I've been looking for my sister for ten years. She is the only family I have."

His arms were folded across his chest, and Lorna folded hers in the exact way. Perhaps because of the way his gaze once again moved to settle on her. She didn't want to admit it, but her fate lay in this man's hands. At least, for the moment it did. The very thing she'd sworn would never happen again.

"You stay," he said.

"Stay?" she replied. "No, we won't. Meg can stay, but the rest of us are leaving."

"No," he said. "You stay. You all stay until Ayashe decides to return to the white world or stay with Tsitsistas."

"No, we won't—"

"Nehetaa'e!"

His fast and harsh snap made a tingle zip up Lorna's spine.

Little One pulled on Meg's hand as she stood. "My

brother has said that is enough. We go now. You come my lodge."

"I don't care if he said that's enough or not," Lorna stated, the tingle in her spine had fused into anger. "We haven't agreed to anything. Nor will we be told what to do."

Betty and Tillie pulled on her arms, attempting to lift her off the ground. Lorna shook them off and told them to sit back down, but they continued to plead with her to get up. The old woman and Black Horse started conversing in Cheyenne again, angrily, which rattled her nerves to no end. This entire escapade was ridiculous. Jumping to her feet, she told Betty and Tillie, "Meg can stay, but we are leaving."

"We can't leave her here," Betty said.

"She didn't leave me, and I won't leave her," Tillie said with more determination than she'd shown since leaving Missouri. "I can't believe you'd suggest we should, Sister Lorna."

Frustration bubbled inside her. "I'm not a sister," she snapped. "I'm not anyone's sister, and neither are you." The sadness on Tillie's face stabbed her. It wasn't as if she wanted to leave Meg, either, but she didn't want to be a prisoner. A captive like Little One.

"A couple of days won't hurt," said Betty softly.

"This won't be settled in a couple of days," Lorna insisted, glancing back to where One Who Heals and Black Horse sat. They had stopped arguing and were glaring at her. Both of them. With eyes full of disgust. The hair on the back of her neck quivered and she turned to watch Betty and Tillie, as well as Meg and Little One move toward the flap doorway. She followed. Convincing the others to leave would be easier outside, away from this beast of a man and scary old woman.

She'd only taken one step, for the area wasn't very large, when Little One blocked her way. "You must stay."

"We'll discuss that outside," Lorna said.

"No."

Lorna turned toward the old woman, who stepped up beside Little One.

"You stay inside," Little One added.

Far more than a shiver rippled her this time. Lorna attempted to push her way toward the doorway. "No, I won't."

For as tiny as she was, the grasp Little One used on both of Lorna's arms was strong. "You stay my brother's lodge."

"No, I won't," she repeated.

"One Who Heals not trust you," Little One said. "Say Black Horse must keep you."

The white woman's hiss filled the lodge as she spun to look at him. Black Horse rose to his feet. White people were trouble, and this one woman was more of a problem than one hundred soldiers. She was not dangerous, but a nuisance. One he did not need. One Who Heals did not trust this *poeso*, said this white woman will cause many fights among his people. He believed that and did not want fighting. A shiver rippled his spine. He did not want her screeching in his lodge day and night, either.

His mind and heart were troubled enough. Little One could choose to leave with these women. It was a decision she must make herself and he would stand by her choice, but he did not want others to influence her during this time. She needed to find the answers inside herself, not from the mouths of others.

He stepped across the center of the lodge and took the white woman by the arm. She started kicking and shouting as he told the others to leave. They left swiftly, but not fast enough. She had caught his shin with her heels three times. Frustrated, he knocked her off her feet, and by the time she'd landed on her bottom, he had retrieved a strip of rawhide from his pile of tools and weapons. He must seek wisdom, and could not do that with disruptions.

"What are you doing?" she shouted as he grabbed both of her hands.

It was not his way to respond, or to be dissuaded by her shouts as he tied her hands behind her back. He used a second strip to tie her ankles together. Once done, he stood, satisfied she would not interfere with his duties.

She flung aside the mass of curls flowing over her face and shoulders with a snap of her head. "What do you think you're doing?"

Not trusting her any more than he would a wildcat, he gathered up one more rawhide strip, threaded it between the one on her wrists and tied the other end to a lodge pole. Then he gave her a satisfied nod.

"You can't do this!" she shouted.

Black Horse said nothing as he left the lodge. Her shouts continued to fill the air while he ordered a young boy to stand guard. No one would enter his lodge without invitation, and no one wanted to be near a screeching *poeso*, but if she did manage to get loose, the boy would ensure she did not get far.

His people were going about their duties, seeing to their chores and homes as usual, but questions hung in the air. The news of Little One's sister arriving had spread faster than if the camp crier had shouted it while running from one end of the village to the other, and everyone wanted to know what he would to do about it.

Black Horse held in a sigh and turned about. The news hung as heavy inside him as it did over the village. Many in his band had feared encounters with the white man because of Little One. They did not want her taken away, nor did they want to be blamed for her capture. As their leader, he could not let such things affect his actions.

He walked around his lodge and past the next row of homes, and the next until coming to the outskirts of the village. Putting one foot in front of the other, he kept going past the large herds of horses overseen by a group of older boys and onward through the tall grass and up the hill where trees grew beside the twisting and turning creek.

The familiar thud of hooves behind him brought a smile to his face. Most often, in times like this, when he needed time to see past his heart, he did so inside his lodge, and Horse must wonder why he was venturing away from the camp. "We do not need these troubles," he told the animal. "The white men are restless, and so are The People."

Black Horse picked out a tree that offered enough shade for both him and Horse and there he sat, resting his back against the rough bark of the tree's trunk. Horse nudged his shoulder and Black Horse ran a hand down the animal's long face before he set both palms upon his knees and closed his eyes.

The white men could use these women as a reason to attack, to kill mothers and fathers and sons and daughters. He did not want that for his people. Yet, in his heart, he did not want Little One to be hurt by his sending her sister away. It was no different than if she had been an Arapaho or Sioux or any other Nation. Little One had the right to know her family.

Horse snorted and then started munching on the grass, and Black Horse allowed his mind to envision the animal eating. They were one and the same, he and this great animal, and he waited for their shared wisdom to fill his body and soul. Animals did not think with their hearts, and he could not, either.

He willed his mind to go deeper, to the earth that provided the sweet grass for Horse and the buffalo that fed his people. He gave his thanks for the grass and for the many other great gifts the earth provided them daily. The food the women gathered that grew wild and lush nearby, the fish gathered out of the stream, the living water collected each morning. Letting his thoughts go, he continued praising all that was given to his people.

When the vision behind his eyes became the image of a black stallion standing on a hill, he drew in a long breath of air in order to become one with the stallion. His mind was now clear and open to accept the wisdom that would be shown to him.

A valley appeared, complete with a great herd of mares grazing peacefully with colts and fillies prancing around their mothers. Pride filled the stallion as he reared onto his hind legs, and a deep sense of harmony filled Black Horse. This was what he sought.

Suddenly the herd of mares erupted. As the horses scattered in all directions, Black Horse's heart started to pound when in the center of the fleeing mares a mountain lion appeared. Sleek and purposeful, it paid little notice to the disruption as it crossed the valley and started to climb the hill. Its glowing eyes never left the black stallion.

One by one, his muscles tightened, like the stallion's as the horse prepared for battle. The lion never slowed in its approached, but it did transform, taking on the shape of a horse. A magnificent mare with a coat of glistening brown and a mane of long curls.

The stallion lifted his head to sniff the air, and Black Horse felt a surge race through him as the mare topped the hill. The stallion stomped a foot and snorted, his nostrils flaring at the mare's intoxicating scent. She tossed her head and stepped closer, nickering sweetly.

Black Horse wrenched his eyes open and jumped to his feet.

The vision had shattered, but left remnants behind. His pulse was pounding beneath his skin, desire burned hot in his loins and the scent of the white woman filled his nose.

Horse nickered behind him. Black Horse turned to glare at the stallion. Animals did not think with their hearts, but other parts of their bodies did drive their actions. Horse snorted and lowered his head back to the grass, and Black Horse turned toward the village. Much like the vision, he was upon a knoll, looking down upon the valley where his village sat. All was calm and peaceful. People moved about slowly. He drew in a long breath of air. He rarely questioned his visions, but this time, he did. Unlike the stallion, a sweet-smelling female could not influence him.

A movement caught his eye, and he squinted to pinpoint exactly where and what. A frown tugged on his brow when he realized his lodge was wobbling. Shaking as if assaulted by a strong wind, and then, right before his eyes, it buckled.

The next moment, much like in his vision, chaos hit. His once quiet village erupted as all ran to see what had caused his lodge to collapse.

He glanced toward the sky briefly, and then, knowing he must leave his place of meditation, started down the hill.

Chapter Six

Panic filled her, but try as she might, Lorna couldn't move. She must have broken something. A leg, an arm, her back. She couldn't even breathe. The weight of the lodge was crushing. It took all she had to twist enough so her face was no longer smashed into the ground. She gulped for air, but very little would go in. The pressure of the pile on top of her was too great.

When the weight shifted slightly, she struggled to shout, "Help me, please."

Her plea came out as little more than a whisper. The weight was too great. Tears stung her eyes and she couldn't hold them back. Not this time. She was going to die. Killed by a collapsing teepee.

Noises filtered past her internal whimpering, and the next moment the weight was gone. Taking in long gasps of air, she attempted to move, but her hands were still tied behind her back. Her shoulders, which she'd thought had already gone numb, started to burn as if they'd been singed by fire.

Lying on the ground, all she could see were moccasin-covered feet, but her sense of dignity returned. "Help me up," she demanded. "Someone help me up."

Someone did. The moment the solid hands grasped her waist, she knew who it was, and started shouting, "See what you did? You almost killed me, you heathen. Tying me up like that."

He set her on her feet, which were still tied together, and she would have tumbled over if he'd completely let go. A fact that irritated her more. She opened her mouth to start spouting off all the insults forming in her mind, but didn't have a chance to let them out before familiar faces gathered around her.

"Goodness, Lorna, are you all right?" Betty asked patting her cheeks.

"No, I'm not all right," she answered, twisting her face away from her friend's touch. "My hands and feet are tied and a teepee just fell on top of me." Setting her gaze on Meg, she said, "Tell your sister to make this heathen untie me."

Although there was anguish on her face, Meg shook her head. "I can't."

"Yes, you can," Lorna insisted.

"It wouldn't do any good for me to ask," Meg said. "He doesn't trust you."

Lorna twisted to glare at the man keeping her upright by holding her arm.

"He probably doesn't trust you even more now that you knocked down his home," Tillie piped in. "Thank goodness you aren't injured. You could have been crushed."

"Could have been? I *was* crushed."

"But you aren't injured," Tillie said.

"I won't know until I'm untied," she screeched, looking at Black Horse.

His hands once again grasped her waist. Without a word he picked her off the ground and carried her a few feet away from the mass of commotion near the remnants of his teepee. A group of ten or so women were dismantling the poles from the hide.

Wanting him far away from her, Lorna shook at his hold. "Let go of me, you beast!" When he didn't, she asked, "Aren't you going to help them?"

His expression, a stern, hard one, didn't change. There wasn't even a flicker of his eyes to say he'd heard her.

"It's *your* teepee," she told him, glancing in the direction of his gaze.

"Women take care of the lodges," Meg said. "Just like in our society."

Somewhat amazed, Lorna couldn't pull her eyes off the Indian women. They reminded her of a hive of worker bees. Without a word, as if each one already knew exactly what to do, they had the poles separated from the hide and were already re-erecting them. It was astonishing how quickly and efficiently they worked; however, she didn't want to be astonished. Turning to Meg, she pointed out, "Women in *our society* don't *build* houses."

"Maybe not in England," Betty said, "but here we do. I helped…"

Lorna stopped listening and turned her full attention on Meg. They had been friends. Best friends from the day they'd met, and she felt deceived. Hurt.

Meg reached out a hand and laid it on a shoulder that still stung. Still burned.

"I know you're mad at me, Lorna," she said. "And I don't blame you, but can you just—"

"Just what?" Lorna demanded. "Let these savages kill us?"

"They aren't going to kill us," Meg said following a long sigh.

"You don't know that," Lorna insisted. "You aren't the one tied up."

"And you wouldn't be, either, if you would just calm down."

"Calm down?"

"Yes."

Lorna bit back another retort when tears glistened in Meg's eyes. She was still mad, and tears wouldn't ease that. Not even her own, which she refused to allow to take root. "You should have told me, Meg. Told me the reason you were heading west was to find your sister. Are you forgetting I'm the one who paid for all of our supplies? Mine and yours?"

"No, I haven't," Meg said. "And I know I should have told you, but you—"

"I'd have found someone else to partner up with," Lorna said. "Someone who was focused on going to California." Another thought happened then. "This is why you said we'd winter out here, so you could keep looking."

Meg closed her eyes.

Lorna drew in air through her nose. She'd been betrayed her entire life, and had told herself it was over when she'd met these wonderful new friends. The betrayal hurt worse this time, right to the quick.

"I couldn't let you partner up with someone else," Meg said quietly. "And not just because I needed your financial backing. I didn't lie when I said those wagon trains aren't safe for a woman alone. You witnessed that. If we hadn't been dressed as nuns, Lord knows what would have happened to us." Lifting her chin stanchly, she asked, "Where do you think you'd be right now if we hadn't partnered up?"

"I don't know," Lorna answered honestly. "But I sure as hell wouldn't be here."

"Lorna!" Tillie admonished.

Snapping her head in Tillie's direction, Lorna seethed,

"Don't tell me not to cuss." Including Betty in her sweeping gaze, she added, "Don't any of you tell me anything."

Betty's chin quivered as she said, "Fine. Be that way." Spinning around, she marched away.

Tillie, blinking back as many tears as Betty had been, pressed a finger beneath her nose before she said, "I hope you get used to those ropes." She, too, then turned about and walked away.

Refusing to let anything show, especially how rotten her insides felt, Lorna settled her gaze on Meg. Waiting for her to desert her, too.

"I am sorry I didn't tell you," Meg said. "But I'd do it all over again if I had to. I've been looking for Carolyn for years. She needs time to get to know me, to decide if she wants to stay here or leave with me. With us. I'm asking you to please just be patient. To give us a week, maybe two, and then, whether Carolyn stays or goes, I'll do everything I can to see you get to California safely. I promise."

As much as she didn't want to admit the rest of them would be lost in a day without Meg, she did want to point something out. "It's not like I have a lot of choices, Meg. None of us do. This predicament you've put us in is pretty set."

"You're wrong, Lorna," Meg said with empathy filling her eyes. "You do have choices. Lots of them."

Still tied together, her feet were going numb from standing in the same position, and she twisted slightly, which only made Black Horse's hold tighten. Glaring at Meg, she said, "Name one."

Meg nodded toward her feet. "Being tied up is because of a choice you made. How would you react to someone coming into your home and calling you names and saying hurtful things?"

That had been exactly what had happened in her home

on a daily basis, but, in this instance, Lorna saw the point Meg was attempting to make, therefore, she pinched her lips together.

"We always have choices, Lorna," Meg said. "Sometimes they aren't the ones we want, but we still have them." Nodding toward Black Horse, Meg said one more thing. "You can choose to believe the Cheyenne are savages, as you called them, or you can choose to believe they are kind and peaceful people who took my sister in and loved her when other tribes would have killed her."

Lorna wasn't sure if it was Meg's words or the way Black Horse nodded at Meg that sent a little tingle up her arm and into the vicinity of her chest. Maybe Meg's words made a lot of sense. Well, in a sense they did, but it could also be that she had come close to dying when that teepee had collapsed on her. Either way, she didn't want things to continue the way they were.

It felt as if she was swallowing her pride, the little bit she'd scavenged when she'd left England, but what had to be done had to be done. Glancing toward Black Horse, she asked, "What do I have to do in order for you to untie me?"

He glanced around.

She bit her bottom lip while waiting.

Meg leaned forward and whispered, "You can start by not expecting him to speak to you in English while others are near."

Lorna held back a growl. This was going to be harder than she expected.

Still whispering, Meg said, "Gaining trust is much more difficult the second time around."

As if she'd had a chance the first time? There, too, Lorna kept her mouth closed. The teepee was standing tall again. It appeared nothing had been damaged when it had toppled. As the other women left, Little One walked up beside Meg. No words were passed, not between the Indian woman and Black Horse or Meg, but the silent communication was clear.

Meg and Little One walked away, and Black Horse once again hoisted her into the air. Lorna didn't appreciate being carried any more than before, but she didn't squirm this time, or protest verbally. When he ducked to carry her inside, she leaned closer, just to make it easier on both of them, although the brush of his bare skin against her cheek sent a fiery shiver down her spine.

The inside looked just as it had before, including how the robes were laid out, and this time, that was where he set her down. On her bottom, which she was grateful for considering her legs probably wouldn't work if how they were tingling was any indication. Accepting what would happen was partially her choice, she said, "Thank you."

He chuckled and the twinkle in his eyes had her pinching her lips together. This time to keep a smile at bay. An oddity. One she didn't want to fathom.

"That irritates me," she said instead.

He lifted a brow.

"That," she said. "How you understand every word I say, but pretend as if you don't. You're even convincing at it."

Sitting down in front of her, he pulled a knife from his waistband. "My people would not understand why I not tell them I know the white man's words."

Assuming he would use the knife to cut her bindings, she stretched her legs out. "Why?"

He frowned slightly.

Lorna bowed her head to accept her own punishment. He had no reason to trust her, and she knew what that was like. Unable to trust, unable to believe anyone had your best interests at heart. "I'm sorry," she said, and truly meant it. There were so many things she'd thought she'd left behind, so much pain, but in truth it had just been buried inside her, waiting for a chance to sprout, much like garden seed. "I am. Sorry, that is, and I won't tell anyone. I promise."

The twinkle had left his eyes, but they were still soft when he looked at her.

"I don't break promises," she said quietly. "I've had too many people break them against me."

"Your friend Meg?"

She nodded. "Yes and no. She didn't break a promise as much as she didn't tell me the entire truth."

"There is a difference?"

"Yes, there is a difference." Lorna wasn't about to try to explain that. It would take her too far down memory lane, and that was one choice she did have—not to remember, at least whenever she could help it. "So," she said, nodding toward the knife. "What do I have to do in order for you to untie me?"

The twinkle was back in his eyes, and the grin on his face made him look anything but fierce.

"Hold still," he said.

With a knife that size coming at her, she'd most certainly hold still. An hour ago she'd have been screaming to see such a weapon. Something Meg had said must have struck a chord. These people certainly could have killed Little One, but they hadn't. She was looked upon as the chief's sister. In any society, being the leader's sister was a lofty position.

He removed the leather strap from her ankles and signaled for her to turn around. While doing so, she wondered if perhaps Black Horse didn't look fierce now because actually he hadn't earlier, either. Other than in her mind. That was a perplexing thought. But when she thought on it a bit harder, she clearly remembered the way he'd looked back at the river. He had been fierce looking. Extremely so.

As soon as the leather let loose, her hands began to tingle. Burn actually, as did her shoulders as she brought her arms forward to rub her hands together against the pins-and-needles sting assaulting them.

After setting the knife aside, he took her hands and rubbed them between his palms, which erupted an entirely different kind of sensation inside her.

She pulled her hands from his hold.

"They stop stinging soon," he said.

"Already did," she lied, not wanting him to rub them again. She didn't like to be touched. Up until she'd started traveling with Tillie and Betty, she'd never been hugged. Not since she was a child and her father was alive. Those two were always hugging, and touching. It had taken her some time to get used to it. Her father had hugged her, but that had been so long ago, she'd forgotten how it felt, and for some reason, didn't want to remember.

Throwing those thoughts aside, she once again asked, "So why haven't you told your people you know the white man's language?" Shaking her head, she added, "It seems odd to call it that."

"Why?"

She shrugged. "Because I've never thought of it that way. Where I come from people speak many different languages."

"You are not from this land."

"I haven't been in America very long, but I was born here."

"You come across the great water?"

She nodded. "On a ship with many other people."

"Why you go to California?"

The way he said California, almost as if it had more syllables and was part of a song, made her smile. He grinned, too, and there was the faintest hint of red on his cheeks. It made him appear more approachable, and she chose to use that. "I'll make you a deal. You tell me why your people don't know you speak English, and I'll tell you why I have to get to California."

He shook his head slightly, not negatively, but more like he was amused she was willing to bargain with him. *"Epeva'e."*

"What does that mean? *Epeva'e?"* She mangled the word worse than he had *California.*

"Epeva'e," he repeated slowly.

"Epeva'e," she tried again, getting closer to it sounding like how he'd said it.

He nodded as if he approved. "It is good."

"It is good that I can say it?"

He smiled. *"Epeva'e* means it is good. All right."

"Oh, *epeva'e."* Complete understanding hit her then. "Oh, so you will tell me?"

"Heehe'e," he said. "Yes, I will tell you."

She couldn't help from pointing out. "That is the oddest word for yes."

His smile increased. "The English have odd words."

The ease that had grown between them was relaxing, and welcoming. "We could argue over odd words for a year," she said. "And how people keep coming up with new ones." She'd discovered that upon landing in New York. Words she'd known her entire life meant different things over here than back in England. More interested than before, she said, "You go first."

He appeared thoughtful before saying, "When Little One was left here by the Southern Cheyenne, she had to give up her old ways."

"Why?"

"It is the way."

Lorna waited for more, when it didn't come, she asked, "That's it? It is the way?"

"Yes, she needed to become one of us."

"Just like that?"

He nodded.

"Isn't that asking a lot?" In her mind it certainly was. "I mean, she was kidnapped off a train, and then told to no longer be that person. That's impossible. And wrong."

He frowned slightly, but then shook his head. "The Southern Cheyenne have much bitterness against white men. The Northern Cheyenne want peace with all."

The conversation was detouring slightly, but she found it interesting. "I read books about Indians, and it said the different tribes have been fighting not only the white man, but other tribes for years. Centuries."

"This is true," he said. "Some societies kill. That is what they do."

"And you just accept that?"

"Do you not have soldiers?" he asked. "Those who kill?"

Looking at it that way, she had to agree. "I guess we do. I guess we just accept it, too."

"Little One had to find peace and harmony to live here, which meant she had to give up her old ways."

Surprisingly, some of what he said was true, but not all of it. "But you didn't make her give up her language? Instead, she taught it to you, didn't she?"

He lifted a brow. "You…" The word trailed as if he was attempting to say something else. Then, tapping his temple, he said, "Think."

"I think?" Once she said it aloud, she caught what he was saying. "You mean I'm smart, as in I figured it out."

"Heehe'e."

No one had ever told her she was smart, and the swelling inside her chest was quite delightful. "Thank you."

He bowed his head slightly.

"So why can't she teach anyone else?"

"Everyone believes she left all her old ways behind. To become one of us. If they know otherwise, they may wonder about her."

"Question her motives," Lorna said aloud.

"*Heehe'e.* One Who Heals said one day Tsitsistas, The People—"

"Your people, meaning your tribe? The Northern Cheyenne?"

He nodded. "One day our people will need to know the white man's words, but until then—"

"You want to keep Little One safe," she interrupted, pondering her thoughts aloud. "You learned the language so you'll have it when you need it, but until then, no one will question or distrust Little One."

Again, he nodded.

"Why? Because you are the chief?"

"Not chief. I am a leader of The People."

"Is there a difference?"

"*Heehe'e.* Yes."

She chose not to ask what the difference was at this time. "What about One Who Heals? She knows the white man's language, too?"

"*Heehe'e.* Yes."

The old woman still scared her. She was one of those who had re-erected the tent, and her glare had been even stronger than it had been earlier. "She doesn't like me," Lorna admitted.

"She does not trust you," he said.

"Do you?" It was out so fast she almost didn't realize she'd asked it.

"I do not know yet."

A shiver tickled her spine, and the comfort she'd known just a moment ago started slipping away. "Are you going to tie me up again?"

"I do not know yet."

A deflating sense washed over her, even though she wasn't exactly sure why. "I guess that's a fair enough answer."

"Do you trust me?" he asked.

The question caught her off guard. At least she certainly hadn't expected it. "I don't know," she said half to herself. She hadn't trusted anyone, other than Meg—and look where that had gotten her—in a long time.

"Epeva'e."

Frowning, she glanced up. *"Epeva'e?* It is good that we don't trust one another?"

"Heehe'e," he said. "Trust takes time."

She nodded. "You're right. It does."

He gave another one of his single head nods, like a slight bow of the head. It was more than a nod, and more than an acknowledgment. Almost an agreement or affirmation.

As odd as it seemed, that little action of his was powerful. At least to her it was. She opened her mouth, assuming he'd expect her to complete her share of the bargain, tell him why she had to get to California. She was willing to do so, but shouting outside stopped her before she could start.

He rose to his feet and held out a hand.

Startled, she asked, "I can go outside with you?"

"Heehe'e."

He said no more, but Lorna understood this was a test. One she was determined to pass.

Chapter Seven

Black Horse didn't release Lorna's hand until they were both standing outside his lodge. He told his mind her name was Lorna, not Poeso, but it was hard. Just like the mountain lion in his vision, she'd transformed, and that affected him in a way he'd never experienced before. That scared him, too.

He did not trust her, but right now he did not trust himself as much as he should, either. She resembled the mare in his vision more and more. Especially when she smiled, and much like the black stallion, his nostrils were full of her scent. It was stimulating, and that he did not need. It had been a long time since he had been with a woman. More than that, he liked this woman. Her pride and determination. She spoke her mind, but listened, and was smart. Very smart.

The camp crier drew closer, and was followed by a crowd of people cheering.

Lorna was glancing from the crowd to him and back again. He smiled at the joy building inside him, and again at the relief on her face.

"Epeva'e," he shouted when the camp crier stopped before him. *"Epeva'e."*

The scouting party arrived moments later, their ponies

covered in sweat and breathing hard. Black Horse spoke with Crazy Fox, the leader of the party, learning where the buffalo herd had been spotted and the number of buffalo gathered together. The answers he received were most welcome. Crazy Fox claimed the herd was the largest he had seen in his lifetime. The crowd cheered at the news.

Black Horse cheered with them, and ordered all to prepare for the celebration commencing the hunt.

Among the jubilation he heard a whispered "What's happening?"

The two white women who had stormed away from Lorna earlier now stood behind her, peeking around her mass of curls. He could understand why they sought her protection. She had the qualities of a leader.

"I don't know," Lorna answered, glancing at him. "But it must be good."

He made no acknowledgment she had spoken, even though his heart smiled. Much like the mountain lion, Lorna did not trust easy, but she wanted to. She just didn't know how. Understandably. Few white men could be trusted.

"How do you know that?" one of the other women asked.

"Look around," Lorna answered. "Everyone appears happy."

"You're right," the other said. "I wonder what happened."

He made no response. Little One along with the white woman Meg were pushing their way through the crowd.

"It is a sign, my brother," Little One said in his native tongue. "My sister's arrival is a good thing for our people. She is good medicine."

Black Horse offered no immediate verbal opinion. Signs the buffalo hunts would be fruitful this year had been given to him, but the joy on his sister's face was because of her sister, not the hunt. He did not like that.

Little One as well as Meg both shifted their gazes to Lorna, and he saw the questions in their eyes. It was not expected that he explain why she was untied. Using the Cheyenne language, he told Little One to take the women and go prepare for the celebration.

"Even that one?" she asked in Cheyenne.

"Heehe'e." He had to prepare for the hunt, and could not do that with the woman in his lodge. She made him want to smile, and that should not be.

Cautious, Little One whispered to Meg, telling her Lorna was to go with them, and when she told that to Lorna, she looked at him with a question. He turned to enter his lodge, and experienced a fleeting sense of disappointment when there was no argument outside. He wanted to believe he could trust her, but did hold doubt. She was white. His band might question his knowledge of the white man's language if they knew, but they would accept his judgment. The other bands that had gathered with them for the hunting season would not—they already questioned why he did not want to fight the white man. Many knew Little One was white, and assumed that was why he had not voted for battle last winter when several other leaders had. They would question his motives more with white women staying with his band. That could put them all in danger. He did not wish to fight the white men or other tribes, and he had given permission for these women to stay with them. Therefore, it was his duty to protect them as he would his own people.

Black Horse picked up his bow and tested the tension. It was also his duty to feed them.

Lorna went along with Meg and Little One, but kept looking over her shoulder at Black Horse's teepee. Not just to make sure she could find her way back this time. He'd said he didn't trust her, so why had he let her leave?

The conversation between Meg and Little One drew her attention once she could no longer see Black Horse's lodge. "What is *hotoa'e*?" she asked, having heard the word several times now.

"Buffalo," Meg answered. "A scouting party found a large herd. Tonight there will be a big celebration."

"Tonight?" Lorna shook her head. "It's too late in the day to plan a celebration."

"A lot of the preparations have already been made," Meg said. "It's what they've been waiting for and it'll be an honor for us to be a part of it."

"An honor?"

"Yes," Meg answered. "To help prepare and participate."

Shivers were tickling Lorna's spine. "Help prepare?"

"Yes, that is what Black Horse told Little One," Meg said. "To take us with her so we can help with the preparations."

Lorna glanced around at the Indian women bustling about, adding sticks to the fires in front of their teepees, stirring the contents of bowls with their hands, and other such cooking activities. "Why?"

"To celebrate the start of the hunt."

Still glancing around, Lorna asked, "What are we supposed to help them do?"

"Whatever they need," Meg said, grabbing her hand.

Hours later, Lorna figured she'd done more work that day than all the others since they'd started traveling west. She'd gathered firewood, hauled buckets of water from the stream, dug roots with several young girls and completed numerous other chores requested of her. Tillie and Betty had disappeared, and she wondered why. They were the two who liked to cook. The ones who knew how to cook. When left to their own devices, she and Meg had eaten some pretty awful meals. Meg was better at cooking than she was, but her skills were also very limited. In fact, they'd lived mainly on beans the first few weeks. Not that she was expecting an appetizing meal tonight. Truth was, it didn't matter. The dozens of trips to the creek to haul water had left her too exhausted to worry about eating. Sleeping was what she was looking forward to, especially now that the sun was setting.

Little One handed her a bowl full of something so foreign-looking she couldn't have described it if her life depended on it. "What am I supposed to do with this?" Lorna asked.

"Follow us," Meg said, her own hands full.

"Where to?" Lorna asked.

"To Black Horse's lodge," Meg answered, already following Little One and One Who Heals.

Lorna followed, too, but kept her distance from the old woman. From the time they'd started preparing for this celebration that had the entire camp running about like chickens with a fox in their pen, One Who Heals had been on Lorna's heels. The old crone had smacked her across the shins with a switch when she'd slopped water out of the bucket on one trip. It had taken all the control she'd had not to grab the stick and smack the old woman back. If not for the fact the old crone would have tattled to Black Horse, she would have.

"Why are we going to Black Horse's lodge?" she asked Meg.

"Because he's the head of the family."

"He and Little One aren't real family," Lorna said as they walked through the maze of teepees and campfires releasing a plethora of scents. "She's not his sister. She's your sister."

"He accepted her into his family from the time the Southern Cheyenne left her here," Meg said. "She loves him like he was family."

There was an underlying tone in Meg's voice. One Lorna had never heard, and for the first time, she wondered if Meg was worried that Little One wouldn't want to leave with her. Didn't want to be her sister.

Betty and Tillie, carrying pots from their wagon, met them near Black Horse's lodge. "Where have you been?" Lorna asked.

"Making things for the celebration," Betty said.

"Isn't it exciting?" Tillie asked.

Lorna kept her opinion to herself and followed Meg through the doorway flaps. The contents of her bowl sloshed as she caught sight of Black Horse. He was sitting in the center of the lodge, surrounded by people, and greeted them with one of his little nods.

She was bustled forward, the bowl was taken from her hands and before she knew it, she was seated on the ground next to Black Horse. The oddest sensation washed through her. She certainly wasn't happy to see him again, but she was the tiniest bit happy to be back in his teepee. As strange as it was, there was familiarity here, or at least a hint of safety. That was something she'd need to ponder. This man had flung her over a horse, thrown her into a wagon, tied her up and let his teepee almost crush her to death. None of that signified safety.

Conversation filled the space, as did laughter as bowls were passed about. They were laden with boiled ribs, stew that included the wild turnips she'd dug up earlier, and several other things she didn't recognize. Everything was cut into bite-size pieces, and there were no utensils. No forks. No spoons. That didn't stop anyone from eating, using their fingers. Betty was seated on her other side, and Lorna leaned closer. "There is a serious lack of table manners here."

With a shrug, Betty said, "I suspect that is because there are no tables."

Lorna didn't have a retort for that.

"Eat," Betty said. "It is very delicious. Especially these ribs Moon Flower made. They are so tender."

Not as interested in the food as she was other things, Lorna asked, "Which one is Moon Flower?"

"The tiny woman next to Little One."

Lorna found the one Betty indicated. The woman was indeed tiny, and was feeding food to a small child. "How do you know her name?"

"Little One told me. Moon Flower lost her husband last winter, and Black Horse has been providing for her family—her and her two children—ever since."

"Why?"

Betty finished chewing and swallowed before answering. "Because she has no one to feed them. No one to hunt for food. The Cheyenne are very generous to each other. They let no one go hungry or cold. Black Horse is very rich, and shares his fortune with others."

"Rich?"

"As in horses, and hides, and robes, and other things he's traded with the white man. His lodge is large and he is a great hunter, so his larder is always full.

"Being the leader of the band, he takes care of the poor, or those down on their luck, until they are able to fend for themselves again." Betty shook her head. "It surprised me to learn their society was much like ours. Those who are rich, and those who are poor. However, unlike our society, the poor are not shunned. No one is looked down upon."

"How did you learn all that?"

"Little One told us much about the Cheyenne, and introduced us to many others."

"When?" Lorna asked. "We've only been here for a few hours."

"While you were tied up, and before and after." Betty stripped the meat off another rib bone with her teeth. After swallowing, she said, "I believe what is written in books does not apply to all Indians. That most of it is simply what the writer wants people to think. Not at all the truth." She picked another rib off her plate. "You should eat before it gets cold."

Using her fingers, since there was no other option, Lorna picked up a rib. It was very tender and flavorful, and she counted heads while she ate. There were a total of sixteen people in the teepee, counting the three children who were extremely well behaved. They sat next to their mothers, opening their mouths like little birds in a nest.

Besides Black Horse, there were three other men. One was elderly, and the younger woman next to him fed him much like the mothers of the children. The other two men were younger, closer to Black Horse's age, which was hard to guess. Older than her twenty years, but not aged. She didn't recognize any of the men as ones who had been at the river earlier.

The men talked much more than the women, and laughed. Their chortles were practically nonstop. As was their eating. The women kept filling the men's plates, and they kept eating, and eating.

Her own plate seemed to have gone empty on its own. She licked off the lingering bits from her fingers—her mother would have beaten her had she done that at home, but here it seemed to be what everyone else was doing. She couldn't name all she'd eaten, but nothing that had hit her taste buds had been revolting. Her palate had changed drastically this past year. There had been a time when she'd have refused to taste anything she couldn't name, or hadn't eaten before.

The tent once again filled with laughter, and Lorna was wondering what they found so funny when Betty reached around and pulled something from behind her.

Recognizing one of Betty's prized pans, Lorna asked, "You've been to our wagons?"

"Of course," Betty said.

She'd left England with nothing more than what she could carry. New York, too, but in Missouri, she'd followed Meg's advice in outfitting their wagon for the trip to California. "Is everything still there?"

"Of course," Betty repeated. "I hope they like this."

Betty took the top off the pan, and the scent of molasses wafted upward. "What is it?" Lorna asked.

"I wanted to make something they would not normally have," Betty said. "Something special, so I made a molasses cake. I usually bake them as cookies, but I couldn't do that in my Dutch oven."

Betty had brought along a spoon and started serving out pieces. She placed the first one on Lorna's plate and whispered, "Happy birthday."

Having forgotten hours ago that this was still her birthday, Lorna felt tears prick the backs of her eyes, and silently admitted her friend's thoughtfulness had touched a vulnerable place inside her.

Plates were passed around the circle, and one didn't need to know the Cheyenne language to know how much the Indians liked the cake. Even the children made little appreciative moans.

Lorna took a bite and was reminded of some of the sweet treats from back home. There had always been plenty of them. Her mother had insisted on having delicacies with tea each afternoon. The bite she'd taken seemed to double in size and she had to swallow twice to get it down.

Laughter once again filled the air, and Lorna glanced up to see why this time. It was over the cake, the two young men were obviously vying for second helpings. Everyone was laughing at their antics, how they were trying to put their plates closest to Betty, who was blushing red.

Being pushed aside by the bulk of the men, Lorna found herself up against Black Horse. He was laughing, too, and his plate was empty.

"Do you want more?" she asked very quietly, for only him to hear.

"There will be no more when they are done," he replied just as quietly.

Making sure no one was watching, for she wouldn't want to hurt Betty's feeling by not eating the cake, Lorna carefully slid her piece onto his plate. "I'm full."

He didn't question her actions and ate the cake before anyone noticed. At least she'd thought no one had noticed until she felt eyes on her. One Who Heals's glare was hot enough to leave blisters.

The old woman said something to Black Horse. Lorna had started to think of their language as inoffensive, but the older woman had a way of making it sound harsh and ugly again. Although it goaded her that she didn't know what the woman said, Lorna ignored her and rose to her feet. Much like in the white man's society, the women began to gather the dirty dishes. It was odd how she'd started to define things as *the white man's*. They had only been here for a few hours. That certainly wasn't enough time to alter a person's thinking.

With so many women helping, the cleanup was done in no time, and Lorna turned to Meg as everyone started to reenter the teepee.

Before she had a chance to speak, Meg said, "It's not polite for us to be conversing in front of them. They can't understand what we say."

"They do it to us," Lorna pointed out.

"And how does that make you feel?"

Lorna couldn't say it didn't bother her as much as it used to—other than the old crone. Meg wouldn't believe that, and Lorna wasn't ready to tell her friend why. She wasn't sure herself. Other than, just as Little One would answer any questions of Meg's about what had been said, Black Horse would answer hers. Lorna couldn't say how she knew that to be true, but she did, and that felt good.

Which was also extremely odd.

The men were passing a pipe among themselves, and though they still laughed, it was quieter now, as was the way they spoke to one another. Their conversation held a rhythm, almost like the cadence of someone reciting a poem. There was no harshness, and that made her glance to where One Who Heals sat near the door, as if she was a guard of some sort. The old woman didn't speak, but her stare was as severe as ever. Perhaps out of defiance, or maybe defense, Lorna crossed the small area and once again sat down beside Black Horse as if it was her rightful place.

He nodded at her, and her heart fluttered oddly. Whether it was because the action felt like an approval from him, or because the old woman huffed, Lorna didn't know, but she lifted her chin and let her gaze land on One Who Heals.

The old woman might as well know that their dislike of each other was mutual.

Once again seated, the women chatted quietly among themselves, using a large amount of sign language to include Betty, Tillie and Meg. The subject was clearly Betty's cake, and she was blushing all over again at the praise she received.

Used to seeing the others dressed in their nun outfits, Lorna hadn't realized she'd never pulled her habit back over her head until the conversation changed. With hand gestures again, the others were asking why hers was hanging down her back. She waved her hands near both cheeks. "Because it's hot," she said.

"Ehaoho'ta."

She glanced at Black Horse.

"Ehaoho'ta," he repeated.

"Hot?"

He nodded.

"Ehaoho'ta," she repeated, feeling an uncanny sense of pride when she didn't mangle the word.

The others nodded and the conversation moved on to another topic. Lorna didn't try to follow. Her gaze had gone to Black Horse. He wasn't looking her way, and she studied the sharp features of his profile. Some might consider him handsome, for his dark complexion was intriguing and pleasant to the eyes. His long hair no longer scared her, either. Not that it ever should have. She'd seen men with long hair before, especially on the ship that brought her to America. She must have just been startled back at the river, for there truly wasn't anything frightening about Black Horse. Not any more than any other man.

People, although their lives might be different, were surprisingly the same. They still needed food, clothing and shelter to survive. They all had families. That was common sense, yet for some unknown reason, she'd never seen it that way before.

He turned then, and Black Horse's thoughtful gaze caught her off guard. Heat rushed into her cheeks as she turned away.

No command was given, not by Black Horse or anyone else, yet one by one people began to file out of the teepee, including her friends. The women with children gathered the two that had fallen asleep, and once they left, it was just her and Black Horse. He'd already moved to the opening, and gestured for her to exit before him.

She pinched her lips to withhold a grin. There may not be table manners, but there was chivalry in their culture. "Where are we going?" she asked.

"To continue the celebration."

One Who Heals was holding the flap open from the outside, making Lorna bite down on several other questions. Others were leaving their teepees, too, and a gaiety filled the air as everyone headed toward the center of the encampment. She walked alongside Black Horse, amazed by the number of people. The gathering was immense, and while people were still arriving, music started.

She couldn't call them musicians, for they didn't resemble what she'd seen in the past, but there were men pounding on drums and others blowing into flutelike instruments. The singing that soon began was more of a rhythmic chanting to the beat of the drums.

Most of the men, including Black Horse, headed for the open area around a huge fire and began dancing. Here, too, it was nothing like she'd seen before. Darkness had long ago descended upon them. The flames and sparks of the fire haloed the dancers, and the eeriness sent a definite shiver down her spine. Standing near her friends, Lorna couldn't pull her gaze from Black Horse. He was leading the band of men, hopping from foot to foot, and the deepness of his chant could be heard above the rest.

Following suit of those around her without really realizing it, Lorna sat on the ground. A large circle had formed all around the dancers. It was odd how everything they did was symmetric. There were no rows of people. No trying to see over the heads of those in front of you. Nothing blocked her view of the men and their primitive dancing. It was nothing like the ballets she'd attended. The music of those events hadn't affected her the way this did. The continual beating of the drums seemed to enter her bloodstream, making her heart beat in harmony with the unorthodox concert.

One by one, women joined the dancing and chanting. Their higher notes complemented the low tones of the men and their gracefulness was admirable. Some steps had people leaping into the air much like the sparks of the fires, while other times they dipped low to the ground, their backs bent forward and their heads down as they continued around the circle. There appeared to be no right or wrong way, yet all were in perfect unison with the music.

When Meg, encouraged by Little One's repeated, *"Ho'sooestse,"* joined in, Lorna was torn. Part of her was amazed by her friend's courage. Another part was appalled that Meg was so willing to unite with these people. There may have been a small part of her that was jealous, yet she couldn't fathom why. Dancing like a gypsy beneath a yellow moon was not something she wanted to do, nor ever would. *Right?*

Another pang stung her stomach as Tillie and Betty were invited to join the dance. She wasn't used to being a wallflower. Most every ball she'd ever attended, her dance card had been full long before the music started. Her mother had made sure of that. Whether she'd wanted to be at the ball or not—and she hadn't wanted to be at any of them—it was expected that she smile and dance until blisters covered her toes. The punishment of not doing so was worse than the blisters; therefore, she'd danced, often well beyond her full card.

Memories of such events brought up a rawness that she'd believed had been deeply buried. Until leaving, she hadn't understood how deeply imprisoned she'd been. The control others had had over her. If not for that night a year ago, she'd still be there—obeying others as if she had no say in her own life.

It wasn't that way now, not for her or her friends.

The three of them, Meg, Tillie and Betty, wearing their black dresses and nun's habits, looked extremely out of place among the hide dresses and fringed leggings. They, however, didn't seem to mind. Nor did anyone else.

Except for a few older men and women, most of those still sitting on the ground were children. They were participating in their own way, clapping their hands and tapping their feet to the beat of the music with rapture glistening in their eyes as they watched the others circling the fire. Ones that young would have long ago been put to bed back home. However, there wasn't a yawn to be seen. The dancing seemed to have rejuvenated the entire camp. And they all were here because they wanted to be, not because they had been forced into participating.

The beat of the music changed again, as did the chanting, and her attention once again landed on the leader of the band. Though the dancing moved around the fire, with no beginning or end to their line, it was clear Black Horse was the leader, not just of the band, but of the dancing.

Lorna glanced around, wondering if anyone would notice if she slipped into the darkness. Her gaze went back to the dancers, including her friends, and she sighed. One for all. All for one.

Black Horse's heart should be full. The spirits of those who had gone before him and those who would follow in his path for many generations were among them tonight.

He could feel them in his footsteps, see them in his head, hear their chants mingling with those around him, yet there was a longing inside him that grew more prominent with each step he took.

Long ago he'd discovered he wasn't meant to walk this world alone. Hopping Rabbit had made him whole, and the void left inside him when she had gone from this world to the other had never been as strong as it was tonight. Nor had the desire to know his children, offspring from his loins, would one day be dancing in such celebrations. That should not be. Just as his eyes should not keep finding Poeso. She sat alone and that bothered him. The other white women were dancing; their long black dresses had melded in and looked as if they belonged among the others as much as Crazy Fox's long buffalo robe.

Poeso had been invited to join in. Moments ago She Who Smiles had offered her a hand. Poeso had shook her head, had chosen to sit on the ground, watching. There was longing in her eyes. If she wanted to dance, why did she not?

The spirits led him around the flames again, his moccasins barely touching the ground as steady beats of the drums carried him forward. He listened to voices whispering in his ears, telling him of the great and successful hunt to come, and tried to ignore the ever growing longing inside him. The celebration would last for hours, until the great Cheyenne moon overhead would fade behind the blue sky that would mark the beginning of their move. Some of his people would retire, dreaming of the hunt in their lodges, while others would remain awake all night, refreshed as much from the dances as those who would find it from their sleep.

He had danced until the moon sank many times, and had retreated to his lodge to dream on just as many occasions. The calling inside him dictated which it would be. Maheo—the Great Creator—had gifted him the powers to be a great hunter, a dedicated leader and a fearless warrior long ago and the medicine within spoke to him often.

Black Horse continued to dance until the desire was no longer there, and then he quietly left the circle. Some warriors would fall upon the ground when they were full. He had never had that reaction, but was joyous for others when they found their medicine so strong it sapped the strength from their bodies. It was a sign of many buffalo kills to come, and that meant no one would go hungry when the snow settled upon the earth, allowing the grasses to sleep and grow strong until the sun once again brought warm winds and long days.

He spoke to no one, not even Poeso, but did stop next to her and held out a hand.

She shook her head. "I don't want to dance."

Back in his lodge, One Who Heals had said this woman was trying to trick him into speaking her language in front of others, trying to trap him. He could not deny the medicine woman's wisdom any more than he could forgo his duty. He had never wished not to be a leader of his people, but right now, he had to consider how much easier it would be to be just a warrior. *"Enhoota,"* he said.

"What does that mean?"

Gesturing in the direction of his lodge, he repeated, *"Enhoota."*

"Leave?" she asked. "Leave the dance?"

"Heehe'e."

She rose and started to walk, but veered in the wrong direction. Taking her arm, he guided her around the lodges and onto a path that would eventually take them to his.

The beating of the drums faded as they walked, and

when the quiet of the night settled around them, she asked, "Will you show me where our wagons are?"

"Why?"

"Because I'm tired and I would like to go to sleep."

"You will sleep in my lodge," he said.

She dug her heels into the ground like a horse coming to the edge of a cliff. "No, I will not."

Chapter Eight

Black Horse wasn't pleased with the idea, either. Having a woman in his tent would only increase the longing in his heart, but it was his duty to protect his people. One Who Heals had insisted this woman would cause trouble, and though she had done nothing wrong throughout the celebration, that didn't mean she might not at any time. Ignoring the fast beats of his heart, he explained, "It would not be safe for you to sleep in your wagon."

"Why? You and Meg keep saying the Cheyenne are peaceful. That you won't hurt us."

"My people are good, and tomorrow we begin the buffalo hunt."

"That doesn't answer my question."

He knew that, but was trying to not frighten her. "Not all here are my band."

"So?"

"Many come together to hunt. Some not welcome white women."

She turned around to look back toward the celebration. "What about my friends? Will they sleep in your lodge, too?"

"Hova'ahane," he answered.

There was a hint of fear in her eyes, but the darkness

of her glare came from mistrust. "Why not? If it's not safe for me, it's not safe for them."

"Others will keep them safe."

"Why can't I stay with others, too? Why can't we all stay together?"

He would welcome that as much as she would. "Because One Who Heals does not trust you."

"I don't trust her, either," she said. "She smacked me with a switch earlier."

He once again steered her in the direction of his lodge. "Why?"

"Because I spilled water."

"You will be more careful next time," he said.

She dug her heels in again. "There won't be a next time. I guarantee you that."

If he had ever believed something a white person said, man or woman, he believed that. It made him want to smile. That should not be. One Who Heals had great powers and would use them against opposing forces. Poeso was as opposing as one could get.

"Furthermore, I have been on my best behavior all night. I hauled water and wood, dug up roots and did every other little menial chore someone grunted for me to do. I have done nothing to make anyone not trust me." She flung her arm about. "I sat over there and didn't move an inch, even when everyone else was dancing. I could have walked away and no one would have noticed. I could have—"

"Come," he said. "You are tired."

"No, I'm not."

"You said you wanted to go to sleep."

"In my wagon," she said. "Not your teepee."

No one, other than Hopping Rabbit, had ever argued with him like this. That annoyed him as much as it tickled his insides. "My protection is great."

"Give me my gun and I'll have great protection, too."

Arguing with her was giving him more pleasure than it should. He took her arm and pulled her toward his lodge. "No, it will not."

She struggled, but could not break away. He almost grinned, until she went limp and dropped to the ground. Startled he released his hold and knelt down.

Crossing her arms, she said, "I'm not going anywhere with you. I'm not sleeping in your teepee. I'm not—"

He lifted her off the ground and flipped her over his shoulder. Her stubbornness was greater than a boulder. "Then, I will tie you again."

That stopped her screeching as quickly as it started. "No, you won't," she said. "I won't let you this time. I'll fight and—"

"You are weak," he said. "I am strong."

"I am not weak!"

She pounded her fists against his back, and though it stung, it did not hurt. He laughed. "You not injure Black Horse."

"Oh, yes, I will," she insisted, hitting him faster. "I will hurt you! I will kill you!"

He let her continue pounding on his back and shouting of her strength. It made him grin, until they had entered his lodge and he set her on her feet. It was dark inside, but the yellow light of the moon was bold enough for him to see her clearly, and the tears that ran from her eyes. Stepping back, he reached out to wipe them away from one cheek. She twisted her face away and swiped at the tears with both of her hands.

"Why you cry, Poeso?"

"I'm not crying," she said. "My eyes are watering from hanging upside down."

"That does not make eyes water."

"How do you know? Have you ever been hauled around like a sack of flour?" She hurried across the lodge, to where many furs covered the pine boughs he slept upon. Tossing things about, she asked, "Where's my gun? Where's that little pouch you were wearing?"

After everything was tossed about, she spun around. "Where is it?"

Tears fell from her eyes, but what struck him like a knife was the fear on her face.

"Where is it?" she shouted. "I need it so no man can get within three feet of me. No man. Including you!"

He took a step closer.

"Don't!" she shouted, backing up. "Don't come any closer."

Being filled with fear was more dangerous than being filled with anger. That went for people as well as animals. Black Horse held his arms out to his sides as he would while approaching a cornered horse. "No one will hurt you, Poeso," he said quietly.

"I know they won't," she shouted. "I won't let them! I won't let anyone hurt me ever again!"

The way she shook entered his heart, made it pound with an unknown anger. She had been mistreated, badly, at some time, someplace. "I won't let them, either," he whispered.

"I won't let you hurt me."

"I will not hurt you," he said. "I will protect you. I will stop all others."

Still crying, she shook her head. "No, you won't."

"Yes," he said, moving forward very slowly. "I will. My protection is great and powerful. All listen to Black Horse."

She glanced around, but upon realizing he was in front of her, giving her nowhere to go, she slid downward, onto the ground as slowly as leaves fall. The fear was still in her eyes and tears on her cheeks, but the fight was leaving her. He didn't like that. Kneeling down, he asked, "Who did this to you, Poeso? Who hurt you so deep?"

She shook her head.

He wanted to touch her, to wipe away her tears, but she would not accept that. Understanding came to him as a whisper from his heart. There was no room for trust in her. Had not been for a long time. Twisting, he gathered some of the buffalo hides she'd tossed about and laid them flat. Patting the bed he'd made, he said, "Lie down, Poeso. Your day was long. You are tired."

Her glance was weary, and wary, and she shook her head.

"Black Horse protect you." Gesturing toward the doorway, he said, "No one will enter my lodge."

Still shaking her head, she whispered, "Who will protect me from you?"

Another whisper of understanding angered him, turned his insides dark. A man had hurt her. A bad man in a bad way. "Black Horse protect you from all." He backed away and then moved across the lodge to repair his bed. Afterward he retrieved his pouch from where it hung on a lodge pole, and pulled out the gun. Trust had to be mutual or it was nothing.

"Here is your gun, Poeso," he said, holding it out for her to take.

Her eyes were big and full of surprise, and her hand shook as she reached for the little pistol.

He laid it in her palm and wrapped both of his hands around hers. "I trust you, Poeso. You trust Black Horse."

She looked from him to their hands and back up at his face. "Are the bullets still in it?"

Her voice was soft, and the words cracked, but he understood she had to say them. "Yes." Letting go of her hands, he pointed to the buffalo hides. "Go to bed, Poeso, you are safe."

He waited, hoping his heart was right, that he could trust her, and then watched her scoot onto the furs. She kept the gun clutched near her chest, even after lying down on her side.

Black Horse moved to his bed. This may become a sleepless night. He had never slept next to a woman holding a gun. Once stretched out on his back, he listened for any movement she might make.

"What does *poeso* mean?" she asked quietly.

"Cat."

"Why do you call me that?"

"Because that is what you remind me of. The sleek mountain lions that roam the hills."

"Is that bad?"

"Hova'ahane," he answered. *"Epeva'e."*

"Epeva'e," she repeated. "It is good?"

"Heehe'e," he said. "It is good."

After several quiet moments, she whispered, "Good night, Black Horse."

He stopped the smile forming on his lips by telling himself she was a white woman, one he may regret trusting. "Good night, Poeso."

When her slow and steady breathing said she was sleeping, he quietly found his knife and laid it next to him, just in case. Then his mind worried no more. He closed his eyes and welcomed the dreams of the great hunt they would embark upon with the sunrise. Such dreams were slow to come. They could not get past the sound of Poeso's breathing. The way that made him think like a man instead of a leader.

* * *

It took Lorna a moment to remember where she was when she awoke. Sunlight filtered through the sides of the teepee, and that reminded her of the crisp parchment paper her mother liked to write notes on. That reminded her of her own diary. For the first time in a year she hadn't scribbled upon the pages before falling asleep.

And that reminded her of exactly what had transpired last night. Yesterday. She sat up with a start and quickly surveyed the rest of the area. The teepee was empty. Feeling the fur mat beneath her, she found her gun and instantly inspected it. Finding it intact, and loaded, she stood before tucking it in her pocket. There was a bowl near her makeshift bed, holding dried bits of meat and grain of some sort. Breakfast no doubt, but left by whom, she wondered.

She ate a few bites while finger combing her hair and twisting her dress into place, discovering it wasn't grain but dried berries, which had a sweet, unique taste. When the bowl was empty, she moved toward the opening.

What she saw had her blinking and checking her vision.

"There you are, sleepyhead."

Lorna turned at the sound of Betty's voice. "What's happened? Why are all the teepees…gone?"

"They aren't gone," Betty said. "They have been dismantled for traveling. Black Horse told Little One we weren't to take his down until you awoke, and we were starting to wonder if that would ever happen."

Lorna's heart skipped a notable beat. "Where is he?" she asked. "Black Horse?"

"Around somewhere, I'm sure," Betty answered. "Getting his herd of horses ready to travel most likely."

Lorna had many more questions, but nature was calling. "I need to relieve myself. Will you come with me?"

Yesterday, while preparing for the celebration, she'd discovered an area a short walk away from the camp that everyone used. Young boys were assigned to maintain the area by immediately covering any deposits with dirt.

"Of course," Betty replied.

Lorna was thankful for that, because she wasn't certain she'd be able to find the area again by herself. The few things she'd pinpointed as landmarks yesterday—the teepee with the buffalo hide covering its doorway and the one with a deer painted on its side—were gone.

Once she'd completed her business with as much privacy as the few trees in the area provided, she and Betty started back toward camp. In more of a condition to converse, Lorna asked, "What is happening? Why are all the teepees down, and what were you saying about herding up the horses?"

"The bands will start traveling today, to where the buffalo were spotted," Betty answered.

"I thought the men hunted while the women stayed home."

"I did, too," Betty said. "But I have learned differently. The entire tribe will travel, following the buffalo for as long as the hunt takes. It's so fascinating, learning all about the ways of the Indians."

"Well, we aren't traveling with them," Lorna pointed out. "We need to get back on the trail to California."

"That's the best part," Betty said. "The herd is northwest of here, which is the same direction we were traveling. We can travel along with the Cheyenne, giving Little One and Meg time to get better acquainted, and for Little One to make her decision whether to leave with us or to stay. It's a grand solution, wouldn't you say?"

No, Lorna wouldn't say that, but merely nodded because something else had caught her attention. "Don't

look behind us," she said. "But I think we're being followed."

"We are," Betty said. "That's Stands Tall. Black Horse
told him not to let you out of his sight."

"Why?"

Betty's lifted brow said more than words.

Anger zipped through Lorna. "I have done nothing for
him not to trust me. Good heavens, he gave me my gun
back."

"He did?" Betty asked with astonishment.

"Yes, he did."

"When?"

When didn't matter. Her gun was in her pocket and
would never leave her person again. Lorna increased her
speed, marching toward Black Horse's teepee.

The structure was on the ground by the time they arrived, parts of it already loaded on a travois. She'd read this
was how the Indian tribes traveled. Loading all they owned
on a simple structure made of poles and leather ropes and
tied behind a horse, they traversed the plains like nomads
with no homes, no permanent place to call their own.

Black Horse was nowhere in sight. The tall young man
who had been instructed to stay close to her shrugged his
shoulders when she asked him where his leader was. He not
only ignored her when she told him to go away, but stayed
at her heels while she looked for Black Horse.

Before long, the entire camp was broken down and
ready to travel. The long line was much like a wagon train,
except there were no wagons, other than their two. Lorna
insisted upon driving one, and Tillie took control of the
other. Betty sat next to Lorna, and an Indian woman ac-
companied Tillie, grinning at the prospect. Meg was riding a sleek red roan horse, and she looked happier upon the
animal than she'd ever looked driving a wagon.

If she had been able to locate Black Horse, Lorna would have protested. He, however, seemed to have disappeared, and she understood being left behind would not be beneficial.

Much like last night, when everyone left the tent without being commanded, the train of people began to move with no audible or visual signal. She couldn't see the beginning; it had already disappeared over a knoll, and the end was far behind their two wagons. Betty pointed out the dozens of horses ahead of them were all Black Horse's. Several pulled travois, loaded with the makings of a teepee or household belongings, and others had huge packs strapped over their backs. Women walked beside some of the horses, keeping them in line, and others road upon them. A large number of horses simply followed along as well-mannered dogs would their owners. She'd never seen anything like that. Or like the dogs here. They ran alongside the line with young children chasing and playing tag with them, and at times, jumping on their backs to ride a distance. Who would ever have imagined that? Riding atop a dog! Yet these animals didn't seem to mind, nor did the children.

They were headed west. She knew that by how the sun shone on her back, much like it had each morning since she'd left Missouri. As long as that continued, she wouldn't protest. As it was, there was no one to protest to. Even Betty had climbed off the wagon in order to walk among some of her newfound friends.

Again, like the wagon train that had left Missouri, there were riders that paced from the front of the line to the back, asking how people were getting along. Of course they didn't ask her, but they spoke with Stands Tall, who rode next to her wagon on a black-and-white horse.

As the sun rose higher, so did the heat, and Lorna pulled her habit over her head to protect it from the penetrating blaze. The material was hot, but saved her head from pounding and her face from burning.

Unlike the other wagon train she'd been a part of, this one didn't stop for a noon meal. They just kept moving westward, nibbling on bits of food they carried with them. Betty had returned to the wagon in order to share some meat and more of the dried berries Lorna had eaten for breakfast.

"We'll stop by midafternoon," Betty said.

Lorna didn't ask how Betty knew that. Nor did she ask if the other woman knew where Black Horse was; that would only irritate her further. He had been kind last night, understanding, and by giving her back her gun, she had assumed that meant he trusted her. But the appearance of Stands Tall said otherwise. There wasn't even any solace in the fact he hadn't made One Who Heals her watchdog.

That was fine. He didn't need to trust her. She didn't need to trust him, either. He had no way of knowing what had gone through her mind last night, of how terrified she'd been to be alone with him in his tent. Had no way of knowing that last night had been an exact year from the only time she'd been alone with a man in such a setting. No one knew about how Douglas had followed her to her room after the last of her partygoers had left, or how he had forced himself upon her. Well, one other person knew. Her mother. Who had claimed Douglas wasn't to blame. That Lorna had encouraged him.

Douglas's cruel treatment had hurt, had left her feeling ugly, dirty and violated, but her mother's blame, her lack of belief, had been crushing. Shattered into a million pieces, Lorna had left later that night, with nothing more than she could carry. She highly doubted either her mother or Douglas cared. They would, though, once she got to California and claimed the secret fortune her father had amassed, unbeknownst to anyone except Elliot Chadwick and his brother, William, whom she'd met back in New York.

Her father had been the only person she'd ever trusted, and that was how it would remain.

The heat was taking its toll on the mules and Lorna was about to pull out of the long line of travelers to let them rest when one of the riders, the same one that Betty said was a camp crier, rode past them shouting a long length of words.

Within a short distance, a camp was already taking shape. Those at the beginning of their long line of travelers were well into the process of unloading their horses and setting up their homes. This was all done by the women, and Lorna discovered she was expected to help. She had every intention of doing her fair share, just as she had all along, but not knowing what she was supposed to do made it difficult. She turned to Betty for instruction.

"Because Black Horse doesn't have a wife, the women he supports take down, transport and set up his lodge," Betty said. "And because you are now sharing that lodge, it will become your responsibility to help."

"I don't know how to do any of that," Lorna said. "And I don't want to. We can stay in our wagon like before."

Betty shook her head. "That wouldn't be safe. There are other bands traveling with Black Horse's band for the hunt, and some of them might believe we are free for the taking if we are alone in our wagons at night."

The explanation was in line with what Black Horse had said the previous night, but to Lorna, accepting responsibility to assist with his or any lodge gave an impression their time here was permanent. It wasn't.

"Little One has agreed to show you everything you need

to know," Betty said. "And to help until you can manage it on your own."

"I will never be able to manage it on my own," Lorna said, "because we won't be here that long."

"We traveled more miles today than we would have on our own," Betty said.

"But the tribe won't go all the way to California," Lorna pointed out.

Betty had never been one to argue, but the pinch on her lips said she might now. She didn't have the chance because Little One waved them both over to a travois. Lorna considered objecting, but knew it would get her nowhere, other than perhaps tied up again. This time by the old crone who stood nearby, glaring at her.

Lorna would never say it was easy work, but with so many hands, the laborious tasks were not the burden they might otherwise have been. Within hours the camp was set up identically to the one they'd left that morning. Circles inside circles—which actually were family circles that intertwined, just as the families who lived in them were intertwined by blood and by marriage. She also discovered each lodge flap was to face the east, as did the entire village, in order to draw power and wisdom from Father Sun. The placement of the teepees, or the reasons behind it, didn't interest her as much as getting the task done. However, as soon as Black Horse's lodge was complete, and all his possessions neatly set about inside, everyone moved on to the next lodge, and she was once again expected to help. And with the next one, and the next.

Once all the teepees were reconstructed and the horses led away by young boys, the women began building fires and cooking. Lorna's stomach clenched on the idea she might also be expected to provide Black Horse with meals. He would starve. She'd never accomplished those tasks when a full kitchen was laid before her, and would fail miserably with nothing but an open fire.

Too hot and tired for a cooking lesson, Lorna sought out Meg. They both had pulled the habits off their heads while laboring with the long poles, and Lorna was once again reminded how much Meg looked like Little One when her black hair was fully exposed. Tossing the thought aside, Lorna said, "You know I don't know how to cook. I don't even know where to start."

"Yes, I do," Meg answered with a grin. "Little One says others will provide Black Horse his meals, as always."

Lorna recalled the conversation last night, about how Black Horse provided others with the food they ate and considered pointing out that the least the others could do was continue to cook it for him.

"Thank you, Lorna," Meg said, disrupting other thoughts. "I know this isn't what you expected, what you want, but thank you for agreeing to it. I didn't realize how hard of a decision it would be for Carolyn, or for me." Meg shrugged. "Thank you for not arguing and for making the best of the situation. And thank you for…well, just thank you."

An uneasy sensation welled in Lorna's stomach. Before this trip, she couldn't recall anyone ever thanking her with such genuine emotion. Sure, friends had offered their appreciation for gifts and such, and Tillie and Betty gushed their thanks of saving their lives—as they put it—but no one had ever thanked her the way Meg just had. Not with sincerity shimmering in their eyes.

Lorna had to clear her throat. "You're welcome." Uncomfortable, and not liking it, she spun about. "I'll go gather firewood."

Chapter Nine

The buffalo were still far away, but their trail was easy to follow. It was Black Horse's duty to lead the way and to find a spot to settle for the night. When they got close to the herd, the village might stay in one place many days, but until then, it would only be for one moon.

Worry hung heavy with him all day. Although he trusted Stands Tall to watch over Poeso, she might not. Never one to question his decisions, for they were always made with considerable thought, he was reconsidering whether he should have given the gun back to her. He would have to punish her if she used the gun against Stands Tall, or anyone else.

Black Horse rode into the camp faster than usual, and the stares that brought about made him slow Horse to a walk. He raised a hand, signaling all was well, and slowly made his way to his lodge, grateful all seemed peaceful. He had never found it difficult to be a leader as well as a man, but this day his mind was more on Poeso than on the buffalo hunt. Had Maheo sent her as a test, or perhaps as a punishment for not agreeing to battle the white men as so many others had wanted?

The sun was still in the sky and the camp was complete, fires burned and food cooked, except near his lodge. He did miss that. Having Hopping Rabbit preparing his meals and warming his bed at night.

He forced that thought to leave him, but could not stop from scanning the area for Poeso. His heart thudded when she was nowhere to be seen. Not among the women of his family, or by her wagons that had once again been placed near the outskirts of the camp. He urged Horse forward, pretending to be inspecting the village until chatter near the water drew his attention.

Her black dress didn't make her stand out as much as her mass of curls. Near his herd of horses, Black Horse dropped to the ground and turned Horse over to a young boy, and then walked toward the river. Two of her friends were there, too. All three in the water.

A smile made his lips twitch. Perhaps he should call her water woman after all.

Several young girls were with the women, scooping up fish and tossing them onto the bank. They greeted him as he approached, telling him the water was good, full of fish. He answered positively, but he was not looking at the fish. Standing in the knee-high water, Poeso was laughing, and the sound entered him. Made his chest full.

She tried to catch fish, and kept missing, but that only made her laugh harder. When she turned, as if just realizing others had stopped fishing, her laughter stopped.

That saddened him. So did the way her eyes stopped shining.

Black Horse walked into the water and told the young girls to keep fishing. The two other women moved away as he walked closer, but Poeso stayed, watching him. She was mad; her eyes told him that.

The young girls scooped out fish again, and her friends joined them farther upstream. Poeso crossed her arms over her chest. Water dripped from her sleeves and the ends of her curls.

"I know you can't answer me in front of others," she said. "Or won't. But I don't appreciate having a watch guard. I thought you trusted me. I have my gun. I don't need a—"

"I promised my protection," he said. "Stands Tall gives that when I not near."

She frowned.

He bent to put his hands in the water. "Stand quiet," he said. "Like this."

"What?"

"Stand quiet to catch fish."

"I—" She closed her mouth, and shrugged. "I tried that."

He planted his heels in the sandy bottom and bent his knees. "Like this."

A twinkle returned to her eyes as she copied his action. "I've been standing like that," she said, "but they swim away before getting close enough to catch."

"Your dress scares them," he said, watching how it floated around her legs. "Hold it quiet."

"How? I need my hands to catch the fish."

He moved behind her and crouched over her back in order to pull her skirt tight. She shivered. "You are safe," he whispered. "Stand quiet and wait for the fish."

Fish soon swam closer to investigate what was in their water. Feeling her twitching, getting ready to move, he cautioned, "Wait…"

When a fish darted closer he lifted her skirt, scooping the fish out of the water with the material. She squealed and laughed, and tried to catch the fish squirming about in her skirt.

After several tries, she managed to get hold of it, and

held it up. "I caught one!" she shouted to her friends. "I caught one!"

The others shouted back, acknowledging her abilities. He had stepped away from her and she spun around, still holding the fish. "I've never caught a fish before," she said. "Never went fishing."

"Then, put it back," he said.

"Put it back? Why?"

"So it can make more fish for you to catch."

"What if I don't catch more?"

"You will. Now you know how."

She looked at the fish before glancing back up at him. A smile grew on her lips until her eyes danced in the sunlight. Nodding, she agreed, "I do. I will." Gently, she lowered the fish into the water and let it glide out of her hands. Once again looking up at him, she said, "Thank you."

He nodded and watched as she turned around, bent her knees and held her skirt tight like he had shown her. She was smart and soon scooped another fish out of the water. Her laughter filled the air like birds singing with each fish she caught.

"You have many fish, Poeso." He had stood nearby, but had not helped again. He had stayed because he liked watching her. Liked seeing her joy.

She glanced up the river, to where the others had been. They were now gone.

"Yes, I do," she said. "What am I going to do with them?"

"Eat them."

"I don't know how to cook them," she said. "I don't know how to cook anything."

He had never heard of such a thing. "Did your mother not teach you?"

She let go of her dress and walked toward the bank.

"My mother doesn't know how to cook," she said. "That is why she had servants."

"Servants?"

"Others to cook for her, clean for her, drive her around." She shrugged. "They do everything. And if they don't, she fires them."

"Fires them? She burns them?"

She finished wringing the water out of her skirt before looking up. "Not fires like that, fires also means to make them leave. So they don't work for her any longer."

He nodded, though it didn't really make sense to him. The white man's ways were hard to understand. Black Horse found a stick, hooked each fish lying on the bank through the gills and handed the stick to her. "Little One teach you how to cook."

She carried the stick by both ends as they walked toward the village. "I don't want to learn."

"Then, how will you feed your husband and children?" Last night, upon understanding she had been hurt, he wondered if it had been by her husband, and wanted to know where that man was. Why he was not taking care of her.

"I don't have a husband or children. Never have and never will."

Her words were spoken fast and hard. He chose not to question why. "How will you feed yourself?"

"I'll hire servants when I get to California."

"So you will be like your mother," he said.

She stopped and the look on her face was thoughtful, but slowly turned angry.

"No," she said. "I will not be like my mother."

Black Horse did not follow when she started walking again. He recognized a mad woman when he saw one, and right now, she was madder than when he had tied her to his lodge. She would be no danger to anyone else, though, and that lifted his spirit.

The next time he saw her was in his lodge, where many had gathered to eat. Anger no longer lived in her eyes, and he nodded before sitting down next to her. One Who Heals sat on his other side, and as the food was passed around, she told him Poeso had wasted many fish trying to cook them. He ignored the scorn in the older woman's words, and in how she called Poeso Woman Who Sleeps in Black Horse's Lodge. Others had called her that today—warriors from the other bands, they also asked how long the white women would travel with them.

It was not their way to scorn someone for learning, and upon reminding One Who Heals of that, he said it was good that Poeso learned how to cook. One Who Heals hissed and said a woman who couldn't cook was no good.

"Nehetaa'e!" He would not listen to any more. *"Meseestse. Nahaeana."* He was hungry and wanted to eat.

One Who Heals pinched her lips, and then hissed, "Don't eat the fish. It will make you sick."

Usually he headed her warnings, for it was her job to foresee things, but on this day, he did not believe her. Nor would he argue with her. Others, though, stared his way, having caught the other woman's words. No one would disobey the medicine woman, not without his permission. He had never defied One Who Heals in front of others, but he must, for Poeso's sake.

"Meseestse." Eat, he told the others. As they appeared hesitant to obey, he added that they could eat the fish. No one would become ill. To prove it, he ate all the fish in his bowl first, and then asked for more.

The tension between the old crone and Black Horse was so thick, Lorna swore it filled the entire teepee, and

her pride at having cooked at least one fish without burning it faded with her suspicion that she was the cause of
the strain filling the teepee. It shouldn't matter—the old
woman made no attempt to hide her dislike, and she hadn't,
either. Yet it soured her stomach. For no reason. She'd
never gone out of her way to please people, and wasn't
about to start now. No one had ever gone out of their way
to please her. No one had ever cared one way or the other
what she wanted or didn't want. It had been that way her
entire life. At least since her father died. He'd cared about
her, and she about him, but that had all died along with
him.

"*Meseestse*, Poeso," Black Horse said under his breath.

She understood *meseestse* meant eat, and picked up a
piece of the fish she'd been so excited about earlier. Why?
There was no need for her to learn to cook. She could hire
all the servants she'd need upon arriving in California
and acquiring her inheritance. Except she was not like
her mother. Never would be. So self-centered and cold
she didn't even care what happened to her own daughter.
Her very own flesh and blood. She'd told herself that her
mother had started hating her upon marrying Douglas, but
in truth, there had not been any love between her and her
mother long before Douglas arrived.

An eerie sensation had Lorna looking up, across the
circle to where Meg and Little One sat side by side, their
heads tilted toward one another as they spoke between
themselves. Her stomach hiccupped. The truth was, she
already was like her mother, wasn't she? Never caring
about anyone other than herself.

The food in her mouth would have choked her if she'd
have let it. She didn't. With great effort, she forced it down,
and then another piece, and another one after that. Her
gaze roamed the circle as she ate. She'd never really sym-

pathized with Tillie and Betty. It had been because of her own goals, her own reasons, that she'd allowed them to join her and Meg. Even when it came to Jacob Lerber following Betty, it hadn't been Betty she'd been thinking about. It had been because she'd never let a man violate another woman the way Douglas had her.

A round of chatter, or little cheers of delight, had her lifting her gaze from her plate. Once again, Betty had pulled out her Dutch oven, and the people around the circle, even One Who Heals, were looking her way with anticipation sparkling in their eyes.

"It's just fried bread," Betty said, "topped with my strawberry jam."

Although most of them hadn't understood what Betty had said, they nodded eagerly.

Passing out the bread, Betty said to her, "I feel we need to contribute to the meals, even if it's just in a small way."

Lorna nodded, and then said, "Thank you, we do need to. And thank you for the dessert you made last night."

Betty's hand stalled and her eyes glistened. "Oh, Lorna," she whispered. "Thank you, and you're welcome."

That evening, when the meal ended, after Betty received much praise for her contribution, the men left the lodge. Meg explained they went to the sweat lodge to further prepare for the hunt they'd soon commence.

"For the whole night?" Lorna asked.

"I don't think so," Meg replied. "I've never heard of that."

As the other women started gathering up and carrying away the dishes, Meg held up a hand when Lorna attempted to follow. "Little One says you are to stay here."

"Why?"

"Black Horse said so."

Lorna sat back down. Some time to think would serve

her well. When Meg sat back down, she was surprised. "He told you to stay, too?"

"No, I just thought I would, at least for a few minutes. Do you mind?"

"No," Lorna answered, yet was unsure of what else to say. Her thoughts had made a full circle, and landed back on Black Horse. Wondering how long he would be gone. Eventually, the silence became uncomfortable when she began to fear Meg might know what she was thinking about. "Do you think your sister will miss these people when we leave?" she asked.

"Of course she will," Meg answered. "They are her family, more than I am even. She's lived with them longer than she lived with our family. She doesn't remember much about our parents, or me."

"But you remember her," Lorna said.

"Yes, and I promised my father I'd find her." Meg huffed out a long breath of air. "I don't know what to think now, though."

"What do you mean? Think about what?"

"About making her leave. Or asking her to leave. She will be as confused by our ways as we are by hers." Meg waved a hand. "By all this. I never thought about that. I just thought about finding her. They have treated her very well. They love her."

Meg had never let her feelings show, not like she was now. There were tears in her eyes.

"You love her, too," Lorna said.

"But will it be enough?" Meg asked. "I'm only one person. Here she has many. Many people who love her." Shaking her head, she sniffled before saying, "I don't know what to do, Lorna. I truly don't."

She'd never had anyone love her, or loved anyone, other

than her father long ago, and couldn't offer any advice. "You will figure it out."

"I have to figure it out," Meg said. "Figure something out. You and Tillie and Betty are counting on me to. Counting on me to get you to California."

She'd never comprehended the pressure Meg felt in leading them all west until that moment, and that made her stomach gurgle. It didn't seem fair. That Meg was responsible for so much. "That's true," Lorna said. "We are, but you forget." She held out a hand. "We are all in this together." Holding out her other hand, she waited for Meg to set her hand on top of her other one. "One for all and all for one."

Meg grinned and slapped one hand and then the other atop Lorna's.

They both laughed for a brief moment.

"Who came up with that anyway? I don't remember." Meg asked as they pulled their hands apart.

"I think it was Betty."

Meg nodded. "When we left the train to take Tillie to the doctor."

"This trip sure has been different than what we planned, back in Missouri," Lorna said.

"Yes, it has," Meg answered. "I'd hoped, but truly never really expected to find Carolyn." She sighed again. "It could be worse, though. Would have been if the Southern Cheyenne hadn't left her with Black Horse. I don't know what I would have done then."

Lorna didn't, either, and couldn't think of a thing to say about that.

After a short silence, Meg asked, "Will you be all right here alone?"

"Of course," Lorna nodded toward the door flap that had been left open. "I have a watchdog."

"Stands Tall is very proud to have been chosen to watch over you in Black Horse's absence. It is an honor."

"I'm sure," Lorna replied drily.

"It is. The camp has named you Woman Who Sleeps in Black Horse's Lodge."

A shiver rippled her spine. "Really?"

Meg nodded. "There are many women here who would like to be called that."

"Says who?"

"Little One. His wife died over two years ago, but he has not shown interest in taking another one."

"Why should he?" Lorna asked. "He already takes care of half the band."

"That is his job. As their leader, he's responsible for everyone. But that doesn't mean he can't take another wife. Have children." Meg bit her lips as if she wanted to say something, but wasn't sure if she should. Then, glancing about, she asked, "What did he say to change your mind?"

"Change my mind?"

"Yes, after he tied you up, he then untied you. Why? What did he do?"

"He didn't say or do anything," Lorna said. "I decided to…to give you and your sister the time you needed."

"Just like that?"

It did sound unbelievable. "Yes," Lorna said. "Just like that."

"He didn't—"

"No," Lorna interrupted. "He didn't do anything."

"I didn't think so," Meg said. "Little One said he would never do anything like that, but more so, I knew you'd never let that happen."

Lorna bit the tip of her tongue inside her mouth, half expecting Meg to add the word *again*. They both knew what Meg was referring to, and that somehow Meg knew what had happened to Lorna in the past. What Douglas had done.

Unwilling to go down that road with anyone—for there were times a person couldn't stop things from happening—Lorna changed the subject. "Why do you call her Carolyn sometimes and Little One at other times?"

Meg shrugged. "I guess because she is two people to me. The little sister I've been searching for and the woman I found."

Lorna accepted that for what it was. The truth.

"Have you heard what they've named Betty and Tillie?" Meg asked.

"No."

"They call Betty White Woman Cooks Good."

"That's fitting," Lorna answered.

"And Tillie is White Woman in Black Dress."

Lorna thought that was pretty simple, but Tillie was simple and it fit her. "What about you?" she asked. "What do they call you?"

"White Sister."

"That fits."

Meg agreed and left shortly afterward, explaining they would be traveling again the next day, much like they had today. Lorna had questions about that, like why had they reassembled everything just to tear it down again in the morning, but chose to hold such queries for Black Horse. There were several things she wanted to talk to him about. Her Cheyenne name being one of them.

Many hours passed before he returned to the lodge. If not for the familiar scent, she might have slept through his entrance. Actually, she *had* slept through his entrance. When the smoky smell of burned sage woke her, he was already stretched out on his bed on the other side of the lodge. The smell wasn't offensive. She recognized it from when Meg had thrown sage on their fires at night to chase away the hungry mosquitoes.

Lorna sat up, and listened, trying to make out if he was sleeping or not.

"It is not time to rise, Poeso."

"I know," she said. "I want to talk to you."

The pine boughs beneath his bed rustled as he sat up. "What is it you want to ask?"

His tone wasn't angry or impatient, and that made her heart flutter strangely. "Do you know what your people are calling me?"

"Heehe'e."

She heard the smile in his voice.

"It's not funny."

"I not laugh."

"But you are smiling."

"Heehe'e."

"Why?"

"It is a good name."

Lorna bit her lips for a moment. "Why can't they call me Poeso, like you do?"

"Poeso is my name for you. I tell no one."

"Why?"

His long silence made her wonder if he would answer or not.

"I not want to."

Pretty sure she would get no further on that subject, she asked, "Why did we set up all the teepees and unload the packs if we are leaving again in the morning?"

"We find buffalo."

"I know, but why didn't we just unload what we would need for the night?"

"Would you like to be feast for many hungry *hoema*?"

"For what?"

He chuckled. "Biting bugs. Without our lodges the *hoema* would bite us, drink our blood. Without fires we would not eat."

While she pondered that, he said, "It is our way, Poeso."

The teepees certainly kept more mosquitoes at bay than the wagon and blankets had, and she certainly didn't miss those annoying creatures or the welts they left behind. And she had been hungry.

"Why you go to California?"

She wasn't done asking questions, but she did remember that she had promised to tell him that. "To find a man named Elliot Chadwick."

"Who is this man?"

"That is a long story," she said.

"It is a long night."

Lorna grinned. He had a way about him that did that to her. Made her unable to keep from smiling sometimes, and it felt nice. His attitude was gentle, too. Unlike other men she'd known in the past. Most of them had been demanding and self-centered. Like Douglas. It was comforting to know that not all men were like her stepfather. "Elliot has much money, and some of it is mine. I'm going to get it."

"Why you need much money?"

"Everyone needs money," she answered. "To buy clothes and food, a house."

"The Cheyenne have clothes and food and many lodges. We no need money."

"That is true," she said. "But I'm not Cheyenne."

He was silent again and she heard his pine boughs rustle before he asked, "Why does this man have your money?"

"Many years ago my father told me that if I ever needed something and he wasn't there, that I should go to New York and find Elliot Chadwick."

"Where is your father?"

"He died when I was young, and my mother remarried. Douglas is my stepfather's name, and he was mean to me. Very mean, and my mother said it was my fault, so I left. My father was born in New York, I was, too, but we moved to England when I was a baby." The need to tell him more was so instinctual, she didn't question how fast the words flowed from her mouth. "When my father told me about Elliot, he said I should never tell my mother, and I didn't. When I arrived in New York, Elliot wasn't there, but his brother, William, was. He said Elliot was in California, that he'd gone there when the gold rush started years ago. Elliot had started a business hauling gold for the miners, and my father had invested in that business, meaning he gave Elliot money and therefore owned a portion of the business. Over the years, the business was very successful, and Elliot partnered up with another business named Wells Fargo. William said since my father died, his portion of the business now belonged to me. William said he would contact Elliot for me, and that I could stay with him until we heard back from Elliot, but I wasn't going to stay with a strange man. I had to find Elliot myself. When he gave me money to stay at a hotel, I left instead. Took the first train heading west. It went as far as Missouri, where I met Meg and bought everything we needed for the wagon train."

"You leave many times."

She frowned before catching his meaning. "I had to leave both England and New York."

"Your mother not try to stop you?"

The Cheyenne were so family centered, his question didn't surprise her. However, her answer might surprise him. "No, I didn't tell anyone I was leaving. She wouldn't have stopped me, though. I was never wanted. They—she and my stepfather—were glad I left."

"How do you know?"

"I just do, but they will be sorry. Douglas and my mother like to spend money, and our property was highly mortgaged. That was the reason I was supposed to marry Andrew Wainwright. Douglas had arranged that. Andrew's father must have learned how broke we were and sent Andrew to Scotland before our engagement could be announced, and Douglas made sure no one else would want to marry me. I think he thought I had told Andrew's family, because he knew I didn't want to marry him."

Her throat had grown thick and she had to close her eyes to ward off the ugly anger churning inside her.

"You have been hurt, Poeso, but carrying so much hate is not good for you. The hate will scar your heart."

Lorna hadn't heard him cross the lodge, but opened her eyes to find him crouched in front of her. "It already has," she whispered.

"This man you were to marry, why did he not protect you?"

"Andrew?" She shrugged. "He didn't want to marry me any more than I wanted to marry him. I agreed only because it would get me out of my mother's house." Sighing, she added, "He agreed to marry me because his father told him to."

Black Horse's hands were warm and gentle when they cupped the sides of her face. "You are safe here, Poeso, and have no need for much money."

"I *do* feel safe here," she said, realizing it was true as she spoke the words. "But I'm not Cheyenne. I'm white, and I need to get to California. I'm going to buy back my father's property from the bank, and put Douglas and my mother out in the cold. Make them pay for what they did to me."

Black Horse didn't say anything; instead, his hands slid

down to her shoulders and he pulled her forward, until she was fully encompassed in his arms. Her entire being trembled before she surrendered to the protectiveness and comfort of his hold.

Chapter Ten

Black Horse told himself to lay her down on her bed and go back to his, but he couldn't. He could feel the pain inside her. She needed to be held, needed to know she was safe, needed to heal. He said nothing, and did not move, just held her while she cried, and wondered what it was about this woman that touched him deep inside. Others were still wary of her, likely because One Who Heals continued to claim Poeso would bring trouble to all.

He did not believe that, and had told One Who Heals that Poeso had much power. Much power over people, and that Maheo had sent her here. He was convinced of that, but did not know the reason why. It was not his way to question such things, yet he could not stop his thoughts. Not only as a man, but as a leader. To befriend a white woman so soon after refusing to fight would diminish him in the eyes of other leaders. Why would Maheo do that to him? Had he not obeyed all the rules? Had he not outfought and outhunted others in order to be deemed a leader? Had he not thought of The People first when Hopping Rabbit had died? Was he not thinking of them now? Again, he thought, *Is this a test?*

A shiver rippled his spine and he looked down upon

the woman who had fallen asleep in his arms. Anger had burst inside him when he'd learned who had hurt her. A father should never hurt his child, not one born from his seed, nor one he had accepted as his own. Such things did happen in both the Indian's and white man's worlds, and that angered him. He banished such men from his band, but some leaders did not, because they did not want to interfere. In his mind, and in the minds of his people, children were cherished, much loved. They were the future and needed to have full hearts to keep the bands alive for many generations to come. Hurt children became angry children and angry children became angry adults who made wars continue.

Poeso's heart had much healing to do. Perhaps she would find that healing in California. She was a white woman, and like white men, they cherished the thing they called money.

He had no use for money, no use for any of the white man's ways, and thinking about such things made him yawn. When his eyes wanted to close and his mind slip into dreams, he twisted to lie down, but kept his arms around Poeso. Perhaps Maheo had sent her to him in order for him to remember what it was like to be a husband, to once again want a wife and family, children who would populate the earth after his time here was over.

The early signs of Father Sun awoke Black Horse, and sleeping beside Poeso meant great longings filled his blood. He eased away from her and left his lodge, heading straight for the river where he stripped down and walked into the cooling waters.

Other men soon joined him, as was their routine, to bathe in the early-morning light. Before the sun fully appeared, they'd completed their ritual and left the river to prepare for another day of trailing buffalo. He knew that was the task before him, yet concentrating on it was difficult.

The camp was awake and full of life. He stopped at Little One's lodge and ate breakfast while filling his pouch with dried meat, berries and nuts to eat throughout the day. Purposely not going near his lodge, he made his way to the horse herds. If Maheo was attempting to tell him it was time to take a wife again, she would be Cheyenne. Or perhaps Arapaho. Not a white woman.

Much like the day before, Black Horse led his people westward, but unlike many hunts in the past, they came upon the buffalo before the sun was fully overhead. The heard was large and spread out over many miles. The Sweet Medicine was with them, and he lifted his hands to the sky in thanks. After giving his blessings, and knowing that when the hunt began the buffalo would scatter, Black Horse urged Horse forward in order to find land and water that would serve their village for the many days they would hunt.

It would take a long time for all of the families to arrive at the new site, including his. A smile grew in his heart as he scanned the water nearby. It was wider and deeper here, and he wondered if Poeso would attempt fishing again. He had not fished much since becoming a warrior, but remembered the fun and had liked watching her find that joy.

Forcing his mind to return to the buffalo, he signaled for other warriors to follow him.

Black Horse led the way back to the buffalo. There they spent many hours scouting the land and herd, planning the hunt that would start in the morning. When he returned to the village, he did not go to his lodge. Instead, he went to the sweat lodge to prepare his mind and body to lead his warriors on a great hunt, and to ask Maheo for a beautiful Cheyenne maiden better suited to his needs.

Days later, Lorna sat in her usual spot next to Black Horse while everyone ate. Buffalo meat, something she might never have tasted had they not been rescued from beside the river that day, reminded her of the beefsteaks that had often sat upon the table back in England. Since the hunt had started, they'd consumed a large amount of the fresh meat. She'd gotten used to eating what had been put in front of her since leaving her childhood home. In fact, she'd gotten used to a lot of things. She had learned a lot, too. Not just things about the Indian way of life, but about herself. It felt like much more than a week since they had become a part of the Cheyenne community.

For instance, she hadn't known she was capable of butchering a buffalo. Yes, butchering! The animals were massive, and though most of the men in the camp had dedicated themselves to hunting the beasts, it was the women of the tribe who butchered them and completed all the tasks that followed the harrowing experience. Oh, yes, the first time she'd been instructed to assist in that bloody experience had been distressing to say the least. The sights and smells had been enough to send her to the latrine area—that was the word she preferred to call the dedicated space downwind from the camp—and heave for the rest of the day.

She hadn't, though, mainly because she'd sensed how happy that would have made One Who Heals. The old crone still didn't like her, even though she'd been trying to make the best of the situation by staying as far away from the old woman as possible.

Even now, as they ate, she felt the evil glare of those narrow eyes on her every move, and was counting the minutes until the meal would end.

Every night since the hunt had started five, or maybe six days ago—she had lost track of time—Black Horse had spent little time in the lodge. He not only chased and killed buffalo most of the daylight hours, but upon returning to the village, he spent hours with his horses. He rode several different ones while hunting the buffalo and each one was as well trained as his big black one.

There had been days when she'd hoped he wouldn't kill another buffalo because each carcass packed into the camp was more work for her. Along with all the other women in his family. She wouldn't spare an ounce of breath to claim they all hadn't done far more work than she. Teaching her how to not only butcher, but then separate the meat into what had to be eaten fresh and what had to be dried, had to have been more work for them than just doing the tasks themselves.

Then there was the skinning and taking care of the hides and bones, and, well, everything. There was not a piece of the buffalo that went to waste, although she still refused to think of exactly what some parts were used for. There was still too much of her old self alive and well to go that far.

The good thing about all this work, even though she'd become capable of many tasks, was that she still wasn't expected to prepare meals. That was still beyond her. Meals. There were no set mealtimes. Food was cooked all day long and when people were hungry they ate. The only meal ritual was when Black Horse returned to his lodge at the end of the day. Out of respect, everyone gathered there to eat with him, whether they were hungry or not.

It was part of the ritual, and that was why they were all gathered in his teepee now, as the sun was setting. Again, he'd proved his hunting skills were superior to other warriors by downing several buffalo, and again, she'd worked until her body ached and called for the soft hides to lie upon.

Her wish came true when Black Horse signaled the meal was over. Lorna wasted no time in helping the others with the evening chores, and then gladly returned to the lodge and collapsed upon the hides.

Each night since the hunt had begun, some of the people of the visiting bands had celebrated their successes with music and dancing, and tonight was no different. The sounds of such were still filtering into the tent when her eyes snapped open. Sitting up, she witnessed Black Horse leaving the lodge. The speed of his departure and commotion from outside had her scrambling to follow him.

Several lodges away, two men were crouched down facing each other, with knives drawn. The moonlight glistened on the metal as they swiped the blades at one another. Black Horse didn't slow his pace as he bounded in between the men and grabbed one of the men by the wrist, forcing him to drop his knife. The other man who had stepped back she recognized as Sleeps All Day.

Black Horse picked up the knife with his free hand and spun the other man around, then forced him to walk away. Few words had been spoken. None that she understood anyway. She took a step to follow Black Horse, but Little One stopped her.

Betty rushed to her side. "Sleeps All Day caught that warrior trying to sneak into Moon Flower's lodge."

The crowd quickly departed. Several women, including Betty, entered Moon Flower's lodge, while Lorna watched Black Horse take the warrior across the river and as far into the neighboring village as the moonlight allowed her to see. Then she slowly returned to Black Horse's lodge, and sat down, awaiting his return.

It seemed hours passed before he entered the lodge.

* * *

Black Horse drew in a breath at the site of Poeso sitting with her arms crossed. He had hoped she would be asleep, but it was no surprise to find she was not. "It is late," he said, while walking toward his side of the lodge.

"What did you do to that man?" she asked.

"He will not be back."

"Why? Is he dead?"

Usually he would say no more, but the quiver in her voice forced him to answer, "No, he has been banished from our village."

"Banished?"

A Cheyenne woman would understand what that meant. Then again, a Cheyenne woman would be asleep and would not question his actions. Stretching out on his bed, Black Horse closed his eyes. Silver Bear would punish the brave; there was no more to worry about. No more he needed to do. "It is done," he said. "Go to sleep."

"How can I do that?" she asked. "Knowing you could have been killed."

He opened one eye to peer across the lodge. The moonlight made her curls shimmer. The ability not to think about touching her, about mating with her was getting harder with each moon.

"You didn't need to put yourself in the middle of that fight," she said.

He closed his eyes. "It is my duty."

"Is it your duty to get stabbed?"

"I not get—"

"You could have been," she said. "You could have been killed."

He held his breath at how she interrupted him, telling himself she did not know better. "There are many things you do not understand about our ways, Poeso. You are not Cheyenne."

"No, I'm not Cheyenne," she said with anger. "But I've been working as hard as any Cheyenne woman here, and I know danger when I see it. That brave could have killed you."

"A Cheyenne woman would not remind her husband of such things."

"Husband? Who said anything about a husband? Not me. Or is that why you banished that brave from your village? Does he like Moon Flower? Do you want her for your next wife?"

Black Horse wanted to squeeze his head between his palms. Normally he did not mind Poeso's questions, but this night he did not want them. The brave had not been after Moon Flower. He had wanted the one Poeso called Betty. He had told Silver Bear that if Black Horse could have a white woman in his lodge, he could, too. Others had said as much. Handing the brave over to Silver Bear, Black Horse had said that none of the white women were here to become wives. That they would leave as soon as the buffalo hunt was over. Go to the white man's fort. That thought left his stomach sour.

"Is that why?" she asked again. "You want Moon Flower as your wife?"

"How can I think of another wife with you sleeping in my tent?" he growled. "And talking, talking, talking until Father Sun arrives."

"I don't—" She huffed out a breath and threw herself onto her bed with a thud. "Fine. I won't talk. You can have any wife you want. It doesn't matter to me."

"Because you will soon go to California," he said in order to end the conversation.

"That's right, I will, and then I won't care one way or the other who you marry, or if you get stabbed or not."

Black Horse bit his lips together. She made him want to argue, and that was not his way. Not the way of his people. He had said his piece, and that should be enough.

Many heartbeats later, while he was still staring at the stars though the open top of the lodge, she whispered, "Moon Flower is pretty, and smart. You could do worse."

"Go to sleep, Poeso," he growled. Marrying Moon Flower had never crossed his thoughts. No other woman had entered his mind since this *poeso* had entered his village.

When Father Sun arrived, Black Horse left the lodge with enough frustration to kill buffalo two at a time.

Although they had taken many buffalo during this hunt, the winter would be long and the band was large. Riding upon Horse, Black Horse led the charge into the mass, bow drawn to make the first kill of the day. He fired arrow after arrow, and Horse never missed a step as buffalo, one after the other, fell to their deaths in his wake. Others would gather the fallen animals. The markings on his arrows piercing the buffalos' hearts would signify they belonged to him. His mind stumbled slightly when he thought of how many more Poeso would have to assist in butchering. It was the way, he told himself, and she must learn that, even if she was only here for a short time.

She had not spoken again after he'd told her to go to sleep last night, but she might as well have. Listening to her tossing and turning had made sleep impossible, and made him question again why Maheo had brought her here.

Sweat ran down his back and stung his eyes along with much dust and dirt as the buffalo turned, running in yet another direction. Movement on top of the hill told him a group of women had arrived to assist with the buffalo being taken. He did not need to see her to know Poeso had joined them this day.

Urging Horse to follow the buffalo, Black Horse caught sight of a warrior falling from his horse. Buffalo were smart and fierce contenders, and a large bull had already spun around to take advantage of the warrior. Black Horse steered Horse around and reached for an arrow, but realized there were too many buffalo between him and the bull to make a clean shot. Hooking his bow over one shoulder, he pulled out his knife and raced through the heard. The buffalo surrounding him were a blur as he kept his sight on the one charging toward the fallen warrior. The bull, so focused on the brave, did not notice as Black Horse rode up beside it. Bearing down on the animal, pinpointing the exact spot he aimed his arrows at, Black Horse plunged the knife between two ribs on the side of the bull, and then deeper into the animal's heart.

The bull's front knees buckled and its large body followed, landing near the fallen warrior. Spinning Horse around, Black Horse rode back to pull his knife out of the bull, and then gestured, telling the warrior to claim the kill as his own before turning Horse about and riding into the herd again. It was the warrior he'd banished from his camp the night before. The one who must learn from his mistakes, not dwell upon them.

The buffalo were soon as exhausted as those hunting them, and Black Horse called a halt to the hunt. It had been a good season and his people would not go hungry when the snow fell. The rest of the herd would be allowed to roam away, and, like Poeso's first fish, produce more buffalo for another hunt, another season.

* * *

Lorna was fully worn out by the time Black Horse arrived at the lodge that evening, but she refused to let it show. She worked as hard as the other women, and would continue to, whether Black Horse recognized that or not. And she was determined he would answer one more question that evening. Entering the lodge behind him, she asked, "Why did you save that warrior from being gored? He was the one you banished last night."

He had already gone swimming in the creek, washing away the sweat and dirt from the hunt, and his skin was still glistening with drops of water. She attempted to ignore that while keeping her stare steady on his face, which was drawn into a frown.

"It is the way," he answered.

She wanted to know more, but stopped herself from asking, and for once that didn't bother her. Unlike all the other men she'd ever known, he didn't like talking about himself. Didn't boast about good deeds, his bravery, skills or successes. Much like all of those in his band, she'd come to respect Black Horse, and realized those traits were just a few of the things that made him a great leader. The Cheyenne were indeed different from white men, and not all the ways were bad.

Her insides had been tied in knots all day, and she knew the only thing that would help was to apologize. "I'm sorry I angered you last night, asking so many questions."

"You did not anger me, Poeso."

"It seems like I did." Black Horse now knew what Douglas had done, and she wondered if that made her ugly in his eyes. Contaminated. That was how it had left her feeling.

She also wondered if Black Horse regretted what he'd done. The way he'd held her, comforted her and slept beside her all night. That hadn't happened again, yet she couldn't erase the memory of how different she'd felt the next morning. As if something inside her had become whole again. It was perplexing, and she questioned it over and over, but couldn't deny she felt different inside since that night. Thought about him differently, too. It had been those thoughts that had driven her to ask him about Moon Flower last night.

"Well, either way, I'm sorry." She had come to appreciate many of the people here, including him—another change inside her that she was noticing—and truly didn't want him to be angry.

"The warrior was shunned from his clan, too."

Lorna had turned and was about to leave the lodge until he'd spoken. Twisting about, she waited, wondering if he would say more.

"Without that buffalo, he would have nothing to eat."

Not exactly sure why her heart started racing, Lorna nodded and slipped out of the lodge. Thoughts of how strong and brave yet also how caring and kind Black Horse was occupied her mind throughout the evening, to the point she barely spoke to anyone, or listened to their gossip. Who would have thought she could be so quiet, so obedient!

After everyone had eaten and left the lodge, her mind was still a tangled mess.

"Your friends told you," Black Horse said.

He still sat in the center of the lodge, having not left with the others or shared the pipe with them as was the ritual. "Told me what?" she asked.

"The hunt is done."

She searched her mind, wondering if someone had mentioned that. Now that she thought about it, others had been extremely quiet tonight, including her friends. "No, no one mentioned that." Many things were different here, and maybe the end of the hunt was depressing for them. "I'm sorry you killed all the buffalo, but isn't that what you wanted to do?"

The hint of a smile on his lips caused her heart to thud.

"There are still many *hotoa'e*," he said. "Many buffalo."

Thinking harder about how quiet everyone had been, she asked, "Then, why was everyone so gloomy?"

"Gloomy?"

"Sad, depressed, acting like their dog just died."

"No dogs died."

"I know that."

He chuckled then, and she realized he'd been teasing her. She shook her head, knowing full well he had a thorough grasp of the English language. "You know what gloomy means, but I still don't understand."

"The other bands will leave. As soon as their meat is prepared to travel."

Traveling with fresh carcasses would be difficult, even for Indians, but she hadn't expected to learn the other bands' departures would sadden anyone. Meg said the bands gathered together a couple times a year to hunt and then separated as if those were just normal activities.

"We, too, will leave this place," Black Horse said.

"To follow the buffalo west?"

"Hova'ahane," he answered. "We have enough buffalo."

His answer didn't surprise her. The Indians were not a greedy lot. They never took all of anything. Not fish, or roots or berries. They always left some behind for the earth to replenish what had been taken. The hair on her arms shivered, but she refused to admit what it meant. "Where will you go?"

"To make winter camp," he said.

"Where will you make this camp?"

He shifted slightly to look her directly in the eye. "South."

"South," she repeated.

He nodded. "To hunt deer and elk in order to have plenty to feed our people this winter, and to trade with the white man."

"South," she said again.

"Heehe'e."

It dawned on her then why everyone had been so somber. They would be parting. "Has Little One said she will leave with Meg?"

"She has not told me her decision."

Lorna had a distinct sense Little One's decision was not the reason a hard knot had formed in her stomach. There was an aspect of safety being among so many, and returning to the trail, just the four, or possibly five, of them seemed frightening in a way it never had before. That had to be because of all the changing she'd done inside. "Well," she said, "she doesn't need to make her mind up tonight. It will be a few days before all the hides are tanned and all the meat is dried."

The way Black Horse pinched his lips together said he was trying to hide his smile. She saw it though, in his eyes. There was no way he could hide that twinkle.

"It's true," she said. "It'll take a few days."

"Heehe'e," he said. "It will."

"Well, then, there is no reason for everyone to be moping." Including her. She pushed off the floor, but once standing, wasn't sure where to go. There was a distinct stinging in her chest. "You must be tired," she said. "Good night."

"Where are you going?"

She had no idea, and voiced the only excuse she could think of. "The latrine."

He stood. "I will come with you."

"You will not." There wasn't enough privacy as it was, and she certainly wasn't going to relieve herself with him around.

"Stands Tall has gone."

"He knows better than to follow me there," she said.

"I know."

Lorna didn't doubt he did know. Some people made a habit of pointing out her every move. When the first buffalo had been brought into camp and she'd turned away from the gruesome sight, One Who Heals had wasted no time in pointing that out to Black Horse that evening. A somewhat heated exchanged had followed. Meg had said he'd told One Who Heals it was her job as the eldest family member to teach others, not criticize them. Hearing that, Lorna had become determined to learn how to butcher that animal, and the ones that followed. Just to show the old woman what a good student she was.

She was just as determined to go to the latrine by herself right now. "I don't need a watchdog."

"Come," he said, pushing open the flap door. "It is dark."

"I know it's dark."

"Then, I will not see anything, will I?"

Her cheeks burned at how he'd read her thoughts. Trying to hide her embarrassment, she ducked and exited the teepee.

The area was a significant distance away, and her fortitude dissolved the farther they walked from the heart of the camp and its fires. Night guards were on duty, making their rounds. Much like in the white man's world, there were many different jobs in the camp. Sleeps All Day was known as that because he was awake all night, overseeing a large number of men who protected the camp so others could sleep without worries.

Not wanting to dwell on what had happened the previous night, she asked, "Do you know that Sleeps All Day can sleep on his horse?" Without waiting for Black Horse to answer, she said, "I saw it. He was lying on his horse's back, with his head on the animal's neck, and slept while we traveled. Tillie and I laughed about it, and were amazed."

"You have seen many new things since you arrived, Poeso," he said. "Things no longer frighten you."

She let that settle for a moment before answering. "You're right. I have seen many things, and they no longer frighten me, but I probably wouldn't have been frightened of a sleeping Indian anyway."

"You still have your gun?"

"Of course," she said. "It's in my pocket."

"You have on a different dress."

She hadn't thought he'd noticed. "I had to wash the black one after my first encounter with a bloody buffalo," she said. "It's in the wagon. I figured I'd wear my other dress until we left." Another shiver rippled her arms. That had been her thought when she'd washed the nun's outfit. Once they started traveling alone again, the outfit would be needed, and would be in horrendous condition if she wore it while butchering buffalo every day. She was able to get the job of butchering done, but had yet to master doing so without needing a bath afterward. The women all bathed regularly in the river, and here, too, she'd learned something. They were modest, but not prudish. No one thought one way or the other about stripping down and scrubbing clean after the messy tasks.

A tug on her skirt had her stopping and spinning about. Two children, almost invisible in the dark, were already racing back toward camp. If not for their giggles and whooping noises, she wouldn't have seen them. "What was that all about?"

"They counted coup on you," Black Horse answered. "They will make fine warriors."

She had learned of such acts from others, and frowned as they started walking again. "But I'm not the enemy."

He laughed. "No, but as the Woman Who Sleeps in Black Horse's Lodge, you are untouchable."

"I am?" She rather liked the idea of being untouchable.

"Yes, only the very brave would dare come close. Only those not afraid of punishment."

"Punishment by whom?"

"Me."

She once again stopped in her tracks. "You aren't going to punish them, are you? They are just children."

"Do you want me to?"

"No!"

He chuckled. "Then, I will not."

She shoved at him playfully and laughed when he grunted and faked stumbling. "You weren't going to in the first place," she said. "You can't fool me. You are not the big bad man you pretend to be."

"I'm not?"

In many ways he was the fiercest and most powerful man she'd ever met, but she wasn't going to inflate his ego. "No, you are not." Lifting her chin, she said, "You are about as frightening as a rabbit."

"A rabbit?"

"Yes, you should be called Black Rabbit instead of Black Horse."

He laughed and waved a hand. "Go. I wait here."

They had arrived at the area, and though it was dark, she still found a tree to provide a bit more privacy. When finished, she skirted back around the tree, but paused to scan the area. Nighttime clouds made the night darker, but she should still be able to see his silhouette. "Black Horse?"

The faint sounds of drums and chanting from a few celebrating their day's hunt as they had done every night were all she could hear.

She flinched, remembering the warrior who had been banned, but stopped herself from calling out to Black Horse again. It was highly doubtful anyone else would attempt to anger him with such antics. He probably had to use the facilities, too.

A rustle behind her released a bit of the tension that had started to build. She turned about, and shivered slightly when no one was there.

Unable not to, she quietly called, "Black Horse?"

Nothing but silence again.

Had he left her? He said he'd wait, and he'd never gone back on his word, not once.

Another sound had her spinning in the other direction, but once again, nothing was visible. She eased a hand toward her hip, where she did indeed keep her gun. Just as her hand was about to slip into her pocket, she was seized from behind.

The scream that leaped into her throat, but which she'd been too paralyzed to let out, slowly eased its way back down at the chuckle echoing in her ears.

"That was not funny," she said, slapping at the arms wrapped around her.

"Were you frightened?"

"Yes," she admitted.

"So Black Horse does scare you."

"Because I didn't know it was you," she said. "I didn't see you."

"I hide like a rabbit."

Fully at ease, she laughed, and leaned back against him, not at all opposed to his closeness. "You are too big to be a rabbit."

"You called me Black Rabbit."

Squirming enough so his hold allowed her to twist about slightly, she said, "I was teasing, just like you were teasing me."

"Aw," he said, drawing out the single syllable as he met her gaze. "You like teasing."

The twinkle in his eyes was stronger than ever. That she did like, yet the truth made her pause briefly before admitting, "I've never been teased before."

He released his hold, but only to spin her all the way around. Still holding her close with one arm, he lifted her chin with his other hand. "Black Horse likes teasing Poeso."

His broken English was yet another way he teased her. She'd heard him speak English fluently. There were times he'd pause to remember the right word, but really only spoke it poorly when the subject matter wasn't serious or he was joking.

"Black Horse being silly," she said in an attempt to mock him.

The smile on his face slipped away, and for a moment she wondered if she'd offended him, but then an entirely different thought emerged.

Lorna had no idea where it came from, for such an idea had never crossed her mind before, but she couldn't deny the notion or the reaction it had on her. Her heart was pounding its way up her throat and her lips were tingling.

He bent forward, sending her already out-of-sorts heart racing so fast her breath wobbled. When his lips touched hers, she froze on the outside while jubilation exploded inside her. The connection was shocking, and…amazing.

His lips moved over hers in such a soft caress she went weak in the knees. However, she had the sense to grasp his shoulders. His arms fully encircled her, pulling her close against his bare chest as his lips pressed firmly against hers. There was nothing hard or forceful about it. Just the opposite. His touch, the way his lips met hers, was gentle and ignited a reaction she couldn't control. Delight raced to every part of her body, including her toes that curled inside her boots.

He was a giant of a man, big and powerful, and it was as if, just as he'd used that power to protect her, he was sharing it with her as he had everything else. A force, a vitality she'd never known filled her. She stretched onto her toes in order to increase the connection of their lips and wrapped her arms around his neck. His hold on her tightened, and the mingling of their lips turned into a teasing and lively foray.

Good heavens, but she could have floated away right then and there. She'd never felt so light and carefree, or so vivacious. A giggle escaped and Black Horse leaned back slightly.

Lorna bit her lip, wishing she could have held in the giggle, for she hadn't wanted the kissing to end.

"My kisses make you laugh?"

His eyes were still twinkling, and he was smiling.

She shook her head, and then nodded, confused in so many ways. "Your kisses make me happy." Once again, shock raced through her. How could she have admitted that?

He combed his fingers into her hair, all the way to the back of her head, where his firm grip kept her from dipping her chin. "I like seeing you happy, Poeso," he whispered. "It makes me happy."

Her mind must have stopped working, or figured it was fine and dandy to reveal what she would never normally have. "I like seeing you happy, too," she said. "And I like how you call me Poeso."

His lips met hers again, and this time his kiss penetrated deep inside her, filling her with more light and heat than the summer sun could ever hope to. Although she was utterly engrossed in all the new and wonderful sensations filling her, she silently questioned if she'd giggled again when he pulled way.

"Others come," he whispered.

"Oh," she said, and stumbled slightly when his hold lessened.

He caught her, and kept one arm around her while guiding her toward the village. Toward his lodge. An entirely different sensation erupted at the thought of being alone with him there.

Chapter Eleven

Each step toward the village sent Black Horse's blood pounding harder, faster. The spirit of the future had been fully awakened inside him and yearned to produce descendants to walk upon this earth after his time had ended. It was expected he would have children, those who would take over in leading his band. Many leaders had more than one wife just for that reason.

Upon killing the buffalo for the warrior, his thoughts had focused on expectations, and consequences. Poeso had been included in those thoughts. Others had expected things because he had allowed her to stay in his lodge, and he had lied. He had told Silver Bear and the others last night he would be happy to see her go. That was wrong. He would not be happy. It was wrong for him to tell untruths, both as a man and a leader of his people. They trusted him, believed what he said, and so did she.

Hunting buffalo took much power, and at night he had needed sleep to renew it. This night, he wanted to stay awake, to enjoy the sight of Poeso, to answer her questions, to listen to the sound of her voice, which made him smile.

He should not want that, but could not deny that he did. Other things should be on his mind. His sister. Little One's eyes had been sad when she'd told him she would make her decision to stay or leave before they moved from the hunting grounds. That had been their agreement. That the white women would remain with them while they traveled west, the same direction as California. That would end now that the hunt was over and they would turn south.

Poeso stumbled slightly, walking beside him, and he brought her closer to his side. "Careful of rabbit holes," he said.

Her giggle was like music, how it filled his heart. She had learned much this past week. Much more than he had expected her to. Even One Who Heals had been amazed by Poeso's grit and intelligence. The medicine woman had also shown sadness at the mention of the hunt ending, knowing as well that the white women would soon depart. Knowing Little One might leave with them caused great sorrow for the older woman, but he had seen how she no longer glared at Poeso. Only when Poeso was not looking. That made him smile.

Poeso had gained trust from many, and many would miss her when she left.

He bit the inside of his lip to keep from growling to himself. She had chosen a good name for him. Black Rabbit. He would like to find a hole and hide in it like a rabbit. Not face tomorrow. Not face tonight. Not face the people who put so much trust in him.

He could not do that, and he could not fulfill the yearning inside him. Poeso was not his woman. If he was different, a Crow or Blackfoot, he would not care what she wanted and he would make her his, but he was not a Crow or Blackfoot. He was a great Cheyenne leader, and must follow what he had always known. What was expected of him.

He could not force Poeso to stay. Force her to become

a Cheyenne woman. Nor did he want to. She would not be happy, and that was what he desired most. For her to be happy. That was what Tsitsistas wanted. For all to be happy.

His mind understood that. But his heart could not agree.

The walk back to his lodge ended, and while opening his lodge flap, he hoped hunting had not used up all of his strong medicine. Going against his heart would be difficult.

Poeso had grown silent, and upon entering, she stopped in the center of the lodge to turn around to look at him.

Her eyes held no shine. She would not giggle again this night.

"I—um—I—"

"It is late," he said. "Time to sleep."

She bowed her head and then nodded. "Good night."

"Good night," he repeated.

Another unusual sensation filled his stomach. Guilt. Guilt at telling her she talked too much last night. Why had he been sent a woman who changed so many things about him?

They both went to their beds, across the lodge from one another. Not small compared to many others, his lodge seemed even bigger tonight. The distance between him and Poeso was as great as the land from Father River to the Great Mountain. If she was already in California, his heart could not miss her more.

Tired from many days of hunting, his body longed for sleep, but his mind would not rest. He closed his eyes, but that did not help. Poeso filled the vision that formed. He was a Cheyenne warrior. A leader of many like him. When he took another wife—something One Who Heals reminded him often he must do soon in order to see his children grow into strong warriors—it was expected that it would be a Cheyenne maiden. Many fathers had brought their daughters to him, but he felt no connection to them. No desire to mate.

He could not take a white woman as a wife. People would lose their trust in him. The Tribal Council would lose their trust in him. That could not be. His people needed a leader with strong power. Strong mind and body.

He had killed more buffalo than all the others during the hunt, but that would not happen again if he lost his power. Lost his good medicine. His family would go hungry. Starve.

The air that left his lungs was as heavy as his heart. If he could not believe in himself, others could not. If he could not trust himself, others would not.

His own thoughts twisted, telling him Little One was a white woman and a leader could marry her, if she wanted it. Little One was Cheyenne, he argued in silence. She had been raised with Tsitsistas; she had become one. Poeso would not. She had learned much, but was too proud to change completely. Too much in love with the white man's money. Her money in California.

She could not be his wife. Could not be his woman.

He should not think about things that could never be. That worry was no good. Only a foolish man wanted things he could not have.

Sleep finally took him to dreamland, but the visions there did not make for a peaceful night.

Black Horse left his lodge before Father Sun appeared in the east and bathed by himself. After commanding Rising Sun to watch over the people in his absence, Black Horse mounted Horse and rode up into the hills to find solace and the medicine to end the turmoil inside him. He would not return until Black Horse the leader and Black Horse the man were once again united, as they had been before Poeso arrived. He owed that to his people.

Lorna could not remember being so worried, not ever, and there was plenty of anger rolling around inside her, too. "What do you mean no one knows where he went?" she asked Little One, whose lodge she had just entered. "He is your leader. He can't just up and disappear."

"He didn't disappear," Meg said, stepping up beside her sister. "He went on a vision quest."

"A what?"

"A vision quest," Little One said. "To find answers." She shook her head. "I have hurt my brother. Not knowing if I should leave or stay has hurt Black Horse."

"What?" Lorna asked.

"Shh," Meg said as she assisted Little One to the ground. "Can't you see this is upsetting to her?"

"To *her*?" Lorna said. "What about *me*? I'm the one alone in a teepee. Anyone could barge in at any time."

"Stands Tall won't let that happen," Meg said. "Besides, after what happened to the warrior from the Fox Band, no one would dare attempt to enter Black Horse's lodge."

Flustered in ways she'd never been, Lorna pointed out, "Nothing happened to that warrior."

"He was shunned by my brother," Little One said. "Therefore he is shunned by all. His people now call him He Who Shames."

"He has become an outcast," Meg said.

"But Black Horse saved him," Lorna said. "Didn't let that buffalo kill him."

"It was not his day to die," Little One answered.

An odd quiver touched Lorna's spine. "You mean that warrior wanted to die? Wanted that buffalo to kill him?"

"Death would be easier than being shunned by Black Horse," Little One answered.

"Did Black Horse know that? What the warrior..."

"My brother knows all."

Just when she'd thought she'd figured something out, it twisted. She'd assumed Black Horse had saved the warrior because he was that forgiving and kind, and brave. He was, but— Sighing again, she let the thought go. It would just confuse her more.

"If you'd like, I can ask Betty or Tillie to stay with you," Meg said.

Lorna plunked down on the ground next to the other two. "No, Tillie would miss those kids she's grown so fond of, and Betty would keep me up talking all night. I'll be fine." It was true. Tillie was never seen anymore without a child holding her hand, or a cradle board hanging off her back— which was an interesting sight, her still wearing the black nun's outfit every day—and Betty talked more now than ever. She'd become a self-proclaimed expert on the Cheyenne. "Where did Black Horse go on this vision quest?"

"To a place in the hills where he is alone to pray to Maheo about the problems concerning his band and his family," Meg answered. "Much like we Christians go to church in order pray to God."

"How long will it take?"

Meg shrugged. "Until he receives a vision that will show him the answers."

Lorna propped her elbow on a crossed knee, and set her chin in her palm. "Church services are rarely over an hour long where I come from." A chill made her quiver. "What if he doesn't come back?"

"He will come back," Little One said. "And I must have my answer when he does."

Although she greatly wanted Black Horse to return

soon, Lorna couldn't help but say, "Now, don't go making hasty decisions. That won't help anyone."

Meg frowned.

Lorna shrugged. "I left my home on a rash decision."

"Do you regret that now?"

Lorna shook her head. Regret she would never have—not when it came to leaving England. "No, but I never had a family who cared. Little One does. She has two families that love her. You and the Cheyenne."

"Your family must have loved you," Little One said. "Others, too. You had over a hundred people at your birthday party."

Lorna glanced at Meg, who shrugged.

"I had a hundred people at my party," Lorna said, "because that is what those hundred people do. They attend parties. No matter whose birthday it is, they are there, gifting the same items they gave the year before, the party before. That's not love, it's society. Like counting coup. Something to be bragged about." A great weight filled her chest. "In reality, no one ever cared what I wanted. Didn't care if it was my birthday or not. I could have had ten birthday parties a year and no one would have noticed because they weren't there for me. No one cared if I was happy." Her throat began to burn, and deep down she missed Black Horse more than she'd ever have imagined.

Meg reached over and took a hold of her hand. "You've changed, Lorna."

"I know," she admitted, "and I can't say I like it."

A soft smiled formed on Meg's lips. "You will, eventually, you will. It just takes some time to get used to."

"And then what?" Lorna asked. "I get used to it, then what?"

Meg clearly didn't know. There had been no need for her to shrug or shake her head. Lorna felt the exact same way. She had no idea what any of it meant. However, if the changes inside her meant she learned to care about people only to have them leave without a word of warning, then she'd rather go back to hating everyone. There was a lot less disappointment in that.

The one other thing she did know was that she wasn't looking forward to sleeping alone tonight. It wasn't because she was afraid, either.

Pushing off the ground, she stood. "I'll see you tomorrow."

"Do you want us to walk to the latrine with you?" Meg asked.

"No, I'm fine," Lorna answered, although fine was the very thing she wasn't. "Night."

She told Stands Tall he could go to his lodge, but he refused. But even his reassuring presence did nothing to assuage her loneliness without Black Horse.

The next day it did something it hadn't done in weeks. It rained. Not just a passing shower, but a downpour that lasted all day. However, life went on the same as usual. The tasks were simply moved indoors, including cooking. Except that was, for Stands Tall. He remained within a few feet of the lodge, getting soaked.

"At least come inside and eat," Lorna shouted past the roar of the falling rain. Meg and Little One, along with One Who Heals and a few other women had brought their chores into Black Horse's lodge that morning, most likely knowing she wouldn't have gone to one of theirs. When the rain had started early in the day, her thoughts had gone to Black Horse, alone in the hills somewhere, without shelter, without food. Actually, her thoughts had never really been without him, but they grew more concerning as the weather worsened.

The women, besides their many chores, had brought along food and cooked it over a fire built in the center of the lodge, and the other men of their family roamed in and out to eat every so often. Stands Tall came in to eat, too, but only after One Who Heals had shouted a long line of words at him. He took a bowl of the boiled meat and sat near the flap to eat it while the women went back to their tasks.

Lorna had been assigned to stitching two pieces of tanned deerskin together. The pieces were soft, but sturdy, and the sewing was not the kind she had been forced to learn in her younger years. Here she had a sharp awl, a bone from some animal—she didn't ask what—that had been mounted into a wooden handle in order to punch holes in the hide. She threaded a piece of dried sinew through a hole, pulled it tight and repeated the action again a very precise distance. The stitches themselves were to make an X and needed to be as symmetrical as everything else in the Cheyenne world. This was very important. The women were very proud of their sewing and the slightest imperfection could ruin the entire project. It would be cut apart and used for something else.

Smiles, or She Who Smiles, as Lorna had discovered, was the one teaching her. The woman had also been the one to show her most of the other tasks she'd learned. Lorna appreciated the woman's patience, but after learning Smiles was Black Horse's former mother-in-law, Lorna felt uncomfortable around her. There was no good reason. It was just there—inside her.

Along with many other things. She'd spent most of the night staring at the empty bed across the lodge. One thought hung heavier than others. She wondered if Black Horse had left because he'd kissed her. Because she'd let him kiss her. As much as she didn't want to compare it with what had happened when Douglas had burst into her bed-room last year, she couldn't help it. Nothing about Black Horse reminded her of Douglas. They were complete op-posites, and the events were as different as night and day. Except that Douglas had also said she'd teased him—and other men—for years. That she had gotten exactly what she'd deserved. Her mother had said something very sim-ilar, and she wondered if Black Horse thought that, too. That she'd been asking for it.

They had been teasing each other, but not in the deceit-ful, devious way Douglas and her mother had implied. She hadn't done anything remotely similar. Not back then, and not with Black Horse.

Her old anger, that which had slowly been dissolving until it had almost disappeared, returned and ate at her as hungrily as it had when she'd left England. It made her de-sire for revenge that much stronger and once again made getting to California a burning need, while at the same time, she questioned leaving. It was tearing her apart.

Later, when everyone prepared to return to their own lodges, she asked Meg, Tillie and Betty to stay for a few minutes. They looked at each other cautiously, but re-mained.

"I've been thinking," Lorna said when it was just the four of them. "What if we left now for California?" In-stantly sensing arguments, she held up a hand. "Hear me out. We could lighten our load, hitch all four mules to one wagon so they wouldn't have to work so hard and could travel farther each day. Maybe even buy some new mules at a town along the way."

"Carolyn hasn't decided—"

"I know," Lorna interrupted Meg. "But she doesn't have to decide. Not right now. Once we get to California and I complete my business, we could return. That would give Carolyn time to decide."

"Return?" Betty said. "You want to go to California, and then return here?"

"Yes." She chewed on her bottom lip before adding, "So Meg and Carolyn can have the time they need to get to know each other, and…" The silent reasoning she'd mulled over all day didn't sound as good when spoken aloud.

"That doesn't make sense," Tillie said. "We'd never make the trip to California and back before winter. We'd have to wait until spring, and we'd have no idea where to find the band next summer."

"We could ask them where they'd be."

"They won't know," Betty said. "They follow the buffalo."

"We could ask them to leave a trail," Lorna said.

"One that anyone could follow?" Tillie asked. "That would be very dangerous for The People."

"It won't work, Lorna," Meg finally said. "Thank you for thinking of options, but that's not one." After a long sigh, Meg said, "It's more complicated than any of us realize for Carolyn to make a decision. She's reached the marrying age. No one has hurried her, because that would usually be left up to her parents, and Black Horse said it would be her decision to say when that might be. Normally, her parents would choose a fitting young man from another Cheyenne band, because that would strengthen their relationship with other bands. There, too, Black Horse has said the decision will be hers. During the hunt, while the bands were all gathered, a young man's family approached One Who Heals, asking her to tell Black Horse they were interested in their son marrying Little One."

"Who is it?" Betty wanted to know. "I've met several families from all of the bands. Some very nice families."

Lorna's jaw tightened. It was a good thing Betty had been gifted with the knowledge of how to cook, because sometimes she lacked common sense. Did she not remember the warrior trying to sneak into Moon Flower's lodge?

Meg was already replying to Betty. "His name is Swift Fox, and Little One is torn by this news. She has known Swift Fox for years. His band has joined Black Horse's to hunt many times, and she has a great fondness for him."

Betty's little moan of adoration was almost more than Lorna could take.

"Swift Fox says he will become part of Black Horse's band if Little One will marry him, and if Black Horse will permit it."

"What did Black Horse say?" Lorna asked, a bit miffed he hadn't mentioned any of this to her.

"He left before One Who Heals could tell him," Meg answered. "Swift Fox and his family came to our lodge the night the hunt ended. The night before Black Horse left."

"Maybe Swift Fox had seen him and talked to him after speaking to One Who Heals," Betty said. "And that's what Black Horse is seeking in his vision. The correct answer."

Meg's gaze settled on Lorna. "I don't think so. Neither does One Who Heals. She thinks his vision quest is about something else entirely."

Chapter Twelve

Black Horse had never experienced such discontent, or been so restless. He had spent five moons away from the village, and had many visions, yet still had no answers. At night, when he'd lain upon the earth beneath the towering pines, he had wished Poeso was here with him, just like in his visions when she walked beside him. That had brought joy inside his heart, but he had seen a time of great anger, too. In his vision, an unknown band of warriors had not been pleased by Poeso being at his side and had argued when he'd refused to join them in a battle against the white men.

His heart was heavy when he mounted Horse for the journey home. He had already stayed away too long, and for the first time he was not certain of what he must do. If Maheo had given him Poeso to walk beside him into the future, then that was what would happen, but she would not understand what that meant. She would not understand why he could not allow her to go to California and seek the white man's money.

He accepted many things, as was the Cheyenne way, but he could no longer deny the longing in his heart that told him Poeso was his true mate. Just as it was his duty to lead his people, it would be his duty to make her understand that. It would not be easy. He was used to people obeying his commands without question.

That was one more thing Poeso did not understand. Commands. He grinned slightly. She had learned to fish and cook, butcher buffalo and many other things. He would make her learn this, too. It would not be so difficult.

Black Horse clicked his tongue for Horse to increase their speed toward the camp as a sense of impatience grew larger within him.

The camp crier saw him coming down the hill, and by the time he neared the village, children raced out to meet him. Most of the other bands had left. As far as he could tell, only Silver Bear's clan remained with his. They were not a large band, their numbers much like his. Small groups fared better. It was easier to find enough food for fifty than for one hundred, and easier to hide when necessary. There were messengers who traveled between all of the bands, sharing news of friends and families, and warning of dangers. Word of Poeso and the other white women in his camp had already been carried to other bands, and he would be faced with many questions when the Tribal Council met after the leaves fell from the trees. That did not worry him.

Black Horse grinned and lifted a hand to the children cheering his return, and allowed them to lead him and Horse into the center of the village. His homecoming warmed his heart. He felt whole again. Both as a warrior chief and a man. As he greeted friends and family, his eyes searched for one woman. The wagons were parked on the outskirts of the village, but he had not needed to see them to know she had not left. He had felt her presence inside him during his absence and knew she was still in the village.

When he spied her standing outside his lodge, he bit

the inside of his bottom lip to keep his happiness hidden. There was anger in her eyes and her hands were on her hips. She was mad he had left, and would tell him that. He met her gaze and held it until she glanced away briefly. Like the rest of him, his heart grew whole.

She was glad he was back, but could not accept that. Anger she knew; love she did not.

The visions back in the hills may not have been the ones he had expected, but they had been for him, and he accepted that. They had shown him many things. Poeso would not leave. Here was where she would find the love in her heart.

Black Horse dismounted and greeted his family as Horse was led away.

"I must council with you, my brother," Little One said as she welcomed him home. "Today."

"Heehe'e," he answered, and told her to come to his lodge later. He had not forgotten his sister while on his quest. It was time for her to decide. His thoughts paused to contemplate something he had not considered. Hunting buffalo, finding good land to set their lodges upon, attending councils about wars and dangers to his people were easy things for him. Ensuring the women he cared about were happy was not. If need be, he would seek council from One Who Heals about that. Later. After he was reunited with Poeso.

He greeted others while slowly making his way toward his lodge. Poeso had not moved from her stance, and he was proud of her for that. Her anger made her a brave and fierce woman, like a warrior. He knew how to handle warriors.

When he stopped before her, only her chin moved, so they met eye to eye.

"Epeva'e," he said.

Her eyes darkened. *"Hova'ahane,"* she hissed. *"Epeva'e."*

He grinned at how well she spoke the Cheyenne words.

"I don't know what you're grinning about," she said. "I just told you, no, it's not good."

He nodded and gestured to his lodge. *"Nahaeana."*

"I don't care if you're hungry," she snapped. "I'm not your cook."

The other women of his family had already assumed he'd be hungry and were arriving with bowls. He took one, gestured for her to be given one, and said he and Poeso would eat alone. She did not protest.

He entered the lodge behind her and took a deep breath, letting the air linger in his nose. It smelled like her, like the tiny white flowers that bloomed after the snow melts. He smiled. "It is good to be home."

She stomped around him and sat down. He lowered onto the ground and set his bowl beside the one she'd set down.

"I thought you were hungry," she said.

"No," he answered quietly, "I wanted to be alone."

"Alone? You've been alone for five days."

"Alone with you," he corrected.

"Well, maybe I don't want to be alone with you."

He shrugged. "You may leave."

Her eyes grew wide and her mouth fell open for a brief moment. "Leave?"

"Heehe'e."

Anger returned as her eyes narrowed. "Of course I can leave. I can leave whenever I want, but I'm not. Not until you tell me where you were. What you were doing in the hills."

"I gave my praise to Maheo for many buffalo, and sought guidance as to where to lead the people until the buffalo run again."

"That took you five days? Couldn't you just have said your prayers here?"

"Our ways are different, Poeso."

"You don't have to tell me that." She shifted slightly and tucked her skirt around her bent knees. "I've figured it out."

The pout of her lips and the softness of her eyes stirred him, and he thought of the days to come. Of the nights to come. His throat thickened and he glanced around before pointing out, "You have new moccasins."

She stretched one foot out and twisted it. "I'll have you know, I made these myself." Running a hand over the hide, she said, "She Who Smiles helped me, but I did almost all of the stitches."

"You like them?"

"Actually, I do. They are softer and more comfortable then my boots."

"Epeva'e."

She folded her arm and stared at him. Anger no longer glistened in her eyes. "I'm still mad at you," she said.

"Why?"

"Because you left without a word. I had no idea where you went or when you'd be back—if at all."

"I regret my leaving angered you, Poeso. It should not. I will always come back."

"Not if you get hurt, or—"

"You worry about Black Horse?"

"N—" She bit her lips together and closed her eyes. Opening them, she said, "Yes."

"Why?"

"I don't know. Because you're the leader, I guess. Everyone worries about you. Everyone depends on you."

"Heehe'e," he said. "This is true."

Her teeth chewed on her bottom lip as she glanced

around the lodge. Bringing her eyes back to him, she asked, "Did Maheo tell you to keep leading the band west?"

"Toward California?"

Her eyes lit up. "Yes."

"No," he said. "That is not our land. That is where the Shoshoni hunt."

"Oh. North, then?"

"Crow," he said, shaking his head. "And Sioux."

Her shoulders slumped. "I thought all you Indians got along."

"We do when we respect each other and our separate hunting grounds." The direction he would lead the people followed the traditional route taken by his people after the hunt. They had many buffalo hides and beaver furs to trade at the white man's post. He just liked to tease her. "We will go north, Poeso, and west. But only as far as the fort where the wagon trains stop."

"Fort Laramie?"

There was surprise in her voice, as he'd expected. It would take a few days to get to the post, and by then she would not want to return to the white man's world. He would make sure of that. *"Heehe'e,"* he answered.

"When?"

"We will leave in the morning," he said.

Lorna tried to believe the news made her happy. It should. Yet it didn't. She was also wrestling with how seeing Black Horse had sent her heart dancing. Keeping that to herself had been close to painful when he'd ridden into the camp. She'd wanted to run out to greet him like the children had, or at least surround his horse like the rest of the women in his family. Her stubbornness wouldn't let her. She wasn't part of his family. Nor were Tillie and Betty, but that hadn't stopped them from cheering and racing to the center of the village.

With little else to do, and nothing more to say, she picked up her bowl.

"You are saddened by the news?" he asked as she stared at the food.

"No. Why would that sadden me? I need to get to California."

"To get much money."

She lifted her head. "Yes, to get my money. Lots of it."

"Much money will make you happy?"

Not wanting to talk about what made her happy and what didn't, she pointed toward his bowl. "Aren't you going to eat? You must be hungry."

"Will that make you happy?"

She set her bowl down, not caring how the contents bounced over the edge. "Why do you care if that makes me happy? No one has ever cared if I was happy or sad or angry or worried. Why do you? Of all people, why do you?"

"This, too, angers you?"

"No," she said. "It confuses me, and I don't like being confused."

"What confuses you?"

"Everything." Exasperated, she leaped to her feet. "You confuse me. You are so strong and powerful, yet so patient and calm. Everyone here is patient and calm. She Who Smiles never got mad at me, not once during all the things she taught me and my many mistakes." Pacing around him, she continued, "Even One Who Heals, who clearly doesn't like me, no longer makes me feel unwelcome. And that's confusing. Why do I feel welcome here? Why have you made all of us welcome here? You shouldn't have. It makes us not want to leave. Makes me not want to…" Her breath left her lungs with a slow burn.

He stood and the gentleness of his expression, a mixture of understanding and sympathy, made her eyes burn.

"Leave?" he asked quietly.

Lorna knew with all her being she shouldn't feel this way, yet couldn't help it. She couldn't deny it, either. "Yes," she said. "For some inexplicable reason, I don't want to leave. At least not as badly as I used to. As I should."

"I don't want you to leave, Poeso."

Her heart beat so hard it hurt, and her mind swirled so quickly she grew dizzy. "Why?" Catching herself, she held up a hand. "No, don't answer that. I have to leave. We have to leave. The others and I. We don't belong here."

"Where do you belong?"

"I don't know." She shook her head. "Maybe I don't belong anywhere."

"Yes, you do." He stepped closer and held out a hand. "I will show you."

"Show me?"

"Heehe'e," he answered, taking her hand. "Sit."

"I—"

"Sit, Poeso."

She let out a sigh and plopped onto the ground. He sat down, but not beside her, behind her. Close behind her. He stretched his long legs out around hers and then circled her upper body with his arms.

"Close your eyes, Poeso." His breath tickled the side of her face.

Her heart beat so hard she could barely think. "Why?"

"Just close your eyes."

She did so. Within seconds, she couldn't explain how or why, the tension in her body slipped away and her mind no longer spun. A deep sense of serenity encouraged her to relax and accept the tranquility. Letting the air escape her lungs, she leaned back against him. Much like the last time, she could feel his energy entering her. This time it was peaceful.

"See nothing, Poeso," he whispered. "Hear nothing but my voice."

His presence easily blocked out everything else.

"Think of what makes you happy," he whispered. "See it in your mind. Feel it in your heart."

"I don't—"

"Just think happy, Poeso."

I don't know if I've ever been happy, she finished the statement silently.

"Feel it in your heart," Black Horse whispered in her ear. "Remember it in your heart."

That was impossible. How was she supposed to focus on anything with his arms wrapped around her? It reminded her of the night he'd scared her by the latrine, and kissed her. She'd remembered that every minute he'd been gone. In her mind and in her heart. She had been happy then— when he'd kissed her.

At that her heart thudded so hard it startled her.

"It's there, Poeso," he said. "Your happiness is in your heart."

Lorna thrust herself out of his arms and scrambled to her feet before turning around. "You can't know what's in my heart! You can't!"

He crossed his legs and his arms. "Where you belong is in your heart."

She wasn't willing to agree to that. Her breathing was uneven and she tried to make sense of it all. "I belong in California. It's not in my heart because I haven't been there yet."

Black Horse gave her one of those little head nods and then stood. "I must speak to Rising Sun." A mischievous smile fluttered across his lips. "I will return. Do not worry."

"I won't," she said. "And I wasn't worried before." That was a lie, but no other retort would form. Her mind was attempting to remember a time she'd been happy—other than the night he'd kissed her.

Nothing formed, and as Black Horse left, leaving her in the lodge where she'd already spent many lonely hours, her heart and mind recalled the night they'd kissed with even more longing. Seeing him, knowing he was back also filled her with a unique joy. One she couldn't help but remember.

Black Horse was indeed happy to be home, and happy Poeso had missed him. Showing her where she belonged would be easy, and he once again felt power and pride inside himself. That evening, after many people filled the lodge for the evening meal, he told Little One to stay while the others left. When Poeso stood to exit with the others, he grasped her hand, silently telling her she could stay. She smiled softly, but shook her head.

He watched her go, and waited for the lodge flap to close before turning to his sister. "All was well in my absence?"

"Yes. Rising Sun is a good leader. Not as good as you, but the people respect him."

They were speaking in Cheyenne, and he was surprised how his mind translated the words into English. He'd been doing that more often lately, as if challenging himself to know the language better. When speaking with Poeso, he liked being able to use many words.

"I must tell you something, brother."

"I know," he answered. "It is about Swift Fox and his proposal."

"You know?"

"Yes." He had known before going on his quest. The signs had been there during the hunt. Silver Bear's clan was still here because they were awaiting his approval. "You told him yes."

"No, I have not," Little One said.

"Do you not want to be Swift Fox's wife?"

She bowed her head. "I do, but I also want to remain your sister, and I also want to remain Meg's sister."

"You are only one person."

"I know," she said with tears in her eyes. "I don't know who I love more. Who needs me more."

"There are many kinds of love, Ayashe, and each is different. I love you very much, and you will always be my sister, but a love for your husband is different and you must be prepared to follow him."

"Swift Fox will become a member of our band, stay with my family, as tradition requires."

"For now, but someday he might want his own band."

"No," she argued. "We will not leave you. We will not leave our band."

He chose not to argue that with her. She was too young to understand how things changed. Food had been plentiful, but there could come a time when it was not, and the bands would need to separate into many smaller ones to feed their people. Changing the subject to the other issue hurting her heart, he said, "What of your sister, Meg?"

"I want to be with her, too," Little One said. "But I don't know if I could live in her world. It is very different from ours. Very strange."

An odd tingling made the hair on his arms rise, much like when he sensed someone was near. Yet this was different, like her words made him aware of something inside him. The white world was very different from theirs. He had always known that, but it had concerned him little. Until now. "You remember this?"

"Some, and Meg has told me more."

Centering his focus on Little One rather than on differences he might need to learn more about, he said, "You are very young for such decisions. I have thought about that and will ask something of you."

"What?"

"I will ask Silver Bear to join us in the voyage to the white man's trading post. You will be allowed to visit this post, if you wish." In all the years she had been with the band, she had never been allowed such freedom. Fear she would be taken back had been alive in all of them since she came to live with them, and he wanted Swift Fox to understand if he took her as a bride, she would need more protection than other maidens. He also wanted her to witness some of the white man's world and ways. Things he'd protected her from up until now. He also had to make one final warning. "Sometimes we cannot have everything our hearts desire. We must determine which is most important, or what is best for all."

"That is what you do, decide what is best for all?"

It was harder this time than ever before, but he responded with a nod. His own words were echoing in his head. Just as Swift Fox would need to know Little One would need more protection than others, he needed to understand Poeso would need more protection than a Cheyenne wife.

Little One sighed heavily, and he knew what he had told her had not been what she had expected.

"You will not decide for me?" she asked.

He knew that was what she had wanted. Just as he now understood he had to make his own decisions. The vision could show him what should be, but only his actions would make them come to pass. "No, I will not decide for you." There was pleading in her eyes, and he shook his head. "We will not speak of this again until after our journey to the fort."

Although clearly disappointed, with respect, she said, "Thank you, brother," before leaving his lodge.

Black Horse pushed the air out of his body. He could not have all he wanted any more than Little One could. Although he knew Poeso was his true mate, he could not force that upon her. It was not the Cheyenne way to make others do what was against their will.

The weight inside him made him feel tired and old. He was neither, and there was still much to be done. He left his lodge to council with Silver Bear, and then told the camp crier to announce they would begin their journey to the white man's trading post in the morning. On his way to the horses, he spied Poeso sitting near the water where he'd taught her to fish. The memory was a happy one and he smiled. He would forever remember much about this white woman who swam like an otter and hissed like a cat.

He paused long enough to speak with the young boys assigned to his herd. That was a young brave's first job, to tend to the horses, and they took pride in their abilities. Horse had been rubbed down with grass until his black coat was shinny and slick, and now he snorted, telling him all was well.

Black Horse then made his way to the river.

"I will miss this place," Poeso said, tossing a pebble into the water as he arrived at her side.

He sat and folded his legs. "You will?"

"Yes. It is very pretty. Very peaceful. Is that why you chose this spot?"

He gestured toward the hills. "It is well protected from the wind, and holds much grass for the animals, and water." With another gesture toward the trees, he added, "And wood for fires."

"That is all true," she said. "But it's still pretty. One of the prettiest places I've ever been."

Pointing toward her lap, he asked, "What do you have?"

"This?" She picked the book up off her lap.

He nodded.

She set it on the ground beside her. "It's my diary. I started it when I left England. It made me feel as if I wasn't alone. I had several when I was smaller, but only wrote in them once in a while. When I was mad or hurt. I guess that is why I started this one."

He had seen the books the white man wrote in at the fort and the ones the churchwomen had carried and read strange words from. "What is in your book?"

"My thoughts mainly. I was just reading some of the things I'd written."

"You write about Black Horse?"

She laughed. "No."

"Why? You could say he mighty hunter. Kill many buffalo."

Her eyes were like the sun on the water when she looked up at him. "I could. You did kill many buffalo." She pointed to her moccasins. "I decorated my new shoes with the teeth from one of them. She Who Smiles showed me how to drill holes in them and sew them on." She laughed again. "Now, *that* I should write in my diary. No one would ever believe I walk around with animal teeth on my shoes, and that I like it."

"Why?"

"Well, animal teeth aren't commonly used for jewelry in England."

He did not completely understand, but nodded. "What do you sew on your clothes in England?"

"Lace mainly. My mother insisted on it. Lots and lots of lace."

"You do not like lace?"

Her smile returned, but a frown sat between her eyes. "Do you know what lace is?"

"Hova'ahane."

"I didn't think so." Her smile filled her words. "It's thin, fine thread woven into frilly light material and then sewn on in layers and layers. Sort of like the fringes on my moccasins."

"I like your moccasins."

"I do, too," she said. "I like them a lot."

Her gaze had gone to the sun sliding to sleep behind a hill. He waited, watching as it fell lower, before he asked, "Do you miss England, Poeso?"

"No."

Her response was so swift and harsh he turned to look at her. She still stared at the sun, but he could feel her sadness. "Do you miss your family?" he asked.

"No. Never." She closed her eyes and sighed before turning to look at him. "That's wrong, isn't it?"

"It is not wrong to feel what is in your heart."

"I don't think my heart works like yours does. Like everyone else's here does. Maybe an Indian heart is different from a white person's."

"I do not believe that," he said.

"I don't, either," she said. "But we are different."

"Heehe'e," he answered. "We are different because our lives are different." The wind blew her hair around her face. He reached up and tucked it behind her ear. "Lives can change. Lives do change."

"But do hearts?"

His had changed much in the days since seeing her in the river. Whether he had wanted it to or not, realized it or not, his life had changed. His heart had changed. *"Heehe'e,"* he said.

He could understand the sadness in her eyes, and put his arm around her.

She leaned her head on his shoulder. "I've never sat

and watched the sun set before," she whispered. "Not even while on the wagon train."

Tightening his hold on her, he whispered, *"Ese'he."*

"Is that the word for sun?"

He nodded.

"Ese'he." She sighed. "The Cheyenne words are much prettier than English ones."

"You did not think so before."

She tilted her head to look up at him. "I changed my mind."

The sparkles in her eyes made him smile. *"Epeva'e."*

Chapter Thirteen

Lorna had thought she'd sleep well with Black Horse back home. The long nights alone had been sleepless and she'd assumed that had been because of his absence. It may have been, but tonight, sleep evaded her because of his presence. The pine boughs beneath him rustled as he moved and echoed through the lodge, as did his breathing, which told her he wasn't asleep, either.

"Can you not sleep, Poeso?"

"I'm sorry. I didn't mean to keep you awake."

"Hova'ahane," he said. "You are not. *Ehaoho'ta."*

"Heehe'e," she agreed. *"Ehaoho'ta."* It indeed was hot, but the heat seemed to be inside her. She'd already taken off her moccasins, something she usually didn't do. Since leaving Missouri she hadn't undressed for bed, not even her footwear. In truth, she'd slept in her clothes since leaving England. Douglas had entered her room just as she'd changed into her nightclothes, and after that night, she hadn't been able to don a night rail. Might never again.

"You could take off clothes," he said.

Her heart thudded, but it wasn't because she was afraid. "You have yours on."

"Heehe'e."

"Why?" Chagrin had her face burning. "I mean, do you usually sleep with your britches on? When it's this hot, I mean."

"Hova'ahane."

"Then, why are you now?" She couldn't believe she was having this conversation with him, yet now that her immediate mortification for asking had dissolved, she wasn't embarrassed, and was more than curious.

"Because I do not want to frighten you," he said.

The humor in his voice provoked her, but she could not relate it to fear. She'd seen more bare skin since arriving at the village than she'd ever have imagined. He never wore a shirt. Most of the men in the camp didn't, and almost all of the children, the little ones, ran around as bare as the day they were born. The mothers took precautions by rubbing the youngsters down with a mixture of lard and clay to keep them from blistering beneath the blazing sun. Even the women...

"Why do you sleep in your dress?" he asked, interrupting her thoughts.

Unable to come up with an answer midthought, she said, "Because I don't want to frighten you."

He laughed. "Poeso not frighten Black Horse."

She didn't doubt that.

"I know what is beneath your dress."

She catapulted upright and spun around to face his bed across the lodge. He was sitting up, too. "When?" She'd bathed with the rest of the women, but he'd never been around the village then.

He laughed again. "At the river. When I found you. You were not wearing your dress."

"When you threw me over your horse," she added, although that no longer angered her. Surprisingly, she'd forgotten how close to naked she'd been that day. It hadn't scared her then. Most likely because she'd thought they'd all be dead soon. That had made her state of dress a very minor detail.

"Heehe'e," he answered. "And you bit me."

Another minor detail she'd forgotten about. "I did, didn't I?"

"Heehe'e."

"And you stole my gun."

"Not stole. I gave it back."

"Heehe'e. You did."

Despite the darkness, she saw how he sat straight and tall, as always, with his chin lifted slightly and his broad shoulders square. Proud but not conceited. She liked that. His confidence. And she liked his protection, for that was what she felt when he was near. Like no one could hurt her.

"I grieve that you were hurt, Poeso."

His statement was so out of the blue, her breath caught. "You grieve?"

"Heehe'e."

She bowed her head, not from embarrassment, but a woeful sensation that she couldn't explain. "I do, too." It had been over a year ago, and the pain wasn't nearly as strong. Her desire for retribution was no longer forefront in her mind. "I will forever hate him," she whispered. "Forever."

"Hate can ruin a heart."

"I know." She had already told him more than she'd told anyone, but couldn't stop the words as they started rolling off her tongue. "They, my mother and Douglas, told me to get dressed and meet them downstairs. I knew they were going to send me away, off to some isolated country estate like they so often did, or maybe I knew it would be worse that time. I got dressed and I dug out the envelope my father had given me. He'd told me about Elliot Chadwick only weeks before he had died. Almost as if he knew his time was limited. I didn't realize that then, but do now. He was robbed and murdered on his way home one night. They never found who did it. Anyway, there was money in the envelope he'd given me, lots of it, and a note he'd written, laying down the details of what he'd told me. That I was only to use the money if he wasn't around and I was in danger. I'd looked at that money plenty of times, thinking of the things I could buy with it, but I never used it, not until that night."

"What did you do?"

"I left the house, and stole a horse. I'm not even sure where I found it, but I rode it to the other side of town. I was sure I was being followed, so I let it go and stole another, then another." The blurriness of that time hadn't cleared in the months since. Might never. "I just kept moving, day and night. I rented carriages and took trains, even boats up the coast. Eventually, I found a ship sailing to New York and bought passage. It was January when I arrived in New York, and it took me some time to find William Chadwick. By then I no longer felt as if I was being followed, but I couldn't wait for him to contact Elliot in California."

"Why?"

"I don't know," she answered honestly. "I just couldn't. I didn't trust anyone. Something inside me said I had to go to California, just as strongly as it said I had to come to America."

"You have great will, Poeso."

His words filled her with so much pride her chest puffed. No one had ever paid her compliments like he did, not ones they really meant. She wasn't sure how to respond, and settled for saying a simple "Thank you."

"You greatly desire to meet this Elliot Chadwick and get your money."

An undertone in his voice sent a chill over her heated skin. Of course she did. She had to get to California and meet Elliot and get her money, she had to. Yet the desire wasn't as strong as it once had been. Lorna twisted, about to lie back down. "We should sleep now."

"You are no longer hot?"

"No," she answered. The heat was the least of her worries. Right now, her greatest desire—one far stronger than getting to California—was to crawl over and lie next to Black Horse. To feel his lips on hers again and to sleep with his arms around her.

Despite such foreign desires, Lorna slept at some point, and the next morning was too busy to focus on what had kept her awake. She went about tearing down the lodge and packing it for travel as if she'd been doing it her entire life. Of course, she still had help, and was thankful for that. Black Horse was nowhere to be seen, hadn't been since she awoke, which at least told her she had indeed slept.

Tillie, along with a small child, were on the wagon seat when Lorna climbed up to drive the team of mules into the long line already heading away from the place she'd come to think of as home. An oddity for sure. There was nothing here, now that the lodges had all been taken down. She'd changed during the weeks they'd camped in this little valley and wasn't sure how or why. There seemed to be many things she wasn't sure of anymore.

The line of people stretching out across the prairie was no longer a strange sight. There were far fewer this time, but she still couldn't see the leader. Black Horse. He and his huge horse had long ago disappeared into the horizon. Her heart skipped a beat at the thought of him, as it did regularly these days.

She attempted to pull her mind off him by picking out

others she knew. Besides Meg, Betty and Tillie, there were many, including Stands Tall riding his stocky black-and-white horse next to her wagon. His presence no longer irritated her. In truth, she respected him and his duties, not only in how he watched over her, but how he and the others in his profession stood guard over the entire village.

The children were another group she'd gained respect for. They were very well behaved, and from the time they could walk, they knew how to ride a horse. Many had their own ponies, and rode them proudly. The children were also excellent at amusing themselves. Even the youngest, those swaddled tightly in cradle boards, giggled as they bobbed along, hanging off the side of a horse their mothers rode or walked beside.

She found herself smiling at their adorable actions more often than not.

"What are you grinning about?" Tillie asked.

Lorna shrugged. "Nothing in particular."

"You've been doing that more and more lately. Smiling. It looks good on you."

"I guess there's something to be said for traveling in numbers," Lorna said, looking deep to find an explanation for things she didn't understand.

"There were a number of others on the wagon train," Tillie pointed out.

"Yes, there were," Lorna replied. "An untrustworthy number."

Tillie grinned. "I trust the Cheyenne far more than I did those on the wagon train, too. They are a lot like us."

"Like us?"

"Yes," Tillie answered. "One for all and all for one."

Lorna glanced toward her friend. They were both dressed in their nun outfits, mainly because the habits provided protection from the sun that was sure to accompany them the entire day. Despite the black material surrounding Tillie's face, she looked prettier than ever before. There was color in her cheeks and a shine in her eyes that hadn't been there previously. She, too, had changed. Nodding, Lorna agreed. "You're right."

"I think I'm right about what you were grinning about, too," Tillie said, pointing ahead of them.

Lorna turned to gaze in that general direction. Even before her eyes found him, her heart started beating faster. Far ahead, a big black horse was making its way toward them.

"He likes you," Tillie said.

Lorna's cheeks burned. "No more than he likes anyone else."

Tillie laughed. "Believe what you want, but I've seen a man in love before, and that man is in love."

A shiver, not a chill, but one filled with delight, rippled inside her. "You don't know what you are saying. And you shouldn't be talking about such things."

"Why not? Because he's a Cheyenne Indian?" Tillie shook her head. "Human love is as color-blind as God's love."

"Love is not…" Her train of thought went blank as Black Horse rode closer.

"Not what you want?" Tillie asked.

"It doesn't matter what I want or don't want. We'll soon be heading for California, and may never see any of these people again," Lorna said.

"I know." Tillie sighed. "I can't say I like that thought. I know Betty and Meg don't."

Anger, or something akin to it, rose inside Lorna. "Well, we really don't have a choice, do we?"

"Yes, we do," Tillie said. "There's nothing in California for me. When Adam was alive, we had a dream of making something together, but there's nothing for me alone. There won't be a big farm with cattle and a house with real glass windows and wooden floors. No…"

Lorna had stopped listening. Black Horse was almost to the wagon and he was leading another horse. A black-and-white paint with big brown eyes. Black Horse was smiling, and that increased her heartbeat yet again.

He spoke to Stands Tall before circling around and riding up beside the wagon. *"Monehe'se?"*

"Ready to go where?" she asked.

He grinned and held out the rope reins of the horse he led.

"I'm driving the wagon," she said.

"I can drive the wagon," Tillie said, easily taking the reins from her hands and guiding the mules out of the line. "Go with him," she whispered under her breath. "It'll be more fun than driving the mules all day."

Lorna was attempting to hide an incredible amount of joy and delight. More than once she'd dreamed of riding one of the Indian ponies. They were very well behaved, and she'd longed for the freedom of riding upon a horse's back for ages. The idea of riding beside Black Horse was the most thrilling of all.

"Go on," Tillie said. "Don't keep him waiting."

Lorna climbed down and walked to where Black Horse waited, her heart beating twice as fast as it should. His smile was part of the reason. She had to admit that. That much was as clear to her as the blue sky overhead. He said nothing as he grasped her waist and lifted her onto the paint. When she attempted to settle her legs over one side, as she was used to riding, he shook his head.

"This is how I always ride."

"It is dangerous," he said.

"This is how all women ride," she said, however, without a saddle, she was questioning her ability to stay on the animal's back.

"The horse will not like it," he said. "You ride like Black Horse."

"I'll try." The disappointment of not riding at all was stronger than her fear of falling off. Finagling the yards of black material was not an easy task, but he assisted her and soon she was astride the horse with nothing beneath her but a thick woven blanket. When he handed her the reins, she asked, "What's her name?"

He shrugged. "Horse?"

She laughed. "You can't name every horse that. I think I'll call her Patches."

He grinned while grabbing a handful of his horse's mane and easily swinging up onto the big animal. Side by side they rode along the line of travelers. Black Horse returned many waves, and responded to questions from many people. Lorna understood most of the queries were inconsequential. About the weather, the travel or the land. The Cheyenne language was easy to understand now that she knew the basic sounds. In fact, it was probably far easier to learn than English.

A sense of pride filled her. She wasn't sure if it was because she'd learned their language so quickly, or if it was how Black Horse had mastered the English language so well, or just due to the fact she was riding beside him. He was very respected and esteemed, and she'd missed riding for a very long time. Whatever the reason, Lorna chose to accept the joy inside her.

She rode beside Black Horse all day, at the very head of a line of people that trailed for more than a mile behind them. When they came upon a plush green meadow with soft hills to the north dotted with pines trees and the river to the west with plenty of dead trees for firewood, Black

Horse signaled with one hand that their travels would end for the day.

It took no more than that for the line of people to disperse packhorse by packhorse and embark upon assembling the village. Within hours, lodges were set in their systematic circles, all facing east, food was being cooked over the fires and children raced about. If a person didn't know better, they might believe the village had been there for days, not hours.

The following day was much the same. Lorna rode beside Black Horse the entire time. And again the next day. Once again she wore her nun's outfit, needing the stiff wide brim to block the sun. He wore nothing more than his breeches and moccasins, and lately, she hadn't been able to pull her eyes off his glistening sun-browned skin. Lying across from him in the lodge, that image had been burned into her brain, and she'd longed to caress his skin beneath her fingertips as deeply as she'd longed for him to kiss her again.

"What are you smiling about?"

She snapped her eyes up to his face, hoping the habit hid the heat in her cheeks. "Just thinking how odd-looking we must be. A bare-chested Indian and a nun leading a line of people across the land."

He smiled. "You look happy."

"I am." The words were out before she had a chance to question herself. "Except for this heat," she then added. Happiness was not something she knew, or accepted readily, and talking about it was uncomfortable. "It's hot today, and it's still morning."

"*Heehe'e,*" he said. "We will not travel far."

"Why?" Although she wasn't certain she wanted to know the answer, she still asked, "Are we almost to the trading post?"

"It is too hot to travel," he said.

She didn't press that he had not answered her other question. A knot formed in her stomach every time she thought about the fort. That sense of doom was a sensation she'd known all of her life and she didn't welcome its return. "How soon will we stop?"

"Soon."

Lorna accepted his answer and pressed no further. Sometimes it surprised her how much she had changed. There had been a time when she'd have demanded a more specific answer, more information, but in the past weeks she'd come to understand that time wasn't as important as she'd once thought. The Cheyenne understood that. It was hard to explain, or even understand, but time just really didn't exist for the Cheyenne. It wasn't needed in their life.

She'd found freedom in that mindset. There was never any rushing to get things done, or hurrying to be somewhere at a specific time. Everything just flowed and happened naturally, when it was supposed to, and there was time for everything. Over the past few days she'd watched Black Horse guide the people, but also engage in conversations and even play with the youngsters as if their nomadic travels were just a natural part of their lives. Which they were. That, too, was something she no longer questioned.

It was amazing how easily she accepted things, as was the fact that the change didn't bother her. There was a time she would have been far more defiant, but her life had never been this peaceful. That was what she really appreciated. The constant mistrust that had filled her home had been exhausting and left a person guarded and angry all the time.

She turned slightly to cast a gaze upon Black Horse. Trust. That was what had changed. She'd come to trust him, and he trusted her. Exactly when that had happened, she wasn't sure, but was positive it had happened. That could be the reason she felt comfortable just living, just being.

Black Horse gestured that he was going back to speak with others, and she nodded. The rolling hills had opened into a small valley, making it an inviting place to camp for the night. It couldn't be later than midmorning, but, as he'd said, it was too hot to travel today. The winding river was wide here and inviting. Perhaps once the family lodges were complete, she'd sneak down to the water to cool off.

Black Horse returned shortly, but rather than tell her they would be stopping, he waved for her to follow him. She did so without question, until a glance over her shoulder showed the others had stopped far behind them.

"Where are we going?"

"Into the hills," he answered.

"Why?"

"I show you."

His grin made her heat skip. "What? What will you show me?"

He kneed his horse into a faster gait. She encouraged Patches to speed up and soon they were galloping through the tall grass. The wind caused by their movement was welcomed, and she pushed the top of her habit off her head, letting the breeze cool her sweaty scalp.

They rode across the open valley and then followed a fork in the river that carved a trail up the hill. The pine trees increased, which slowed their trek, as did the rocky terrain. When they topped a small hill, her breath momentarily caught in her lungs.

The stream they'd been riding adjacent to had formed a crystal clear pool before the water flowed over a bed of rocks and down the other side of the hill.

"It's beautiful," she said. "Absolutely beautiful."

Black Horse dismounted while she took in the scenery. The sun glistening upon the water, and the rocks and surrounding foliage were like a picture painted in the pages of a book. An enchanted book, full of pictures one could only dream of seeing.

"Come, Poeso," he said, grasping her waist.

She settled her hands on his shoulders as he lifted her off the horse and lowered her to the ground. The surrounding beauty didn't hold her attention then, he did, and she had to close her eyes to keep from staring at him, from wishing he'd kiss her. It was getting harder and harder to pretend she did not desire him.

Once her feet were on the ground, he let her go, as he always did. She let the air out of her lungs and told herself once again that she shouldn't want to kiss him. Shouldn't want him to touch her. Telling herself such things didn't do much good. In fact, it made her want it more.

They walked to the water's edge, where he sat down.

"What are you doing?" she asked.

"Taking off my moccasins," he answered.

"I see that, why?"

"So they don't get wet."

She glanced from him to the water and back again. "Are you going swimming?"

"Heehe'e."

The consequences shot through her mind, but they weren't strong enough or disturbing enough to slow her down. Plopping onto the ground, she hoisted up her skirt to tug off her moccasins. "Then, I am, too."

He removed all of his clothes, but was so swift in entering the water she barely got a glimpse of his bare backside. She wasn't about to go that far, but did remove her dress and habit. After all, he'd already seen her swimming in her underclothes.

The water was as magnificent as it promised, and she completely submerged herself, luxuriating in the cooling freshness. Coming up for air, she filled her lungs and then flipped onto her back to float atop the water.

Fully prepared to float into a place so wonderful not even thoughts would break through, she closed her eyes. At about that same moment, hands wrapped around her waist. Not afraid in the least, she giggled as Black Horse twisted her toward him.

"Are you still hot?" he asked.

Dropping her feet onto the sandy bottom, she shook her head. "No, this is wonderful. Thank you for bringing me here. I was hoping to have time to go swimming after setting up the lodges today."

"I know."

"How could you know that?"

"I saw it in your eyes."

Her smile didn't falter. For some reason, standing in the water, surrounded by nothing but nature and him, made a strange bit of courage form inside her. "What else have you seen in my eyes?"

He smiled and whispered, "This."

His lips touched hers with such gentleness her knees wobbled. She grasped his upper arms and held on tight as the pressure of his lips increased. An indescribable thrill cascaded down to her toes and instantly shot back up. She stepped closer, pressing against him as his kiss continued. It was all she remembered and more. So very much more.

Lorna didn't want the kiss to end when his lips parted from hers, but the smile on his face dissolved any disappointment.

"Come," he said. "Swim with me."

Her body was far hotter now than it had been before, on the inside. Every spot that had touched him was tingling and burning. Nodding, she stretched out into the water and kicked her feet.

They glided through the water much like they had ridden their horses, side by side, but every once in a while, he would take her hand or her arm and pull her close for a brief kiss. It was as silly as it was wonderful, and allowed her to be more brazen than she might otherwise have been. When he stretched out to swim once again after one such kiss, she jumped onto his back. He didn't stop swimming as she'd expected, but instead glided through the water with her on his back. It was fascinating. The movement, the heat of his skin merging with hers, soon became one more thing she wished would never end.

At the far side of the pool, he lowered his legs and twisted about to grasp her in one easy movement. "I must show you something else."

Her heart was thudding wildly with anticipation, yet she had to admit, "Nothing could be more wonderful than this."

Holding her hand, he led her out of the water and along the rocky shore to where the water ran over the rocks. She fought hard to keep her gaze on the pathway and not on him. He was as naked as the day he was born, and the idea of examining all of him was making her blood rush. The lack of modesty, complete nakedness in some instances, was common among The People. Not in a foul or uncivilized way—it was a natural state that drew little attention from others. The days were hot and it was common to see braves and maidens stripped down and cooling off in the water. However, The People were also aware she and the others were not used to parading around unclothed, and therefore spared them any teasing or taunting when they chose to bathe in their underclothes.

Seeing him bare had other thoughts racing through her

mind. The Cheyenne were very loving people, and right now, she wanted to kiss and caress him as she'd seen other couples doing.

When Black Horse stopped, Lorna stepped up beside him. As her gaze followed his hand gesture, once again her breath caught. "A waterfall!"

"Heehe'e."

The water wasn't rushing over the edge of the hill but flowing gently, making a smooth wall of water that cascaded into a bubbling pool several feet beneath them before once again forming a stream that disappeared into the thick crop of trees. "It's beautiful," she whispered.

Black Horse had his own opinion of beauty and knew he could look at this great land for many years and never see anything as breathtaking as the woman standing beside him. He had accepted what was in his heart days ago, and because of that he had many decisions to make. For himself. For Poeso. For his people.

"Come." Holding her hand, he started down the rocks. When they camped tomorrow, they will be only a short distance from the trading post. Others were wondering if she and the women would leave then, as he'd once proclaimed. He could not tie her up in his tent again, but he could show her he did not want her to leave. Never questioning his decisions before, he did not now.

"These rocks are slippery," she said, holding on to his arm with her free hand.

"I will not let you fall."

"I know," she said.

He didn't stop until they were at the base of the waterfall, and then turned to face her. "You trust Black Horse."

The shine in her eyes was as bright as the sun. "Yes, I trust you. I have for a long time."

"Not so long." He wanted her to recognize how things had changed. How she had changed.

"Maybe not, but I do trust you, and you trust me." She stepped closer and lifted her chin. "Don't you?"

"Heehe'e." Her closeness made his throat thick, and the way her wet clothes molded to her shape made other parts of him react. He wanted her so badly, so completely, his mind could think of little else. Turning her about, he guided her down the hill toward the water. This was a spot he had never shown anyone; it was where he had spent his first vision quest as a young brave. "Careful of the rocks. Some are sharp," he warned.

"I am."

They entered the water together and swam to the center of the pool. Treading water with one hand, she pushed her hair out of her face with the other. "I haven't gone swimming so much in my life."

She then stretched her arms over her head and fell backward to rest upon the water, reminding him of the day he'd first seen her, floating around on her back like an otter.

"It's so wonderful. I truly don't know why I never enjoyed swimming this much before."

"It was not in your heart, Poeso," he said, attempting to float atop the water beside her. It took effort to stay buoyant, and he kept sinking beneath the water. Mainly because the wet material covering her showed far more than it hid.

"It must not be in your heart," she said with a laugh as he resurfaced yet again. "Here, like this. Stretch your arms out all the way and let them go lax, like you're exhausted after a long day of hunting."

He followed her instructions, but still sank. Her nipples were like two snow-covered mountain peaks.

"You have to relax the rest of your body, too," she said. "Your back, your bottom, your legs. Just pretend you are lying on your bed, drifting off to sleep."

He made another attempt at it, closing his eyes to focus on something other than her until his body was held up by the water.

"That's it," she said. "Isn't it wonderful?"

They floated side by side, holding hands. *"Heehe'e."*

"You've mastered it," she whispered. "It must be in your heart now."

"You are in my heart, Poeso," he answered softly.

She was quiet for a long time before saying, "I think you are in my heart, too, Black Horse, or maybe you took the old heart out of my chest and put a new one there in its place, because it doesn't feel the same as my old one did. It no longer hurts all the time."

The water was too deep to hold her the way he wanted to, so he flipped onto his stomach. "Come."

Flipping around, she swam beside him toward the waterfall, but after a few strokes, said, "We are going to swim into the rock wall."

"Trust me," he said.

She followed him beneath the falling water, and once on the other side, clung on to the rocks. The cascading water splashing into their faces made talking impossible. He grasped her waist and lifted her up to see the ledge above their heads. Without further instructions, she grasped the ledge and pulled herself up and over the edge. He followed and they sat there for a moment, their feet dangling over the edge, watching the wall of water falling in front of them.

"It's amazing," she said.

"Heehe'e."

She turned, glancing over her shoulder. Sunlight shone

through the water, and she asked. "It's a cave. How far back does it go?"

He pulled his legs up and stood. When she took the hand he held out, he helped her to stand and then led her into the small alcove.

"It's enchanting," she said. "A place fairies might live."

"Fairies?" That was a word he had never heard.

"Imaginary little people with wings," she said, "who grant wishes."

He grinned at her explanation of spirits. "What would you wish for?"

"That this day would never end." Her eyes dimmed then. "That I didn't have to go to California."

Stepping up beside her, he took both of her hands in his. "You do not. I will make you my wife."

Wrinkles formed between her brows as she closed her eyes. "Don't say things like that."

"I will."

Eyes still closed, she shook her head. "But you can't. You are a leader of Tsitsistas, a great leader. You must marry a Cheyenne woman."

"Why?"

She shrugged. "It is the way."

He sensed anger, even though only sadness lived in her eyes. Imagining others would have told her that, he said, "One Who Heals does not speak for Black Horse."

She shook her head. "One Who Heals didn't tell me that. I just know it. I understand that is how it must be. I've come to understand a lot." Twisting her hands, she pulled them out of his hold and stepped away. "It would not work for me. I've witnessed how the men in your village have more than one wife. I couldn't do that. I couldn't share you with someone else."

He smiled. She was truthful, and correct. Although she

had accepted many things were different here compared to her world, some things she would never bow to, and he found pride in that. He was proud of all the things she had learned. He even liked how she would not accept some things. It showed her wisdom. He had that same wisdom. "I would not like to share you."

"You wouldn't be sharing," she pointed out before saying, "It is the way."

"I am the leader," he said. "I do not share if I do not want to."

She licked her lips and then bit down on the bottom one. The sound of the falling water grew louder during her silence, echoing against the rock walls surrounding them, and the sun shining through the water danced on the side of her face, making her skin glow. He wanted this woman for his wife. Wanted her like he had never wanted anything. "There would be no sharing, Poeso."

He did not know if the water on her eyelashes were tears or from swimming. "There would be no sharing, Black Horse, if I could stay. If I could be your wife. But I can't. I have to go to California."

As much as he wanted her to stay, he could not force her. It would take away her spirit and he did not want that. Yet he could not understand why she still wanted to leave when she was happy here. "To get your much money?"

She nodded, but then shook her head. "It's more than that. Always has been."

A frown still pulled on her face. "I told you once that I thought I was being followed."

"Black Horse will—"

She pressed a hand to his lips, stopping his words. "I know you will protect me. And that is why I must go. I'm still afraid. Money means a lot to my mother and Douglas. If they find out about my money in California, they will find me. They will do whatever they have to in order to get that money. I know they will."

The idea of her being hurt again was like an arrow shot in his side. "I will not let them."

"You will not be with me. You cannot be with me. I know them. They will find me. The only way I can stop them is with money. After that…" She shrugged. "After that I will be free to…" Tears dripped from her eyes as she shook her head. "I wish…"

His throat burned and he squeezed her hands tighter. He could not say he would go with her. He could not go to this place called California. "A part of me will go with you," he said quietly, hoping she could understand that. "A part of me will always be in your heart, just as a part of you will always be in mine." He had never spoken truer words. She filled his heart with much love. More love than he had ever known, and he had to stand by her decisions. Even if his vision had shown him a different path.

There was no more to say. He pulled her against his chest and kissed her. The taste, the feel of her lips against his was like honey still warm from the sun, and filled him with a great and powerful desire. One he could no longer hold at bay.

Black Horse was masterful in everything he did, including kissing. Lorna went weak in the knees and clutched on to his waist. Like the rest of him it was full of muscles, and hard, yet sleek and smooth beneath her fingertips. She found herself surrendering to him long before he gently lowered her onto the cave floor, where the coolness of the rocks was a blessing to her heated skin.

He'd already removed her shift during their kissing that had turned into a battle of lips and tongues that had left them both gasping and going back for more. Her pantaloons were gone as well, and when Black Horse pressed the heel of his palm against her center, a pleasure-filled moan escaped her lips. He'd long ago aroused her, with his kindness, his laughter, his protection and most of all his trust. She held no fear or shame. There wasn't room for such things in her heart or her mind. Not when it came to him.

"I must claim what is mine, Poeso," he whispered next to her ear, after kissing the length of her neck. "But will not if you do not want—"

"I want," she interrupted in a moment of panic. The flesh beneath her fingers was slick and hot, and not touching him right now could very well be the death of her. "I want you to claim me. I want you."

The pressure of his hand between her legs increased, moving in such a way her hips rose off the floor, as if begging for more. She was. She wanted him, all of him, in the way a woman gave herself to a man. It was what she'd wanted for weeks, but hadn't fully understood it until now.

His kisses continued, down her neck, over her shoulders, across her breasts. Her body responded to his every touch, arching upward, welcoming his hands, his mouth. When at last he eased her legs farther apart and entered her, she was so feverish with want and desire that beads of sweat dripped from her temples.

She looped her legs around his and rose up to meet his forward thrust, and at that moment, when they truly became connected, she gazed into his eyes. There was great joy and passion looking back at her, but there was more. Call it trust, call it love; in her heart, in the deepest part of her very being, she knew what she saw. The great leader of Tsitsistas, the great buffalo hunter, the warrior Black Horse, had just been conquered. By her, a simple white woman. And was doing so willingly, as if he desired it as much as she did.

He often seemed to be able to read her mind, and now was no different. "I am yours, Poeso," he whispered.

"And I am yours, Black Horse."

Chapter Fourteen

To Lorna's great delight, they stayed in the cave for hours. Resting and loving, and resting again. At one point, when he asked if he'd hurt her, she snuggled against him and assured him he had not. He truly hadn't, and she couldn't imagine why he'd have asked such a thing. In fact, it wasn't until they were about to leave that her mind tumbled and caught. Not once had she thought of her stepfather and that awful night.

Reaching out, she cupped Black Horse's square jaw and held his face while she kissed him soundly. "There was a time," she whispered against his lips, "that I thought this would never happen. That I would never be able to have a man touch me, but you made me forget everything. I thought of nothing but you."

He kissed her forehead. "You thought of what is in your heart."

She took a moment to contemplate that. Douglas may have stolen her virginity that night, but he had not taken the things that really mattered. Trust and love. Those were hers alone to give as she chose, and she had chosen. Chosen to trust and love Black Horse with all her heart.

"Heehe'e," she answered. "I did. Thank you for making my heart whole again."

He shook his head. "It was always whole. I just helped you see that." She gathered up her clothes with one hand, and he took her other. "Come. It will be dark soon."

Their exit was faster than their entrance. Holding hands, they jumped through the waterfall, and parted only long enough to swim to the shore. Then hand in hand they traipsed over the rocks and down to the other pool, which they once again swam across. She'd never swum naked before, nor had she ever felt so carefree. So happy and content, and she kept glancing at Black Horse, wondering if he felt the same way. His smile was bright and the shimmer in his eyes increased her giddiness. If someone had told her she'd find happiness here, in the middle of nowhere with a man some referred to as a savage, she'd have laughed right in their face. Or gotten angry and told them that would never happen to her. That would have been more true to form for her old self. That was how it seemed lately, as if there was an old Lorna, and this new one. She liked being the new one far more than the old one, but was confused because the two couldn't be the same person. They wanted different things. Needed different things. What if she became the old Lorna again when she left? She wasn't sure she could bear that.

Or would she? There was no anger inside her. No retaliation. The past, what had happened to her no longer mattered. There wasn't room inside her for such things. Her heart was too full.

Getting dressed on the banks of the pool took far more time than it should have. Black Horse was relentless with his teasing and kissing, neither of which she minded. They were both laughing as they ran to the horses that had waited patiently in the shade of the trees. Black Horse helped her mount, and after one more kiss, he swung onto Horse and they started down the hill.

Anticipation rode along with Lorna. She would not be sleeping across the lodge floor from Black Horse tonight. The thrill of that remained with her as they rode across the prairie toward where the new village lay.

The sun was dropping low in the sky, but it was still warm and her dress felt confining after being free of it for much of the day. Or perhaps it was the thought of taking it off again that made her so warm. It was as if her insides were glowing. A tiny part of her mind asked why she wasn't embarrassed or ashamed at what had happened—an old part of her. The new part smiled and silently said there wasn't anything to be ashamed or embarrassed about. Nothing had ever felt more natural, more real in her entire life.

"You are happy, Poeso."

"Heehe'e," she answered, "My heart is happy. I am happy."

"This is a good thing," he said with a nod and smile.

"Heehe'e," she agreed. The smell of campfires and roasting meat filled the air. Glancing his way, she urged Patches into a faster lope. "And I'm hungry."

When the children raced out to meet them, she greeted them with the happiness filling her. It was wonderful to be welcomed home, and pride found room among her joy to rise up inside her as she rode alongside Black Horse all the way to the center of the village.

Their lodge had been erected, with everything completely in order, and soon the entire family was inside, sharing a meal. Conversation flowed easily. Out of choice, Lorna remained quiet. The waterfall had been beautiful and her friends would love to hear about it, but it was her and Black Horse's special place, and she wasn't ready to share even the tiniest bit of that.

Most nights, after the meal, the men gathered in groups, smoking and talking, but Black Horse made no effort to join them that evening. He seemed as anxious as she to be alone together in the lodge.

When that did happen, her anticipation was so high it felt as if her insides were twisted in knots.

Slowly, softly, Black Horse pushed her hair away from her face while looking her straight in the eye. "You will sleep on my robes this night."

"I will like that," she answered, keeping her eyes locked with his. "I will like that very much."

"You are a strong woman, Poeso."

She appreciated the compliment, and admitted, "It took a strong man to make me so." The slight furrowing of his brows had her adding, "You made me strong. Before you I was weak."

He shook his head.

"I was," she maintained. "I acted strong, but I wasn't. I was just scared, and I didn't trust anyone."

His hands spanned her rib cage and his thumbs brushed the undersides of her breasts. The tingling of her skin was as powerful as when she'd been wearing nothing. He pulled her close, and as she laid her cheek against his bare chest she felt him shudder slightly, as if her touch gave him the same thrill his did her. She wrapped her arms around him, and twisted her face in order to nuzzle his chest and kiss his satin skin. The musky wonderful scent of him filled her nose, and suddenly she was hotter than when the sun had been blazing down.

She lifted her head in order to meet his lips, and lost herself in his kisses. Although she had no idea how many hours they'd spend in each other's arms, she knew she'd never forget this night. The moon, big and bright, shone down through the top of the lodge and illuminated the hide walls as Black Horse teased and coaxed her body into responses that left her gasping for air while begging for more. His passion was as relentless as ever, and didn't stop until she was so sated, so exhausted, she couldn't have lifted a finger if the lodge had been burning down around them.

He was also as kind as ever, holding her close as she drifted into dreams full of tranquility. When she awoke to the same moon still shining upon them, as aroused as he, she rolled onto her back, welcoming him to once again take her.

They couldn't have slept much, but when daylight broke, and she rolled over, the smile on his face filled her with more vigor than if she'd slept for a day or more. Her excitement remained as the entire village packed up for the day of traveling. The faster they moved out, the faster they'd find the place they'd camp tonight, and that was what she was looking forward to.

Her friends would not understand what she was experiencing, and she was glad her position of riding next to Black Horse as they headed out meant she didn't have to explain anything to anyone. As The Woman Who Sleeps in Black Horse's Lodge, she was untouchable and she liked that.

They day's travel was longer than the one before, however, they found a lush valley by midafternoon and the rebuilding started as soon as the first horses came to a stop. Lorna busied herself helping others, waiting for the wagons that traveled near the middle of the long procession, until she saw Black Horse wander toward the river.

She caught up with him several feet from the bank, and leaned against his side when he took her hand. "This is a pretty place."

"You say that everywhere we camp."

"I know, but it's true. I never noticed the beauty of the land while we were traveling by ourselves. There was too much to do, too many other things on my mind." Waving a hand toward the water, she said, "How do you always know where to go? Each day you find the perfect place. Plenty of water, wood, protection from the wind."

Looking down at the face smiling up at him, Black Horse's heart had never been so full. The weight on his shoulders had never been so heavy, either. He had not told Poeso the fort was only a short ride over the hill. The desire to spend many nights with her was powerful, and he did not want... A heavy sigh left his lungs. He did not want her to go. Did not want their time together to end. Last night, while holding her close, he'd thought about battling the white men, just to keep her here. When he had accepted the position to lead his people, he had vowed never to put them in danger because of his own wants, yet that was what he had considered last night.

"The Cheyenne have lived here for a long time," he said, turning his gaze to the land. It did not pull at his spirit as usual. Only Poeso did that now. She had changed him, and that did not anger him.

"So these places you've chosen, you've stayed at them before?"

"Heehe'e."

"Including the waterfall?"

His heart thudded as he replied, *"Heehe'e."* The desire for her that had grown stronger each day flared brightly, and he was about to pull her close when shouts sounded behind them.

Disappointment crossed her face as she turned toward the camp. "The wagons have arrived."

He noticed that, but also saw Rising Sun riding toward them. Black Horse instantly knew why, and the knowledge made his stomach churn.

"What is he saying?"

There was no need for him to answer. Rising Sun was now close enough for her to hear for herself.

"Soldiers are coming?" she asked. "What soldiers?"

Once again, there was no reason for him to answer. She knew and the sadness in her eyes filled his chest.

Soldiers had never ridden out to welcome them upon arrival before, and that was not why they were heading for the village now. "Come," he said. "We must greet them."

"I don't want to greet them," she replied while walking beside him to where Rising Sun had stopped his horse.

Despite his dread, Black Horse grinned at her honesty before he used his native language to ask Rising Sun how many soldiers were coming. When Poeso frowned upon the warrior's answer of a dozen, Black Horse wished she had not learned the Cheyenne language so quickly and thoroughly.

After dismissing Rising Sun with a wave, Black Horse turned to her. "Go to the wagons."

"Why?" Her frown increased. "A moment ago you said we were going to greet the soldiers. Why are you sending me away now?"

"Go, Poeso. Now."

She pushed his chest with both hands. "Don't tell me what to do!" Turning her angry glare toward the hill where a dozen horses were raising a plume of dust, she added, "No one will tell me what to do ever again."

He was proud of her determination, but also feared that someday it would cause more trouble for her. He would never tell her that, but he would always protect her, even when he could not see her. "Listen to Black Horse, Poeso. Go."

When she opened her mouth to protest again, he waved at Stands Tall to take her away. She hissed, and struggled against Stands Tall's hold, but soon was behind the line of warriors standing several feet behind him.

Alone, as he should be, Black Horse turned and moved forward to meet the soldiers now galloping their horses across the valley floor.

Crazy Hawk was with the soldiers, riding an army horse instead of a pony. The Crow warrior had become an interpreter for the soldiers many seasons ago. Fluent in several of the tribal languages, including Cheyenne and Sioux, as well as English, Crazy Hawk was known for not translating fairly for either side. One more reason Black Horse did not want it known he understood and spoke the white man's language. Some thought he could read minds. He liked that. It gave him more power against the white man's tricks.

"My brother," Crazy Hawk said in Cheyenne. "It has been a long time."

"Heehe'e." Continuing in Cheyenne, Black Horse said, "I see you are still talking for the soldiers."

"Someone has to help the poor fools," Crazy Hawk answered with a chortle. He turned toward the yellow-haired man on the horse beside him to say in English, "This is the mighty Black Horse. Leader of this band of Cheyenne. He welcomes the soldiers to his village."

Although he did not welcome the soldiers, Black Horse made no comment. Crazy Hawk was correct in calling the soldiers fools. No band welcomed them, nor understood why they followed orders from faceless leaders many miles away. Those men they called Government and claimed they wanted peace. A leader who wanted peace should speak for himself, not send soldiers.

"Tell him I am Sergeant Hudson, and that I have heard of Black Horse."

As soon as Crazy Hawk repeated what the man had said, Black Horse asked, "What do they want?"

"I—we—we've come for the white women they've captured," the army man answered the question after Crazy Hawk repeated it.

Black Horse lifted his chin and replied in Cheyenne. "We captured no one."

Crazy Hawk repeated his words in English before nodding. "I told them The Horse Band did not capture women, but they didn't believe me," Crazy Hawk said. "Some white man said you fished his woman out of the river. Stole her from him. And that you tried to scalp him."

Black Horse ignored the last sentence. All knew the Cheyenne did not take scalps. However, he gave a slight nod. "I did take her out of the river, but stole her from no one. She is now Black Horse's." Claiming Poeso as his would raise questions, but he was not ashamed of loving her.

"He can't claim her," the yellow-haired man said after Crazy Hawk repeated his words in English. "He can't claim any of them."

"I will not say that," Crazy Hawk said in English. "This is Black Horse. All know of his skill with a bow and a knife. If he was Southern Cheyenne, you would already be dead. Me, too."

Black Horse kept his gaze on the yellow-haired man who swallowed and licked his lips. When the man said, "We come in peace," Black Horse almost laughed. Only because he remembered when Poeso had said those same words. Then the idea of her leaving once again turned his insides dark.

"Te-tell him we are only looking for one woman. Lorna Bradford. He can keep the others."

Long before Crazy Hawk translated the words, a shiver raced up Black Horse's. Why would this soldier know Poeso's name? And want only her?

"Tell him her uncles, her family, are looking for her," the yellow-haired man said. "They are at the fort. I must bring her to them."

Black Horse waited for Crazy Hawk to translate the words before he said, "You bring her uncles here." Poeso never mentioned uncles, and he did not trust the foolish soldier's words.

When Crazy Hawk was done translating, the yellow-haired man shook his head. "I have been ordered to bring her to the fort, and that is what I must do. He has my word nothing will happen to her."

Black Horse grunted without waiting for Crazy Hawk to repeat what had been said. A white man's word meant little to him.

The jangle of harnessed horses and wagon wheels had Black Horse turning to glance behind him. Both wagons rolled closer. Poeso drove the first one, White Sister the second one. Each had a friend sitting beside them, all dressed in their black outfits.

Black Horse clamped his teeth together, knowing what she would do, yet knowing he could not stop her. Not unless he captured her and tied her to his lodge pole again, which would start a battle with the soldiers.

"We are who you are looking for," Poeso said.

The yellow-haired man took off his hat, and squinted. "Are you Lorna Bradford?"

"Yes."

"I'm Sergeant Hudson, Miss Bradford. Your family has been looking for you. I've been sent to retrieve you."

Black Horse held his stance as his spine stiffened, and balled his hands into fists.

Poeso glanced at him before she said, "I don't have any family."

"Elliot and William Chadwick are not your uncles?" the sergeant asked.

Keeping his tongue silent was difficult, but Black Horse was relieved to see the surprise in her eyes. She had mentioned those names. Elliot was the man from California, the one who held her much money.

"They are not my uncles. But I do know them."

"Either way, we are here to take you back to the fort," the man replied. "You can discuss your relationship with them there."

"They are at the fort?" she asked.

Black Horse hissed at Crazy Hawk, who had climbed off his horse to stand close and repeat what was being said. With a frown, Crazy Hawk moved back to his horse.

"Who told you where to find us?" Poeso asked.

For the first time in his life, Black Horse felt inadequate. It was as if his hands were tied. Poeso would leave, and he could not stop it. If she was Cheyenne, he could tell her to get down from the wagon, to stay put until he said, but he could not do that to her. Nor could he argue with her in front of his people. She would not listen, and anyone who does not listen to the leader is shunned from their band. Right now, he didn't like her stubbornness so much.

"One of the men from the wagon train you got separated from said you were with the Cheyenne," the sergeant answered.

"We didn't get separated," Poeso said. "We left the train. To get away from Jacob Lerber. The Cheyenne rescued us from him."

"Nehetaa'e," Black Horse said. He'd heard enough and would not be sending Poeso anywhere near Lerber. Speaking in Cheyenne, he told Crazy Hawk, "Tell the soldiers to leave."

Crazy Hawk glanced between the soldiers and him.

A burst of fury raced through him. "Tell them," Black Horse demanded.

Crazy Hawk said nothing, but a dozen clicks filled the air. The soldiers had lifted their guns. All of them were pointed at him. Black Horse did not care. Sweet Medicine had long ago bestowed four arrows upon the Cheyenne. Upon him. Two for power over the buffalo, two for power over men.

"Put your guns down," Poeso shouted.

"Miss Bradford," the sergeant said, "I insist you come with us posthaste. We have come in peace and do not wish a confrontation, but we are not leaving without you."

"I know that," she said harshly, before turning to look at him.

Black Horse said nothing. These men and their guns did not frighten him.

"I must go," she said in Cheyenne. "They will kill you if I don't."

"Hova'ahane," he said.

"Heehe'e," she argued softly.

There was great sadness in her eyes and Black Horse's teeth were clenched so tight his jaw stung. She had said she would leave, and he had accepted that, until now.

"Miss Bradford, you have my word that—"

She hissed and turned toward the army man. "Considering I do not know you, Sergeant Hudson, your word means nothing to me."

"Ma'am, I am a member of the US Army, and—"

"I only recently arrived in America, so your army means little to me, too," she interrupted. "I will go with you, on one condition."

Black Horse bit his lips to keep from smiling. Her bravery never failed to amuse him. Her intelligence didn't, either. She would insist he went with her, and that suited him just fine.

The sergeant glanced around before asking, "And that is?"

Her gaze met his again and Black Horse gave a nod, giving her permission to make her request.

She bit her lips and closed her eyes before turning back to the sergeant. "That Stands Tall will come with us."

"Stands Tall?"

Black Horse wasn't sure who spoke first, him or the sergeant. Luckily the other man's words covered his own outburst. He must remember to keep his knowledge of the white man's language a secret.

"Yes, Stands Tall," she said, indicating the warrior with a wave of her hand. "He will accompany us."

Her eyes were on him again, and they were pleading with him to agree. Black Horse was still full of anger, of worry, but he understood her compromise. She was a wise woman. One who had not lied or tried to trick him. She had kept all promises, and he must, too.

Half full of anger, and half full of frustration, Black Horse turned to face the soldiers.

Chapter Fifteen

Lorna wasn't any happier about the situation than Black Horse, but was also fully aware of the rifles the army men carried. She'd watched Black Horse kill a buffalo with nothing but a knife, but buffalo didn't have guns. Closing her eyes briefly, she willed him to understand she had to leave in order to keep everyone else safe.

His back was to her as she whispered, "I will wait for you at the fort." Her Cheyenne wasn't the best, but he always seemed to grasp what she was attempting to say. "I will have Black Horse's protection in Stands Tall."

He turned slowly.

"You do not have your bow," she said. "You are not prepared to fight."

For several long moments, Lorna feared he would not agree, and her insides quivered. She didn't want to be responsible for a battle, for anyone to lose their life, but also knew she could say no more. He was a leader, and to argue with him would shun her from his band forever. That would be worse than death. She fully understood what a punishment shunning was.

Just when she thought her heart would be broken, he shifted his stance and nodded at Stands Tall. He then gestured for three other warriors to accompany them, as well.

Relief flooded her so swiftly tears stung her eyes. She could tell how frustrating this was for Black Horse, and wanted to assure him all would be fine, but she couldn't. The stirring of her stomach told her something bad was close at hand. She couldn't let anything happen to the Cheyenne. Wouldn't. Not to these people who had been so kind and loving when they didn't have to be. She'd never imagined this would happen to her, that she'd care so much about others that she was willing to sacrifice herself for them. It wasn't as if she was being led to her deathbed, but an inner sense told her that going to the fort would change everything. All she'd come to love.

That, too, was unbelievable. She'd never known what love was. Perhaps that was how she recognized it now. The feelings she had for Black Horse went deeper and were stronger than any she'd ever had before. It couldn't be anything but love.

Swallowing the lump in her throat, she whispered, *"Nestaevahosevoomatse."*

He gave a slight nod and agreed that he would see her again soon, too. Stepping back, he waved for the warriors behind him to let the wagons pass.

There were no long goodbyes. No farewell hugs or wishes of safe travels. It was just as well; the sad faces on the children who rushed forward to gather around the wagons as she drove one, and Meg the other, was heart wrenching enough. Parting words with Black Horse would only make things more difficult, so even though her eyes stung, she kept her head up and offered little more than a head nod as they rolled past him.

Once the children departed, the militia broke into small groups, some riding in front of the wagons, the others behind. Stands Tall and the other warriors rode beside the wagons, one on each side. This was so different from any departure she'd had in the past and she struggled to keep her gaze fixed on the horizon rather than turn around for a final glimpse.

With each turn of the wagon wheels, each bounce of the seat, the beauty she'd seen in the land seemed to fade. Once again, much like before coming to the village, she saw nothing but grassland, hills, and trees. There was no enchantment in any of it.

The sun was hot, and the mules, already tired from their morning trek, were sluggish. Perhaps they, too, were sad to be leaving a life they'd become accustomed to. She thought of the heavy load the animals were pulling. The things packed and piled in the wagons. Things none of them had needed since entering the village. Betty had used some of the cooking utensils and supplies, but for the most part, everything they'd needed to sustain life had been provided by the Cheyenne. Along with other things she'd never known she'd needed. Things she'd lived her entire life without.

Community. Friendship. Love.

Her chest burned and she released the air, an act that left her feeling even more hollow.

"Who are Elliot and William Chadwick?" Betty asked. "Are they your uncles?"

With her focus on leaving, Lorna had forgotten the sergeant had mentioned the men. It had also slipped her mind that her friends still didn't know her original mission. "They aren't my uncles," she said. "But I do know them—I met William in New York, and Elliot is the man I was to meet in California."

"Why are they here?"

"I don't know," Lorna answered honestly.

"I suppose you'll be leaving with them," Betty said.

Lorna clamped her teeth together to keep from snapping

that she'd do no such thing. She had no idea why the men were here, and couldn't truthfully say what she would or wouldn't do. What she wanted most was to turn the wagon around, but that would put Black Horse and the others in danger. She had no doubt the soldiers would make good on their threat.

Her silence stopped any further questioning from Betty. Or maybe the other woman had just as many dreadful thoughts as she did.

Because she felt no excitement about arriving, the travel to the fort seemed short. They'd barely started down the other side of the hill when a large wooden fortress appeared in the base of the valley. The tops of buildings peeked out above the tall fence, and as they rolled closer, men with guns could be seen stationed on platforms near the top of the stockade.

Every detail made her heart sink deeper. Although Black Horse's band was of a fair number, there were far more women and children than warriors. They wouldn't stand a chance against the army men with their barricade and guns. It would be up to her to make sure the army understood the Cheyenne had done nothing wrong.

"Do you think Jacob is still here?" Betty asked.

"Yes."

"They won't make us go with him, will they?"

"No," Lorna answered. "No one will be leaving with Lerber."

"But if you leave with—"

"No one will be leaving with Lerber," Lorna repeated forcefully.

They were still a distance away when the two wide stockade gates swung open and more army men on horseback rode out. Sergeant Hudson spurred his horse and rode forward to meet them. He and the leader of the new group separated themselves and reined their horses to the side of the trail. Lorna couldn't stop herself from staring. The second man had more yellow stripes on the shoulders of his uniform, and tipped his hat her way. Not here to make friends, she made no acknowledgment, but didn't look away, either.

Once the wagon rolled past she turned forward, and took a deep breath. The looming opening in the wooden walls looked like a huge mouth—wide open and ready to swallow them whole.

The army men on horses in front of the wagon crossed the threshold, but others, with guns drawn, stepped around the walls, blocking Stands Tall and the warrior on the other side of the wagon.

"Whoa up!" Lorna shouted to the mules while pulling on the reins and pressing the brake with one foot.

"No Injuns can enter the fort," one of the men said, "except on trading days."

"They are with us," Lorna replied. "We won't enter if they don't."

"What's the hold up, Corporal?"

Lorna turned toward the men riding closer. The one who had ridden out to speak with Sergeant Hudson had asked the question, and it was to him the man on the ground answered.

"Just telling them the Injuns gotta stay on this side of the wall, Captain."

"It was agreed these men could travel with us," Lorna said. "If they can't enter the fort, we won't, either."

"Indians are not allowed inside the fort expect at specific times, Miss Bradford. You have my word you'll be perfectly safe without them," the captain said.

"I'm not concerned about my safety," she replied. "Because these warriors will remain with us at all times."

"That is not allowed, ma'am," he said smartly. "Now release the brake and—"

"What about him?" she asked, pointing at the Indian who had translated back at the village. "Is he allowed inside the fort?"

"Crazy Hawk is a guide for the army and translator. He has special permission."

"Then, give my warriors special permission, too."

"That cannot be done."

"Why not?" The man's face was turning red and his eyes narrowing. She'd seen a man sneer many times and wasn't fazed by it. "They brought no lodges with them. Where do you expect them to stay out here? There's no shelter, hardly any trees."

"Animals don't need shelter," one of the men on the ground muttered.

Her anger was increasing steadily, and the glare she cast toward the man remained when she turned to the captain again. "I will not pass through that gate without these men."

"Miss Bradford—"

The captain's response was interrupted by someone shouting her given name. Lorna turned her attention to the opening in the stockade, but the man who appeared was a complete stranger. The one behind him holding a high-top black hat on his head she recognized from New York—William Chadwick. That meant the one repeating her name and rushing past the mules must be Elliot Chadwick.

"Goodness, William told me you resembled Arleta, but I didn't expect—" He stumbled slightly as he arrived at the side of the wagon. Much like his brother, there was more gray hair on his head than brown and his three-piece suit would have been much more suitable for New York or San

Francisco than Wyoming. "Oh, child, are you all right? Were you harmed?"

"Harmed? Of course I wasn't harmed."

Elliot spun around. "Captain Walcott, what is the holdup? We need to get these women out of the sun."

"The holdup, sir, is your niece," the captain replied rather rudely. "She refuses to enter the fort without her Injuns."

"Escorts," Lorna snapped. She didn't like how the men had sneered using the word *Injun*, and would not allow it to continue. That much she said with her glare.

"Escorts?" Elliot asked, looking up at her with a frown.

She nodded toward Stands Tall. "Stands Tall has been overseeing my safety since shortly after Jacob Lerber attempted to assault us at the river a few weeks ago. I go nowhere without him."

"I've informed her that Indians are not allowed inside the fort," Captain Walcott said.

Once again Elliot turned toward the captain. "I'm sure you can make an exception, Captain. General Hollister will approve. I guarantee it." For an older man, Elliot was rather spry. With little effort, he climbed onto the wagon. "Slide over, child. I'll drive the wagon in. You soldiers move aside." He then turned to Stands Tall and gestured for him to follow. "This way."

Under most circumstances, Lorna would never have slid over, but Elliot Chadwick's authoritative actions had caught her off guard. They seemed to have caught the captain that way, too, for he didn't protest when Elliot drove the mules into the fort with Stands Tall and the other warrior right beside them. Meg's wagon followed, along with the other two warriors.

She hadn't seen anything quite like what sat inside the fort. A small town of sorts, except that most of the buildings built along the back wall were attached. It was like one long line of houses connected to each other, sharing the same long porch.

Elliot stopped the wagon near the center of the buildings and quickly climbed down. He spun around when he hit the ground and held up both hands to help her down. His brother was on the other side of the wagon, helping Betty down.

Lorna waited until her feet touched the ground before asking, "Why do these army men think I am your niece? Why would you have told them that?"

His confused gazed lingered on her for a moment before he glanced across the wagon. "You didn't tell her?"

"I didn't have a chance," William said. "I told you, as soon as I gave her money for a hotel, she disappeared."

Lorna's stomach gurgled. "Tell me what?"

"Let's go inside, dear," Elliot said. "Get out of this heat."

"No, I don't mind the heat," she answered, planting her feet firmly in the ground. "What didn't William tell me?"

Elliot laid his hands on her shoulders. "William and I are your uncles. Your mother's brothers."

She shook her head. "My mother doesn't have any family."

"Not Regina," Elliot said. "She is your stepmother. Arleta, our sister, was your real mother."

Things seemed to spin before her eyes, making Lorna blink long and slowly. "Real mother?"

"Yes," Elliot said. "Let's go inside and I'll explain everything."

Lorna wanted to agree, but even with her thoughts spinning, she had others to think of first. "My friends and warriors—"

"Will be seen to." Elliot turned to the captain. "All of my niece's friends are to be given the best quarters possible, Captain. I will check myself once I've spoken with my niece privately."

"Yes, sir."

Once again, Elliot's authoritative nature seemed to take rank even over the captain. How he did that reminded her of Black Horse. No brute force or weapons were needed. Confidence alone said he expected others to listen. Weeks ago she would not have recognized that, or respected it. She did now, and walked to the door William held open.

As he closed the door behind them, William asked, "Would you like me to request a pot of tea, my dear?"

Lorna shook her head. "No, thank you." Glancing from William to Elliot, her mind went to the idea of them being her uncles. "I don't understand. I—"

"Sit down, my dear," Elliot said, guiding her toward a grouping of chairs. "I can imagine what a shock this is to you."

Lorna sat, gratefully, her knees about to give out. There were so many questions revolving around in her head she didn't know where to start.

"Your mother, my sister and William's," Elliot said while waving the other man closer, "died shortly after you were born. Your father was beside himself. He and Arleta were more in love than any two people ever could have been."

"That's the truth, Lorna. Those two had been in love from the time they were little." William added. "I'd have told you all about it if you'd stayed in New York like I thought you would."

Not sure how to respond, she stuttered, "I didn't—I couldn't—"

"I—we—understand, dear," Elliot said. "William was a stranger to you. We tried to see you many times over the years, but Regina wouldn't allow it. You see, after your mother died, your father was so sad, he truly didn't know what he was doing. Within months, he married Regina and moved to England. He made us promise we'd never tell you the truth, that Regina wasn't your mother."

"Why?"

"I think he wanted to forget himself. Hoped maybe that would take away the pain," Elliot answered. "That's what I surmised over the years anyway." He took her hands. "We loved him like a brother, and wanted to see him happy, so decided if Regina and moving away would do that, we wouldn't interfere. We kept in contact with letters, and when his letters stopped, I traveled to England to investigate. He wasn't himself, barely half the man I remembered him to be, but was still insistent that you shouldn't know the truth. I continued to abide by that, until a couple of years later, when I heard he'd died."

The sadness of both men couldn't be denied, and a vague memory of a man from America visiting when she was very small led her to believe they were telling the truth.

"Regina said if we sent her money, she'd allow us to see you, but when we arrived, you weren't there," William said. "She'd sent you to friends in the country for the summer months. We tried, but couldn't find you."

Lorna remembered staying for months on end with one of Douglas's offshoot cousins—an old woman who never took a bath—and how sometimes, despite the smelly woman and the lack of welcome in her home, she hadn't wanted to return to London.

"I'm assuming Regina never gave you any of the letters we mailed to you?"

She shook her head in response to Elliot's question.

"We figured as much, which is why I was so shocked when you showed up at my office," William said. "I wasn't even sure if it was you, or someone Regina sent over to fool us. At least, not until I got home that evening and pulled out a picture of your mother. Your hair had been covered with a hat that day, but now, with it hanging down, I see you are the spitting image of your mother. Your real mother, Arleta."

"I am?" Lorna shook her head at the delight filling her. There were other questions she should be asking. They could be lying to her. Although she couldn't fathom why. "Why are you here?" Addressing Elliot she added, "Why didn't you wait until I got to California?"

"William wired me as soon as you left his office, and then again after looking at Arleta's picture, which you do greatly resemble. I bought passage on the first stage heading east, but as he was unable to contact me, it wasn't until my arrival that William informed me you'd left New York. We tracked the train to Missouri, and the wagon train." His sigh lingered in the air as he said, "We arrived in the town where your friend had been doctored only days after you'd left. A short time later, your trail dried up."

"We came here to engage the help of the army, and found your friend, Jacob Lerber."

"He's not my friend," Lorna said. "He's evil. You can't believe a word he says."

"He told us it had been his suggestion that you all dress as nuns, to keep yourselves safer as you traveled," William said.

"No, he didn't. Meg came up with that idea before we left Missouri. We gave Betty and Tillie our extra dresses after we left the wagon train. And it was all because of men like Lerber."

"I'm glad to hear you say that, dear," Elliot said. "I have misgivings about that man."

"As you should," she said.

The two men shared a glance that was weighted and caused a shiver to ripple her spine.

"How well do you know Jacob?" William asked.

"Well enough not to like or trust him," she answered. "We were on the same wagon train that left Missouri." The shiver increased. "Why?"

After sharing another subjective glance with his brother, Elliot leaned back in his chair. "We have reason to believe Jacob was hired by your stepparents to make sure you arrived in California."

Startled, and confused, she shook her head. "Hired by— Why?"

"To make sure you claimed your inheritance," Elliot answered.

"They couldn't claim it as theirs if you hadn't claimed it first," William said. "That is our theory."

Her mind was twisting again. "But once I claim it, it's mine."

"Everyone believes Regina is your mother, so she could claim all you own upon your death," William said.

A chill rippled down her spine, yet she wasn't startled. Since running away she'd been looking over her shoulder, fearful Douglas would find her. This confirmed why, and why the only place she'd ever felt safe had been with Black Horse and his people.

Elliot patted her hand. "Don't worry, dear. We are here, and we won't let anything happen to you."

The inability to trust reared inside her. "Why? Why would you have trailed me so far? Why—"

"Because we love you," William said. "We've waited so long to see you again."

The expression on his face, half disbelief, half bliss, startled her as deeply as his statement. "But you don't even know me." Her thoughts shifted again. "And if I never claimed my inheritance, it would be yours, wouldn't it?"

"We understand, imagining the sort of life you must have lived with Regina and Douglas, that you find it strange, but the only reason we are here is because we love you. We have since the day you were born, Lori," Elliot said. "You are our niece. Our family."

Her father had been the only one to call her Lori, and hearing it brought back memories, and the sting of tears. If she hadn't believed these two men, these two virtual strangers, were her uncles, her true family, before, she did now. "I didn't know you existed," she whispered.

Elliot squeezed her hands. "You do now."

She closed her eyes for a moment, wondering how different things might have been if she had known. If her father had told her. If— There were so many ifs tumbling in her mind she had to stop them, and she opened her eyes and said to William, "You offered to let me stay with you before you knew who I was for sure."

"I hoped it was truly you," he said. "I hoped with all my heart, but I saw the misgiving in your eyes, the mistrust of my reason for offering to let you stay with me, and knowing Regina, I could understand why. So I gave you the money for a hotel instead." His grin was a bit sheepish. "I didn't expect you to leave town."

Rather than telling him the cost of the hotel he'd suggested had been beyond outrageous, she said, "I used it for the train. The money my father had left me was running low. I used the rest for the supplies and our wagon." Turning toward Elliot, she added, "His letter only mentioned you."

"There is no reason to explain, dear," Elliot said. "We are glad you are safe and sound."

"That we are," William said, grinning. "Now you just

have to decide if you want to go to California with Elliot or return to New York with me."

"That is not a choice she needs to make right now," Elliot said.

Nodding, William agreed, "I know. My wife, Stella, is so sorry she missed meeting you and is hoping you'll return to stay with us."

"As is my wife, Katherine," Elliot said. "She wanted to travel to New York with me, but settled for preparing a bedroom for when you finally arrive in California."

Once again Lorna's thoughts spun. It was as if these two men were fighting over her. "I don't know—"

"Of course you don't," William interrupted while patting her hand. "This must all be such a shock for you. We are just so excited to have found you." He bowed his head slightly as if ashamed. "I was fearful my actions had alienated you from us forever."

Once again taken aback, she asked, "Actions? What actions?"

His sigh lingered in the air before he said, "Over a year ago, Regina sent a letter demanding money for your dowry. Considering her past antics, I didn't trust that Regina would have found you a suitable man to marry. After asking an associate in England to investigate the man you were to marry, and his family, and learning they were known to be involved in some quite unscrupulous activities, I informed Regina there would be no dowry. I also had the Wainwright family informed that unless they could prove their son truly loved you, there would be no dowry."

Patting her hand, he said, "I'd hoped if he truly loved you, and you him, the dowry wouldn't matter. If I broke your heart in that matter, my dear, I must beg your forgiveness. Both Elliot and I will do everything in our power to reconnect you and that young man, if that is your wish."

Lorna glanced from one man to the other. Their faces held such sincerity a knot formed in her stomach. She shook her head. "I never loved Andrew. Never wanted to marry him."

"That is such a relief to hear," William said. "His family is truly not one you would want to be associated with."

"Lori, my dear," Elliot said, once again taking her hand. "Please believe us when we say we have always had your best interests at heart. Not because you are a very wealthy woman, but because we love you dearly."

A tingling had her throat tightening. She needed time to process all this. Get used to the idea that she had family. People who had traveled mile upon mile to find her, all because they loved her. Cared about her, and who she associated with.

Her throat grew even tighter. "I think I'd like that tea now," she whispered.

Chapter Sixteen

As soon as the horizon had swallowed Poeso, Black Horse ordered a hunting party to follow him in the opposite direction. Traditionally a celebration was held the night before journeying to the trading post. There would be much dancing and singing, and gifts offered to Maheo for the plentiful hides they'd acquired to be traded with the white man. Though his heart was not in it, he must ensure it happened for his people. This day, unlike ever before, being a leader of his people was not in his heart.

He thought of the Tribal Council, and how he'd ordered they wait until the white man's war was over to speak again of battles. Many would agree with his wish if he called them together now and declared an attack. They would be glad his mind had changed.

His heart may have changed, but his mind had not. He could not declare an attack because the woman he loved had chosen to go with the white man.

As his eyes scanned the land for deer and elk for the celebration, his mind was held captive by Poeso. He did not want to put his trust in the army men to keep her safe from Jacob Lerber. He worried, too, about the man Elliot Chadwick. What if this man left, taking her to California before tomorrow? Tracking them would be easy, but there would be no reason to follow. She wanted to go and get her much money. Just like Poeso did not understand his world, he did not understand hers, and unlike her, he was not able to accept some things.

The hill before him was steep, and Black Horse let Horse choose the speed at which they climbed. A buck leaped out of the woods and without thought, Black Horse loaded his bow and shot. He then waved a young boy to join him. This was the boy's first hunt, and Black Horse directed the boy to bleed the deer—a skill that must be mastered before the boy would be allowed to hunt like a man.

The young brave had been taught well and had the carcass ready to be hauled back to the village in a short time. Black Horse praised the boy. Others laughed when the brave declared he'd soon be as good a hunter as Black Horse.

Black Horse handed his bow and an arrow to the boy and pointed to a tree. His bow was very powerful and many wagers had been placed and won against other bands that no one but he was strong enough to bend it.

After several tries, the boy handed the bow back, stating he would start with a smaller one. While others laughed, Black Horse gifted the brave the arrow that had killed the buck, and then swung onto Horse's back. Several more deer would be needed for the celebration.

A short distance up the hill, he spotted another buck. Too far away for his arrow, Black Horse urged Horse into a chase.

They topped the hill and Horse stopped, puffing and snorting. The buck was nowhere in sight. Black Horse scanned the area again. He had not lost a chase in many moons.

The white tail of the buck caught the corner of his eye

at the same time a faraway squeal of a horse echoed. Horse heard it, too, and lifted his head to sniff the air. Black Horse waved for the hunting party to follow the buck while he went in the direction of the squeal. Far below in a box canyon was a small herd of horses, he couldn't make out much more than that, but another squeal made Horse snort and stomp.

It was not the time of year to gather horses. Well fed by summer grass, only the old and lame wild horses could be overtaken by a horse with a warrior on its back, whereas during the time of melting snow, wild horses were skinny and tired easy. Cheyenne ponies never did. They were well fed year-round.

Scanning for a trail that would take them down the hill, Black Horse steered Horse toward an area that wasn't too steep. He would not capture horses, but wanted to check if one was injured. Halfway down, the entrance to the canyon became hidden and he used his instincts to direct their way. It was slow going, and once at the base, he searched to find a narrow opening between the rocky outcropping and high cliffs to take them into the canyon.

Once past the rocky entrance, softer sand displayed hoofprints, and a short distance later, the trail opened into the canyon full of thick sagebrush. He continued following the hoofprints, looking for indentions in the grass when the sand completely disappeared.

The squeal that sounded again said he was closer, and he held Horse back while watching for any movement. Something had a horse scared or cornered. It could be wolves or mountain lions, and he had no desire to be ambushed by either. It could also be another horse. There was a hierarchy in herds, and plenty of fighting.

As they rounded a large patch of bushes, most of the herd came into view. Upon seeing him, they backed away.

He entered the clearing and scanned the area. When his gaze landed on a single horse, his heart jolted.

A brown horse, with a mane of tangled curls, stood near a pile of rocks. Unlike the others, upon seeing him, it didn't run, but let out a loud squeal.

Cautious of his surrounding, Black Horse climbed off Horse and moved closer on foot.

Whispering soft words, he spoke to the animal. It tossed its head and nickered. When he was almost within arm's reach of the mare, he saw one of its back legs was wedged between two rocks. He also noticed the horse's mane wasn't a mass of curls, but only appeared that way because it was full of burrs.

Still whispering, he walked close enough to lay a hand on the mare's neck. She snorted but didn't pull away. While leaning down to examine the rocks, he absently pulled a few burrs out of the horse's mane.

"I will help you," he said quietly while kneeling down to run a hand over the mare's hind legs. There was no swelling, which gave him hope the leg wasn't injured but simply stuck. It appeared as if the top rock had slid across the bottom one, trapping the leg, and Black Horse glanced around looking for a branch for leverage. The rock was too large to just push aside.

After some searching, he found a branch. The mare nickered at his approach this time, now understanding he was there only to help. Many from the herd had moved closer, as if to watch.

Black Horse located a spot and slid the branch beneath the rock. His first try at lifting it snapped the branch, but he wasn't deterred. The wood was brittle, but the branch was long, so he tried again. He put all his strength into it, and the exertion caused him to grunt. The rock slid, and the mare pulled out her leg and took off in a full gallop.

Black Horse continued to push the rock until it slid completely off the one below so another horse wouldn't get caught between the two. While tossing aside the branch, he watched the mare rejoin the herd. Much like people, others in her herd greeted her fondly.

The mare separated herself from the others as he walked toward Horse, and once he was mounted, she came closer.

Horse nickered and the mare responded.

Black Horse forced Horse to turn around. "She doesn't belong to us," he told the animal. "She just needed to be set free."

His heart clenched as the words echoed in his mind. He closed his eyes and shook his head, not wanting to accept it, all the while knowing he had to. A wise leader learned from all that happened. Knowledge wasn't gained only from visions or dreams. The spirits were always about. Always teaching.

Just like the mare, Poeso had only needed him to set her free. For her it had been the fear that had trapped her.

A pain much like what he'd experienced after Hopping Rabbit had died entered his chest, but this time it was far stronger.

He rode out of the canyon swiftly. After reuniting with his hunting party, he killed two more deer and then announced it was time to return to the village. Their homecoming was met with joy, but he could also feel the heaviness hanging over his people, and filling his lodge.

"We must save them," Little One said while the family gathered to eat the roasted venison.

"The army men afraid of Sweet Medicine," One Who Heals said. "I go to fort and—"

"Enough of this talk," Black Horse interrupted.

"I save Woman Who Sleeps in Black Horse's Lodge," One Who Heals said just as firmly.

"She does not need to be saved." Pushing his food aside he stood and walked toward the lodge flap. "Come. It is time for celebration."

Lorna sat on a lumpy bed, staring into the shocked faces of her three friends sitting on the opposite bed in the small room.

"Wells Fargo?" Betty asked. "The stagecoach company?"

"Yes," Lorna answered.

"Wells Fargo is more than a stagecoach company," Meg said. "They transport gold for the mines in California and Colorado, and a bank in San Francisco."

"That's correct," Lorna answered.

"And you own it?" Tillie said.

"No," Lorna said. "I don't own it. I own shares of the company. Elliot went to California when the gold rush happened and opened a gold-hauling company, about the same time Henry Wells and William Fargo started theirs. A few years later, they asked Elliot to merge his company with theirs so there would only be one company. Elliot agreed, but only if he still owned shares and was given a job with Wells Fargo. They agreed and Elliot still works for them. He has been reinvesting the original money my father gave him, and says those shares are now mine. It's more money than even I imagined. Enough for me to share with all of you."

Meg frowned. "Why would you want to share it with us?"

"Because…" Lorna shrugged. "I just do. One for all and all for one."

"That was for the trip west," Meg said. "Not forever."

Lorna opened her mouth but Meg held up a hand.

"It's a nice offer, Lorna, and I appreciate it, but I wouldn't feel right about taking your money. Besides, until

I know what Carolyn's going to do, I don't even know where I'll be living. If it's with the Cheyenne, money won't mean much at all."

Lorna's heartbeat increased considerably. "You plan on staying with the Cheyenne?" That was what she'd been considering, but she'd been afraid to say anything.

"That won't be easy," Tillie said. "It was fun, but think about the winter. Their lodges can't be very warm."

Of everyone, Tillie was the one Lorna thought might be the most interested in permanently living with the Cheyenne. She'd become so attached to the children.

"Tillie's right," Betty said. "I talked with many of them about that. Little Dove says it's very cold when the snow comes. The creeks freeze over, and they have to chop away the ice for water each morning."

Lorna couldn't say she'd thought that far ahead, but Betty had asked about it, part of her determination to be a self-proclaimed expert on the Cheyenne.

A knock on the door ended the conversation.

"Good evening, ladies," Elliot said as he stepped into the room. With a wave of one hand, he said, "I do apologize again for the accommodations, and I can't guarantee the evening meal will be delicious, but I will do my best to entertain you."

Tillie giggled while Betty blushed and Meg lifted a brow.

Lorna stood and crossed the room. "Have you always been so charming?"

He laughed. "You are more like your mother than you'll ever know. That was something she said to me more than once."

"I do wish I'd known her," Lorna said.

"I'm sure that would have been her greatest wish, too." He held out an elbow for her to link her arm through. "I know you're still getting used to both William and me, and I'd be honored to hear you call me Uncle Elliot when you are ready."

She nodded. There was a hint of guilt at how much these two men cared about her while she barely knew them.

"Are you ready, ladies?" he asked the others. "We will dine in the captain's quarters."

The meal wasn't very tasty, and very boring, compared to the Cheyenne food to which they had become accustomed. Captain Walcott monopolized the conversation talking about all the places he'd been stationed. Lorna had been longing for Black Horse since leaving the village, and that longing grew more powerful as she listened to the army man drone on and on.

"Excuse me, Captain," Elliot said. "The ladies are very tired, as you can imagine. I believe it is time we allowed them to retire."

"Of course," the captain said, rising to his feet. "I do hope you ladies will sleep well. The cots are not the most comfortable, but after sleeping on the ground for so long, I'm sure you'll find them a great improvement. You'll also be more protected here than you have been."

Lorna took offense at his words. The buffalo robe in Black Horse's lodge had been most comfortable, and his protection worth more than every man at this fort, yet she understood any comment she made would fall on deaf ears. Therefore, she chose a different subject that entered her mind. "Captain Walcott, is Jacob Lerber still at the fort?"

His neck reddened as he placed his arms behind his back. "No, ma'am. It appears Mr. Lerber left earlier today."

"It appears?" Elliot asked.

"Yes, sir."

"When?"

"Shortly after the women arrived, Mr. Chadwick."

"And when where you planning on telling me about this?"

"Forgive me, sir, but I didn't know that was information you were interested in obtaining."

As Elliot obviously attempted to control his temper, William cleared his throat. "Elliot, I'll walk the women to their room while you and the captain continue this discussion."

They were ushered out before anyone had a chance to say more; however, as soon as they were on the long porch, Lorna said, "Elliot seems to be a very influential person."

"He is, my dear," William answered. "The army utilizes the services of Wells Fargo on a regular basis, and Elliot is in charge of that division. There isn't a general who would risk upsetting him."

"Do you work for Wells Fargo, too?" she asked William.

"Not directly," he answered. "I'm a lawyer and they hire me now and again for specific issues, but for the most part I handle financial legal issues for a number of other clients."

"Who is handling your clients while you are gone?"

"I have an assistant. Anything he can't handle will wait for my return." Patting her hand, he smiled at her. "Family is more important than all my clients put together."

A lump formed in Lorna's throat. She couldn't imagine having someone care so much about her. It was simply too implausible. Too fanciful.

The warriors were standing outside the doors to the two rooms that been assigned to her and Meg as well as Tillie and Betty, and the sight of them increased her longing for Black Horse.

William greeted the warriors affably as he opened the door to her and Meg's room. "Your Indian friends have been given quarters as well, but they refused to enter them."

"They won't leave us unguarded," Lorna replied. "It is their way."

"They are good men," William answered.

She turned to Stands Tall, who stood somber and stoic next to the doorway. Here, too, were people who cared about her. The warriors. Granted, they had been assigned to protect her, but they could have refused and hadn't. "Yes, they are," she said quietly.

William bid them all good-night, and waited until she and Meg entered the room and Tillie and Betty entered the room next door. As she closed the door, she heard him bid the warriors good-night, too.

Sleep evaded her for a long time. The bed was lumpy and the rope stays sagged so profoundly that rolling over was almost impossible. However, she knew the bed had little to do with her sleeplessness. There was too much churning around in her mind. Her uncles had traveled for months to find her. Leaving behind wives, families and businesses. Furthermore, they'd saved her from having to marry Andrew, and by doing that, from the imprisoned life she'd always known—and would still be living if not for them.

How could she ever repay them for that? They both wanted her to live with them. New York. San Francisco. They probably had beautiful homes full of servants to wait on their every whim.

Such things were what she used to dream about, mainly because that was what had been put in her head. Money and how you spent it.

She attempted to roll onto her side, and the comfort of sleeping upon the buffalo hides in Black Horse's lodge crossed her mind again. Thoughts of him were there, too.

Had been all day and evening. She missed him, that was for certain. Missed his arms and his kisses, and love, but she also missed his wisdom. He'd made her think about things differently, understand things she'd never have understood otherwise, and she could use some of that right now. He was a wealthy man by Cheyenne standards, but it wasn't because of what he bought with his wealth. It was how he'd acquired it—through bravery and stamina—and therefore was respected. He shared all he had generously, too, as all of the band had, not just among themselves, but with her and Meg, and Betty and Tillie. Virtual strangers they had fed and clothed and housed without asking anything in return, save a little hard work and elbow grease.

There was no pompousness or conceit in Black Horse, either. He was a wise man and intelligent, but he didn't boast about it, or the many things he had accomplished, like the captain had during their meal.

"Can't sleep?" Meg asked from across the small room.

"No," Lorna answered.

"Me, either," Meg said. "I never thought I'd long to sleep on the ground, but I do."

"Me, too," Lorna replied. "Me, too."

Chapter Seventeen

Black Horse had completed his bathing and was prepared to travel to the fort long before the sun rose. By the time others were ready, his patience had grown thin. Anger ate at his stomach and made him snap and shout at minor missteps and inquires. Little One's tears, when he told her she could not go with them as previously planned, caused more irritation inside him. So did Horse, who sensed his frustration and pranced impatiently beneath him.

All was finally in order, horses loaded with hides and furs to trade, and he gave the signal to leave, yet found no solace in moving forward. The pace would be slow, and that grated as deeply as all else. He should be proud his people had gathered so much to trade. In exchange they would receive many things. Not things needed to sustain life, but items Tsitsistas had grown used to, had learned to desire because of the white man.

He, too, had grown to hunger some of those items, but more so, he now craved something stronger and deeper than ever before.

Poeso.

His lodge felt empty without her, his bed cold. His heart colder.

She had changed him. Changed his heart and his thinking. Something he had thought would never happen. That was why Maheo had brought her to him. In order for him to see things from outside the Cheyenne way. Now he had to decide what to do with that information.

They had not traveled far when three riders emerged from the trees. They were not army men, and Black Horse lifted a hand for those behind him to stop. Then, gesturing for the two warriors riding beside him to accompany him, he tapped Horse with his heels.

Anger inside him increased as he recognized one of the men as one who'd been at the river the day he found Poeso. The one she called Jacob Lerber.

"These men need to speak to you, Black Horse," Talks Good, a Pawnee interpreter, yelled in Cheyenne. "It is about the white woman."

The heart inside his chest turned hard. "What about her?" he asked Talks Good while casting a glare at Lerber.

"The army men have her locked up, and your warriors, in their fort," Talks Good answered.

Black Horse refrained from letting his anger release. Although he might believe what Talks Good said, he did not trust Lerber, or the man beside him with much hate in his eyes.

"Have you seen this?" Black Horse asked.

"What did he say?" Lerber asked. "Did you tell him what I said? That they have the women and his warriors locked up?"

"Yes," Talks Good answered. "I told him. He wants to know if I saw it."

"Tell him yes."

"I did not see this that you talk of," Talks Good answered.

Black Horse did not move while listening to the conversation. Unlike other interpreters, Talks Good took no sides or played favorites. Married to a white woman for many years, he walked in both worlds and wanted peace between them.

"You are far from your home," Black Horse said to the interpreter.

"Yes," Talks Good answered. "I was given many dollars."

"Why?"

"To find you."

"Why?"

"What are you saying?" Lerber asked. "Does he believe you saw it? Believe she's locked up? Tell him he must gather his braves and attack the army fort. Kill all the soldiers so we can rescue her."

Talks Good glanced at the two men before speaking in Cheyenne again. "The older one, he hired me to find you because you stole his daughter out of the river. They want you to attack the army fort. To rescue the white women."

The anger that had been darkening Black Horse's insides was nothing compared to what reared up inside him. Hate filled him. This was the man who had hurt Poeso. To him, that meant one thing. The man did not deserve to live.

His mind was so busy thinking of ways the man would pay for what he had inflicted on his daughter, Black Horse barely heard Talks Good until the interpreter said the name Lorna.

Shifting his gaze from the older man to Talks Good, Black Horse asked the interpreter to repeat what he'd said.

"This man, Jacob, he says he saw the army men tie up Lorna and the others and lock them in a room, along with your warriors. He says the army does not have many soldiers at the fort. That your warriors could attack and win without much bloodshed."

At most times Black Horse would have insisted Tsitsistas were peaceful people and did not wage wars on others, but right now, he was not feeling peaceful. Rage built inside him as considered his options.

A sleepless night left Lorna exhausted the next morning, but she had no desire to lie back down on that lumpy mattress. Her body ached in places it never had before due to the sagging rope stays. Rather than the nun's outfit, she put on one of her other dresses, as did Tillie and Betty. Meg chose what she'd worn when Lorna first met her in Missouri—men's trousers and shirt.

They'd barely finished the morning meal, choking down very unpalatable food—even to her eat-what's-in-front-of-you mindset of late—when the shot that sounded outside had them all jumping from their chairs around the table.

"I'm sure it's nothing," Elliot said already headed for the door. "You ladies wait here while I investigate."

Lorna may have accepted he was her uncle, and acknowledged all he'd done for her, but she'd never accept being told what to do ever again. Therefore, she followed him and William out the door. Despite her second uncle's protests.

"Get those women inside," a solider running past shouted. "Indians are charging the barracks."

Captain Walcott paused in shouting his orders at others to turn toward them. "You heard what he said. The Indians are coming for their captives."

William took her arm to hustle her back inside, but Lorna shook off his hold.

"The Cheyenne are peaceful people," she said. "They are coming to trade their hides and furs. It has been planned for days."

When William frowned, she rushed forward and

grabbed Elliot's arm with both hands. "Black Horse wouldn't attack the fort." As men ran past with guns and ammunition, she squeezed his arm. "Please, Uncle Elliot, you have to believe me. Black Horse wouldn't put me in danger."

Elliot frowned. "Wouldn't put you in danger?"

"No. He wouldn't." Tears were forming and she couldn't stop them. "Please don't let them fire at them. Please."

"Wait here," Elliot said as he stepped off the wooden walkway. "Captain Walcott! Tell your men to hold their fire!"

The captain was but a few steps away and spun around. "This is army business, Mr. Chadwick, and I am in charge."

"And I can see that you are never in charge of an army post again, and I will if a single shot is fired. Now tell your men to stand down."

"We are under attack here, Mr. Chadwick, and I—"

"Tell your men to stand down," Elliot interrupted. "Those Indians are merely coming to trade. This is, after all, a trading post."

"Trading Indians don't approach on galloping horses," the captain shouted. "If you don't believe me, see for yourself."

Lorna hoisted her skirts and ran for the large wall. Uncle Elliot arrived beside her, both of them looking out narrow slits that had been cut in the high wall. The cloud of dust said the horses were indeed running, but she still couldn't believe Black Horse would attack the barracks. Holding that thought, she saw beyond the initial impression.

"Look," she instructed. "There are only a few horses. If they were attacking, there would be many warriors. Many from Black Horse's band and other bands. There are not."

"I see that, dear," Elliot said, "but they do appear to be on a mission."

Swallowing the lump in her throat, she had to agree, "It does appear that way."

Elliot spun around to where Captain Walcott stood shouting orders for men to mount up and the gates to be opened.

"Give me a horse," her uncle demanded.

"I can't do that," the captain answered. "You don't even know how to speak their language."

Elliot might not, but Lorna did, and before anyone could stop her, she snatched the reins from a man leading a horse toward the captain. Shouts echoed behind her, but she paid them no heed as she flung herself upon the animal and kicked it hard. The horse leaped forward and she lowered her head, somehow thinking that would assist in getting through the opening before the men pulling the heavy gates open could push them shut.

There was a thundering of hooves behind her and shouts, but she kept urging the horse to go faster, through the gate and across the prairie toward Black Horse. When she finally lifted her head enough to glance behind her, and then in front, her heart slammed against her chest.

Using all her might, she pulled on the reins.

Hopping, skipping and tossing its head, the horse fought against the bit. Fearing she'd ride right past Black Horse, Lorna tried to get a tighter grip on the reins, but instantly realized her mistake.

The horse reared and then ran right out from beneath her. She hit the ground with such force, her breathing stopped.

Within seconds, Black Horse appeared above her, bent down, and though she wanted to speak, the burning of her lungs wouldn't allow it.

The ground beneath her vibrated, telling her the soldiers were close, and she tried to gulp in enough air to warn Black Horse. It wasn't needed. He knew.

The rage inside Black Horse grew as he picked Poeso up off the ground. He had known the army men would not protect her. Could not. Cradling her in his arms, he turned to face the soldiers holding many guns, all pointed at him.

The one with many yellow stripes on his coat sleeve shouted, "Put the white woman down, Black Horse."

He tightened his hold on her. A great sense of relief entered him as he felt the breath return to her body. His heart could feel hers, and this was good. He turned slightly to command Talks Good to ride closer.

"Is she hurt?" a man not dressed like the army men asked as he jumped off his horse.

Poeso lifted her head off his chest. "No, Uncle Elliot. I'm not hurt." She then looked up at him, and the warmth of her lips touched his cheek before she whispered, "I'm fine."

"What's happened?" the man asked. "Why were you charging the fort?"

Black Horse nodded at Talks Good.

"These men tried to trick Black Horse. Told him the army men had tied up the white women and Cheyenne guards and locked them in a room. They wanted Black Horse to bring many warriors and attack the fort."

"Of course we didn't tie her up," the army man said.

The one Poeso had called Uncle asked, "What men?"

Black Horse set Poeso on her feet, but held her close while gesturing for two of his warriors to lead the horses holding two men tied in their saddles closer.

"That's Jacob Lerber and—" Her voice trailed away as she wobbled.

Tightening the hold he had on her shoulder, Black Horse nodded again to Talks Good. He had told the interpreter what to say as they rode.

"Black Horse says these men are not welcome on Cheyenne land. He says to arrest them, and that if the army does not want them, he will kill them."

Poeso trembled harder. Then she turned around and said to the army man, "If he doesn't, I will."

"Lorna!"

Black Horse felt great pride in the way she turned to the man who had shouted her name. Her back was straight, her shoulders back.

"I will, Uncle Elliot. This man, Viscount Vermeer, is here for one reason. To kill me and claim my inheritance. You know that as well as I do."

"Do as Black Horse ordered," the man shouted. "Arrest them." Then he stepped forward. "I am Elliot Chadwick, Lorna's uncle. I am happy to meet the great Black Horse."

Black Horse nodded at the man, and then picked Poeso up and set her on the back of Horse before he swung up behind her. He needed to speak with this man—her uncle—but not with the army men listening.

"Monehe'se?" he said.

"Black Horse is asking if you are ready to go to the fort," Poeso interpreted.

"Yes, by all means," her uncle replied and climbed onto his horse.

Nudging Horse ahead of the others, Black Horse said, "Black Horse missed Poeso. Missed her much talking."

She twisted and her smiled filled her eyes. "I missed you, too."

"Epeva'e," he answered.

"Epeva'e," she repeated.

Her uncle rode up on one side, while the army man with many stripes rode up on the other.

"I am Captain Walcott. I will need to get an official statement from you, Black Horse, in order to determine punishment."

Black Horse let his eyes fill with hate as he turned toward the man.

The man looked away. "I will get an interpreter."

"There is no need," Poeso said. "Black Horse has said all he has to say to you."

Black Horse nudged Horse into a faster gait, smiling deep inside. She was a good woman. A strong woman. One who made him proud. He then briefly glanced at her uncle, and determined he would wait to see if he was a good man or not. One he could trust.

Their arrival at the wide gates did not follow standard procedure. The guards did not make them take out their knives and leave them and their bows on the ground beside their horses. Instead, they rode right through the gates into the center of their fort. The army man did not approve, but Poeso's uncle declared it would be this way, and so it was.

Her uncle climbed off his horse and held up his arms to help Poeso down. Black Horse was not ready to release her. Would never be. Therefore, he swung off Horse and lifted her down himself.

"I would like to speak with you, Black Horse," her uncle said.

"I will interpret," Poeso said.

Black Horse shook his head. He did not want to be separated from her, but this talk was not for women.

Her uncle nodded. "I—we would prefer it be someone else."

"And I'd prefer it be me," she answered. "So it will be."

Black Horse didn't need to know the white man's language to read the man's thoughts, and was surprised when her uncle nodded.

"This way," the man said.

Black Horse turned in the opposite direction and gestured for Rising Sun to stand guard over the men they'd captured. He did not trust the army to keep them tied.

"Lorna," the uncle said. "Tell him not to worry. The prisoners will be secured."

"His warriors have been ordered not to leave them, even once they are secured," she answered. "And they won't, no matter who tells them to."

After giving Horse's reins to Stands Tall, Black Horse joined Poeso and her uncle. They entered one of the many doors and he waited until the door was closed before he turned to her. "Do you trust him, Poeso?" he asked in Cheyenne.

"Heehe'e," Lorna replied.

Black Horse turned to Elliot Chadwick and said, "I do not need an interpreter."

The uncle said nothing as their eyes met, but Poeso did.

"Very few people know that he can speak English, Uncle Elliot. You must promise not to tell anyone." The plea in her voice was as strong as the pleading in her eyes.

When he spoke, her uncle addressed him. "Thank you, Black Horse, for your honesty. I appreciate that in a man." He then walked back to the door. "We will not need a translator after all, dear."

Poeso shook her head. "I'm staying anyway."

Black Horse lifted his chin and crossed his arms. "I not speak until you leave, Poeso."

Her eyes narrowed. "Don't do this. Not now. I'm not leaving."

He took his eyes off her and stared across the room.

"Lorna, please, it—" her uncle started.

"No," she snapped. "This is about me, and I have every right to be here."

Black Horse was reminded of when he'd first brought her to the village, and had to hold in a sigh. She was a very stubborn woman, but he was a stubborn man. She must remember that.

She huffed and puffed and protested. Just when he thought she would never give in, she stomped a foot and then bolted for the door. "Fine, be that way. I don't want to talk to you, either. Neither of you!"

Lorna slammed the door so hard behind her that wood rattled the length of the building. The joy of seeing Black Horse had transformed into a ball of anger so great her stomach hurt. She had questions, plenty of them, and it wouldn't have hurt him to answer them. Or to speak to Elliot with her in the room. She'd proved she was trustworthy.

Frustration bubbled inside her. She'd wanted to tell Black Horse she was returning to the village with him. That she no longer wanted to go to California. No longer needed to go. She wanted to see his smile, his happiness at that.

"Goodness, child, you scared the life out of me, racing out on that horse."

She lifted her gaze to William. "I've known how to ride a horse since I was a child." Glad he hadn't seen her fall, she added, "My father taught me."

"He taught you to ride astride?"

A heavy sigh left her chest. "No." Black Horse had done that. Still furious at being sent from the room, she crossed the wooden walkway and stepped down on the hard-packed dirt. The compound was a flurry of activity and a shiver tickled her spine as her gaze landed on a separate building in the far corner, where several warriors and army men were gathered in two separate groups.

"Don't fear. Douglas is being well guarded, dear," William said.

She was over the shock of seeing Douglas, and in truth, with Black Horse near, the man didn't frighten her. Jacob Lerber didn't, either. "He doesn't scare me, but I am glad Black Horse captured him. Now I won't have to look over my shoulder the rest of my life."

"Douglas told the captain he'd been searching for you, that he was only here to take you home," William said.

"Lies," she said. "I will never return to England."

"No one expects you to."

Thoughts of Douglas disappeared as she heard her name and saw Betty running across the compound. Moving forward, for the woman was clearly upset, she met her friend in the center of the compound.

"Lorna, you must come to the trading post," Betty said breathlessly.

"Why?"

"They are cheating, clearly cheating."

"Who's cheating?" she asked. "Cheating what?"

Betty waved a hand toward the building near the wide gate. "The army. They are only giving pennies for the pelts and furs we worked so hard on."

Lorna glanced toward the long line of Cheyenne men carrying armloads of furs toward the building, and the anger inside her increased. Everyone had worked very hard to produce excellent pelts, including her, and she wasn't about to be cheated for her efforts. Was not about to let the people she cared about be cheated. Snagging Uncle William's arm, she asked, "Do you know anything about furs?"

"Some," he answered. "I have several clients in the fur-buying and manufacturing business."

"Good," she said, moving forward.

The warriors graciously stepped aside, giving her clearance to enter the building, however, once inside, the man behind the counter didn't even acknowledge her. With one hand, he was flipping over hides and shouting numbers while writing on a tablet with his other hand. She moved closer to peer over the pile of hides, and noticed the only number he wrote was one.

"Excuse me," Lorna said.

The man barely looked up. "This ain't no place for a woman."

Stopping the man from flipping over another pelt by placing both hands on the thick fur, she asked, "How much are you giving us for this one?"

"Us?" The man shook his head. "I'm trading these with those Injuns behind you."

"How much?" she asked without further explanation.

The man was tall and burly, with a thick black mustache that he rubbed with one hand. Letting out a huff, he finally replied, "That one there is worth about a dime."

"A dime?"

Still at her side, Uncle William said, "Now, see here. Tanneries out east pay at least three dollars for a hide of this size." Flipping a corner to examine the underside, he added, "More, considering the condition is excellent."

"Well, you ain't out east, now is ya?" the man replied, flipping the corner back down.

"No, we are not," William answered, "but all the same, we will not be cheated."

"We?" the man spat. "You two ain't with those Injuns."

"I beg to differ, my good man," William replied.

"Beg all you want," the man answered. "Now move aside, I got work to do."

William patted her shoulder. "Wait here, dear."

Lorna nodded and turning to offer the burly man a snide smile, she planted her hands more firmly on the pile of hides. He glared. She returned one just as uninviting. When he looked away, she said, "Have you heard of Black Horse?"

"Everyone's heard of Black Horse."

"These are his hides, his people."

The man nodded. "I know that, missy."

She let out an exaggerated sigh. "The Cheyenne are peaceful people, until they are cheated. I've seen what happens then." The man glanced her way. "The two men Black Horse just brought in, he told the captain they are not welcome on Cheyenne land because they tried to trick him. If he finds them on his land again, he will kill them."

With a frown, and a somewhat shaky hand, the man said, "I don't set the prices, the army does."

Just then William returned with Captain Walcott in hand, and was already arguing a case. He certainly was a lawyer. An excellent one. By the time he finished, the captain, though grudgingly, informed the burly man to increase the rates.

Although they were not given the prices William claimed the furs were worth out east, they were provided much more than the pennies being offered before.

Not in a trusting mood, Lorna moved to the back side of the counter where she retrieved another piece of paper and wrote down every price quoted, ensuring the correct amount would be tallied in the end.

When Uncle Elliot entered the building, her heart jolted and she gestured for Betty to take over writing down the numbers. "Where is Black Horse?"

"He has things to do," Elliot said with a clipped tone. He then turned to his brother. "William, you need to join us."

"What things?" Lorna asked. "With the army? About Jacob and Douglas? Who's interpreting?"

Elliot's hold on her arm tightened as he propelled her out the door. "Don't worry about Black Horse. He can take care of himself. Right now, we need to speak with you."

"About what?"

Scowling slightly, he said, "About Black Horse."

Chapter Eighteen

Lorna had already formed a dislike for the army fort, but right now she hated the four walls of this little room with everything she had. She wasn't too fond of her uncles, either. "What do you mean they have to let them go? Both Douglas and Jacob are mean and evil and—"

"But they have not committed crimes against you," Elliot said.

William appeared a bit more disturbed over the situation. "We both believe what you told us about Douglas, dear, but that happened in England. We can't press charges against him here. I know that sounds unfair, and it is, but there is nothing we can do about it."

Unable to find another argument concerning her interactions with the two men, she tried another route. "They tried to start a war. They wanted Black Horse to attack the fort."

"Yes, they did," Elliot answered. "But that is not against the law, either. If it was up to me, I would let them loose, let Black Horse deal with them."

"He would kill them," she said.

"I know," Elliot said. "And then you would never have to worry about them again. He was afraid you and I had already left for California. That is why he was riding so fast toward the fort. After he captured them, Lerber told him we were preparing to leave last night and that he could lead Black Horse to us."

"More lies," she said. "I wouldn't have left, not without telling Black Horse."

"But you are willing to leave?"

Sensing there was more behind his question, things she wasn't ready to answer, she turned the conversation back to Douglas. "So you are just going to let them go free?"

"No." It was William who answered. "I'll have them transported to New York, where I will personally see that Douglas is sent back to England. I will also have Jacob's past investigated. The likes of him is probably wanted someplace for something. If so, I'll see he's prosecuted."

There was no justice in any of this. Not for her. "Ultimately, they will both go free." As she spoke the words, she realized she truly didn't care. She no longer felt like a victim when it came to Douglas. What he'd done had been evil and wrong, but she'd survived it and had nothing to fear when it came to him. Whether he lived or died didn't matter, and never would. And Lerber was nothing but a thug. He'd eventually get his due, as all thugs did. Furthermore, she believed Black Horse would see the men killed if he found them on Cheyenne land again. He was the only man who mattered to her. Indignation then grew within her. Including both men in one gaze, she said, "Black Horse won't like this."

"He didn't like it," Elliott said. "But he is an intelligent man, wise in the ways of his people as well as the white men. He could have killed Douglas and Lerber on sight, but knew the army would respect him more for bringing them in alive."

With a tremendous amount of pride filling her, she said, "That sounds like him."

After a deep breath, Elliot said, "Fortunately, he also understood what else I had to tell him."

The hair on her arms stood as a shiver ripped through her. "What *else* did you tell him?"

Elliot glanced at William before saying, "That I couldn't accept his offer."

"What offer?" she and William asked at the same time.

"One hundred horses."

"A hundred horses? For what?" William asked.

Lorna had learned many things during her time with the Cheyenne, and her heart started to pound. "To marry me," she whispered. A thrill shot through her. "He offered you a hundred horses for me?"

"Yes," Elliot answered, "I told him I couldn't accept any horses."

Lorna jumped to her feet. "You have no right to tell him—"

"Yes," Elliot said. "As your uncle, I do. He knew that. That's why he asked me."

"No, you didn't," she argued, heading for the door. "You don't have any say in who I marry and who I don't."

Elliot blocked the doorway. "I only have your best interests at heart, Lori."

"My best interests?" Fury was growing hard and fast. "You don't know me! And don't call me that. Don't ever call me that. Move. I need to find Black Horse."

"He's not here. He left."

Momentarily paralyzed, she asked, "Left?"

"Yes, he returned to his village."

She pushed him away from the door and flung it open. There was no line outside the trading post, nor were there any warriors standing near the building holding Douglas and Jacob. Lorna spun, glancing up and down the long walkway. Stands Tall was nowhere to be seen.

Pivoting, she stormed back into the room. "What did you say to him?"

"Sit down, dear, and I'll tell you."

"I don't want to sit down," she shouted. "I want to know what you told him. I want to know why he left. Why he left me here!"

"Here, here, now," William said, handing her a handkerchief. "Let's sit down and listen to what Elliot has to say. He must have good reasons for what he did."

"I do," Elliot said.

Wiping her face with the handkerchief, Lorna snapped, "And what would that be?" She was furious at both Elliot and Black Horse. One was no better than the other. Making decisions about her behind her back. Leaving without her. Asking her uncle instead of her.

"I told him I couldn't accept his horses, because I didn't know if you wanted to marry him or not," Elliot said.

Of course I want to marry him, Lorna was prepared to shout, but Elliot held up a hand when she opened her mouth.

"Let me finish before you speak." He waited for her to nod before saying, "I understand you may believe yourself in love with him because of how he rescued you from Lerber. How the entire band treated you and your friends so kindly. The Northern Cheyenne are known for their generosity, but they are still Indians."

Irritated, she asked, "And what's wrong with that?"

He didn't answer directly, but said, "The country is expanding, Lori. More and more people are moving west every day, and that is only going to continue. Making sure it's a safe place for people to travel through, and homesteading, are high priorities for the government. They have set aside a large amount of land for the Indians southwest of here, and have been encouraging the bands to move there for years."

That was not new information. She'd read about the reservations the government had created, and how the tribes refused to be relocated. "The tribes don't want to move."

"I know. That is why the army has started implementing new strategies, new tactics, to move all the bands to the reservations," Elliot said. "Including the Cheyenne."

Lorna's insides turned dark and hard. "Strategies? You mean battles and massacres. Full-fledged Indian wars like they had with the Sioux in Minnesota, forcing them west." Betty had learned of that incident, and told her all about it during the time Black Horse had been on his vision quest.

"Yes," Elliot answered. "I can't deny there will be bloodshed, battles, deaths. But there is no other way. People need to be able to travel safely. Stagecoaches need to be able to transport people without fear of Indian attacks. It is necessary for progress."

"Stagecoaches, as in Wells Fargo."

"Yes, as in Wells Fargo."

Lorna sighed. Caring about other people was complicated.

Eventually they would have to travel to their summer camp, but Black Horse could not give the command to begin the move. He had told Poeso's uncle he would give her five days. Just as he had declared Little One had to make her own decision, he had to agree with Elliot Chadwick that Poeso had to make her own decision, too.

A smile tugged at his mouth thinking of the last time he'd seen her. She had not seen him. Had been too busy making sure the army gave more for their trades than in the past. His people were very happy with the abundance.

Many spoke about how she and her uncle with the large hat had demanded the army make fair trade. And many missed her. Even One Who Heals sang for Poeso's safe return.

Black Horse told no one of his request to wed Poeso. He did not want them to be saddened if she chose to go to California. He knew, even if she did go, the rope tethering them together would still be there. His heart would be with her forever. She had taught him many things. Things he had not known he'd needed to discover until they were in his mind, in his heart.

Lifting his face to the sky, he emptied his lungs. Never had he watched the sun so forlornly, feeling the time between it rising and setting long and empty. Not even when Hopping Rabbit died had so many days and nights felt bare and vacant. His spirit had not struggled with being the leader of his people then, either. There had been no need. Poeso had put that inside him, and he understood why. The divide inside him, that of being a man and a leader, was because there would soon be a division for all the bands. It had taken being separated from her, to feel as if someone had hunted him down and cut out his insides while leaving his body in this world, to accept the truths he had not wanted to believe.

Black Horse turned from watching the sun fall for the third time since riding away from the army fort. His family would soon bring food to his lodge, where he would pretend to eat and then lie on his bed watching the moon travel across the sky through the top of his teepee, much like he did the sun.

Rather than entering the village, he went to check on his herd of horses corralled within a large grove of trees. He had already separated out the one hundred he would give to Elliot Chadwick. They were good horses. Worth much money.

One of the young boys assigned to his animals met him as he approached. "Horse likes your new mare," the boy said.

Black Horse frowned, and searched the herd for Horse. Mystified, he stared harder and moved into the grove. Horse and a brown mare were separate from the many other animals, and they both watched as he walked closer. The mare tossed her head and nickered. He recognized her as the one from the canyon.

"When did she arrive?" he asked the boy.

With a shrug, the boy answered, "She was here this morning, with Horse."

The happiness that rose up inside him was great, and he lifted his arms into the air, giving thanks to Maheo. It was a sign. Poeso would soon arrive. He had not doubted her, but he also knew Poeso. She could be stubborn.

She would make a good mate. A strong wife for him, and because of her, many Cheyenne lives would be saved.

Shouts from the camp crier filled the air, but the distance and the excited replies from others made it impossible to understand the crier's words. Black Horse hurried toward the village, but stopped near the edge. The setting sun made what he saw look like a vision, an image that wasn't real. Yet, in his heart, he knew it was real. Very real.

The single wagon rolling closer was pulled by two mules. Two women in black dresses sat on the seat. Keeping his stride slow and steady was difficult, but he did it as any dignified leader would. Because of Poeso, he was once again the leader his people needed. She had challenged him. Made him see with both his mind and his heart.

He stood in the center of the village, surrounded by many happy people, when the wagon rolled to a stop.

Poeso looked at no one but him as she climbed down and walked forward.

Keeping his hands at his sides, he nodded toward Meg. "Where are the others?"

Poeso bit her bottom lip, but kept her head up. "Tillie is on her way to California with Uncle Elliot, and Betty is going to New York with Uncle William."

"Why are you here?"

"Because I need to talk to you."

They spoke in Cheyenne, and pride at how closely she continued to uphold his secret filled him with love. He also held much excitement and joy at seeing her. She had given him much trouble, but also much happiness. It was the way. He should never have questioned that.

"I will be in the lodge when you are ready," she said.

Black Horse bit the inside of his lip to keep from smiling as she walked around him and toward his lodge. He would forever feel pride in this white woman who thought she could defy him. Taking big steps, he caught up with her and took her arm to propel her faster to his lodge.

Once inside, he spun her around to face him. "Why are you here?" he asked once again, this time in English.

Sparkles as bright as stars appeared in her eyes. "Because I love you," she said.

His throat burned as he withheld the words. He loved her very much, and though his band would accept her—a white woman—as his wife if he proclaimed it, he had to respect what her uncle had said. How the white men would disown her.

As if she knew his thoughts, she said, "My uncle should not have told you I would not marry you."

"You uncle did not say you would not marry me," Black Horse corrected. "He said it was your choice." Pushing down the regret rising inside him, he continued, "And that you do not understand the consequences of that."

"He was right," she said. "It is my choice. But he was

also wrong. I do understand the consequences, both of marrying you and not marrying you."

She stepped closer and the touch of her hands on his face made his heart thud.

"I love you, Black Horse, and I always will. I want to be with you every day of my life."

He had many things to say to her, and questions. He chose to start with the ones she would understand. "What about your uncles? California? The much money waiting for you there?"

"My uncles will continue to oversee my money, and send it to us as needed."

"I have no need for money."

"Not now, but someday we will."

"Hova'ahane," he answered.

She smiled. "My uncles also understand how much I love you. How only you will make me happy. You showed me what is in my heart, and what I see is you."

He did believe that. She filled his heart, too. "There are many things that could change that, Poeso," he said. "The white people would not like you married to me."

"I don't care," she answered. "The white people were never as kind to me as the Cheyenne. They never allowed me to be me. To live without walls confining me, without a ceiling over my head or a floor beneath my feet. That is how I feel here. Free. Free to live. Free to be me. Whatever the future brings, whatever people say or do, we will face it together. Because I am strong when I am with you."

The smell of her was filling him, making his blood swirl and fueling desires so strong his insides quaked. The idea of kissing her, taking her to his bed, was so strong his thoughts grew cloudy. He had to warn her before he could take her. "There will be divisions, Poeso, great divisions of the people."

"I know, and I have brought you much information about that."

He frowned, and opened his mouth to question what she meant.

She put a finger against his lips. "I'll tell you all that later. Much later. Right now, I want you to answer one question."

He pressed his heels into the ground for power from mother earth, the strength to contain his desires as she asked her many questions.

"Do you still want to marry me?" she asked.

"Heehe'e."

She closed her eyes briefly, and when they opened, she said, "I want to marry you. You showed me the happiness in my heart. Now it is time to show me how to keep it there."

Her request was one he could not deny. Now or ever. He leaned down, and the touch of her lips broke loose all the love in his heart, all the desires he'd been holding back.

As Black Horse's arms encircled her, held her tight, Lorna knew she'd made the right choice. Despite all the warnings and reasons her uncles had declared, this was truly where she belonged. The only place she'd ever be happy.

Their kisses grew demanding, and wild, and sent a heated thrill clear to her toes.

"I will protect you, Poeso," he said gruffly as their mouths separated briefly. "From all others. All dangers."

"I know," she gasped before pressing her lips to his again.

Their shared desires took precedence over all else, and the next thing she was fully aware of was lying on his bed, completely unclothed. He was poised above her, having already tempted and teased every part of her body into a desperation that left her with no control. Here, though, she didn't need any. Not with him. Not when it came to loving him.

"Claim me, Black Horse," she whispered. "Claim me as The Woman Who Sleeps in Black Horse's Lodge forever."

Surprisingly, his entrance was slow, exceedingly so, and she arched her hips upward, accepting him with the perfection of two beings created for one another.

"You are mine, Poeso," he whispered. "You have been mine since I claimed you in the cave, and I shall proclaim it to all, until the end of time."

His words were a ceremony in themselves, a declaration of their love as binding as any vows ever spoken. "I love you, my husband." Fully committed, she began to move beneath him, rising up and lowering back onto the buffalo robe with an age-old knowledge that came from deep within her. Planted there upon her birth for this very moment. Pleasing him, making their union a joyous, fulfilling venture for both of them, she increased her boldness while pinpointing all of her awareness on nothing but the two of them, the love they shared, and forever would.

Later, much, much later, as they lay with their arms and legs still tangled, their bodies once again heaving from yet another amazing excursion, Lorna's gaze roamed upward, to the moon shining brightly down upon them. The smile on her lips increased as she turned to Black Horse. "What is the Cheyenne word for moon?"

"Taa'é-eše'he," he answered.

"Taa'é-eše'he," she repeated. "I like how that sounds."

He chuckled. "I like how you sound." Kissing her neck, he added, "Especially when I do this."

She giggled. "Are we going to get any sleep tonight?"

"Hova'ahane," he answered.

Looping her arms around his neck, she whispered, *"Epeva'e."*

Epilogue

There were no flakes, but the light of the moon reflected in the tiny particles of moisture in the cold and crisp winter air, making it look as if stars fell all the way to the ground. Standing on the porch of their home, Lorna leaned back against her husband as he wrapped his arms around her. It had been more than thirty-five years since this amazing warrior had saved her life, and the love she felt for him had never faltered. Just as she'd known it wouldn't.

"It has been a good life," he whispered in her ear as if reading her mind.

"Heehe'e," she replied. Although he never appeared to, she asked, "Do you hold any regrets?"

"Hova'ahane," he answered.

It would soon be midnight, at which point not only would the year end, but the century, too. "Many things have changed," she said. "And will continue to do so."

"Heehe'e," he answered. "This will be the world of our grandchildren. The next generation. Just as Maheo promised."

All four of their children were married now, and providing them with grandchildren each year. Two lived on this very land, but the other two and their families lived in

California. Despite the distance, they visited often. "One that is very different from what we knew."

"But it is good."

Lorna twisted about to look up at him. He was now in his sixties, or around there, and still as handsome, as strong and proud, as the young warrior chief he'd been when they first met. "Do you ever wonder what might have happened if we hadn't come here? If we'd joined the others to fight the soldiers?"

"I do not wonder, Poeso, I know." His gaze went back to the moon. "If we had survived, as many did not, we would be on the reservation, with few resources to feed and clothe our family. It is because you entered our village that The Horse Band survived and has land for the next generation. We have much to be thankful for."

She laid her head against his chest. Upon returning to his village from the fort all those years ago, she'd told him what Elliot had told her about the government, the reservations, the wars that were coming. He hadn't been surprised and had willingly listened to her suggestions. Others, though, had not. Black Horse had held many Tribal Councils with leaders of several bands and tribes, had tried to persuade everyone to follow their example, but many had chosen differently.

In the end, only members of his band had followed them to Montana that fall, where her uncles had arranged the purchase of twenty thousand acres of land.

Just as Elliot had predicted, the army had attacked many bands that year, and in the years that followed, herded Indians down to Oklahoma like cattle. Others had been sent to small reservations in Colorado and Montana, on land that wasn't rich enough to provide sustenance for so many lives.

It had been hard to hear what had become of so many they'd known and loved, but never once had Black Horse blamed her, nor had he complained about the changes to their life. Instead, he had put all his efforts into making it successful. He'd accomplished that beyond her expectations, and he was as generous as ever. Over the years they had purchased more acreage, and had deeded it over to extended family members as well as their children.

In the beginning, they had only sold the horses they raised to Uncle Elliot, for Wells Fargo, which, with all their stagecoaches, had been enough, but as time went on others wanted the superior horses raised at The Cheyenne Moon Ranch. Black Horse and his horsemanship skills were now widely renowned even beyond the shores of America.

Part of that could be due to the many books her longtime friend Betty had written. Lorna had read every one of them, and though she questioned Betty's memory of a few events, she never told her friend that. Betty's efforts and her books had made a difference in the treatment of Indians nationwide, and for that, Lorna was grateful.

The other women she'd started this magnificent journey with were still two of her closest friends. Tillie had stayed in California, married a man Uncle Elliot knew, and acted as if Lorna's grandchildren living out there were her very own. She often traveled with them to visit. Meg, however, was close by. She had married Stands Tall and lived on a neighboring ranch—land Black Horse had deeded them. Meg also had her sister nearby. Little One and Silver Fox were on another nearby ranch.

Black Horse kissed the top of her head. "It is done."

Lorna stepped back to look at him. "What is?"

"The century has arrived," he said. "It is now nineteen hundred."

"I didn't hear—" She stopped as the chimes of the mantel clocked echoed from inside the house. "You'll never need a clock, will you?"

"I have no need."

She stepped closer again and pressed up against him.

Nipping at an earlobe, she whispered, "I know something you need."

He grasped both her hips, holding her firmly against him. "I need, or you need?"

Kissing his neck, she said, "I think it's mutual."

"Epeva'e." He spun around then. "Come, my wife, I will show you how a great leader treats his woman."

She laughed. "I think you mean that I'll show you how a great leader bows to the woman he loves."

He shook his head. "It's fortunate you are a good lover, because you will never make a good translator."

Marching past him through the open doorway, she replied, "Only because I never wanted to be a translator." As he shut the door, she pivoted about and looped her arms around his neck. "I only ever wanted to be your wife, and that I am very good at."

"Heehe'e," he answered, and then kissed her as if they were back in his lodge, or under the waterfall, or in the hayloft, or…

* * * * *

If you enjoyed this story, you won't want to miss these
other great reads from Lauri Robinson:
THE WRONG COWBOY
A FORTUNE FOR THE OUTLAW'S DAUGHTER
SAVING MARINA

And for a taste of the 1920s, try her rip-roaring
DAUGHTERS OF THE ROARING TWENTIES
miniseries!
THE RUNAWAY DAUGHTER (UNDONE!)
THE BOOTLEGGER'S DAUGHTER
THE REBEL DAUGHTER
THE FORGOTTEN DAUGHTER

COMING NEXT MONTH FROM

H HARLEQUIN®

⛪ HISTORICAL

Available June 21, 2016

THE INNOCENT AND THE OUTLAW (Western)
Outlaws of the Wild West • by Harper St. George
Innocent Emmaline Drake knows Hunter Jameson is trouble the second he
walks into her saloon. He's on the path of revenge, but she can't escape his
captivating gaze!

THE UNEXPECTED MARRIAGE OF GABRIEL STONE
(Regency) *Lords of Disgrace* • by Louise Allen
Gabriel Stone, Earl of Edenbridge, resolves to help respectable
Lady Caroline Holt. But then his mission takes him somewhere he *never*
thought he'd end up—down the aisle!

UNBUTTONING THE INNOCENT MISS (Regency)
Wallflowers to Wives • by Bronwyn Scott
How can Jonathon Lashley concentrate on his French lessons with
Miss Claire Welton when all he wants is to claim her delectable mouth with
a heart-stopping kiss?

COMMANDED BY THE FRENCH DUKE (Medieval)
by Meriel Fuller
Alinor of Claverstock risks her life to rescue Bianca d'Attalens. But when Alinor
encounters Guilhem, Duc d'Attalens, it's not just her life that's in danger...

Available via Reader Service and online:

THE OUTCAST'S REDEMPTION (Regency)
The Infamous Arrandales • by Sarah Mallory
Wolfgang Arrandale has lived as a fugitive for ten years, until the
revelation that he's a father changes everything. Can parson's daughter
Grace Duncombe help him prove his innocence?

CLAIMING THE CHAPERON'S HEART (Regency)
by Anne Herries
For Lord Frant, haunted by his experiences in India, love is definitely the last
thing on his mind! Until, that is, he meets his ward's beautiful new chaperon,
Lady Jane March...

**YOU CAN FIND MORE INFORMATION ON UPCOMING HARLEQUIN® TITLES,
FREE EXCERPTS AND MORE AT WWW.HARLEQUIN.COM.**

HHCNM0616

REQUEST YOUR FREE BOOKS!

HARLEQUIN®

ℋISTORICAL

Where love is timeless

2 FREE NOVELS PLUS 2 FREE GIFTS!

YES! Please send me 2 FREE Harlequin® Historical novels and my 2 FREE gifts (gifts are worth about $10). After receiving them, if I don't wish to receive any more books, I can return the shipping statement marked "cancel." If I don't cancel, I will receive 6 brand-new novels every month and be billed just $5.69 per book in the U.S. or $5.99 per book in Canada. That's a savings of at least 12% off the cover price! It's quite a bargain! Shipping and handling is just 50¢ per book in the U.S. and 75¢ per book in Canada.* I understand that accepting the 2 free books and gifts places me under no obligation to buy anything. I can always return a shipment and cancel at any time. Even if I never buy another book, the two free books and gifts are mine to keep forever.

246/349 HDN GH2Z

Name	(PLEASE PRINT)
Address	Apt. #
City	State/Prov. Zip/Postal Code

Signature (if under 18, a parent or guardian must sign)

Mail to the **Reader Service**:
IN U.S.A.: P.O. Box 1867, Buffalo, NY 14240-1867
IN CANADA: P.O. Box 609, Fort Erie, Ontario L2A 5X3

Want to try two free books from another line?
Call 1-800-873-8635 or visit www.ReaderService.com.

SPECIAL EXCERPT FROM

♦ HARLEQUIN®

℣ISTORICAL

*Claire has always loved Jonathon Lashley from afar,
but when he asks her to tutor him in French, she soon
realizes how little she really knows him and how much
he has to teach her…about the art of seduction!*

*Read on for a sneak preview of
UNBUTTONING THE INNOCENT MISS,
the first book in* **Bronwyn Scott***'s sensational
new quartet,* **WALLFLOWERS TO WIVES**

He was leaving? No. Unacceptable. She was not losing
him after one lesson. Jonathon Lashley could learn to
speak French and she could teach him. But she had to act
fast. He was already halfway to the door. Something fiery
and stubborn flared inside Claire. He was not leaving this
room.

She fixed herself in the doorway, hands on hips to take up
the entire space, blocking the exit. He would not elude her.
"I never figured you for a quitter, Mr. Lashley, or perhaps
you have simply never met with a challenge you could not
immediately overcome?"

"Do you know me so well as to make such a
pronouncement?" Lashley folded his arms across his chest,
his eyes boring into her. This was a colder, harsher Jonathon
Lashley than the one she knew. The laughing golden boy of
the *ton* had been transformed into something dangerously
exciting. Her pulse raced, but she stood her ground.

What ground it was! She'd never been this close to him before—so close she had to look up to see his face, so close her breasts might actually brush the lapels of his coat without any contrivance on her part, so close she could smell his morning soap, all cedar and sandalwood and entirely masculine, entirely him. She'd waited her whole life to stand this close to Jonathon Lashley and, of course, it was her luck that when it happened it was because of a quarrel—a quarrel she'd provoked.

She'd never thought she'd fight with him, the supposed "man of her dreams." She'd been thinking *never* a lot since this all started. Yesterday, she'd never thought they would have desperation in common. Today, she'd never dreamed his French would be this bad, or that she'd have trouble teaching him or that she'd quarrel with him.

"You are a very bold woman, Miss Welton." His tone was one of cold caution. "Yesterday you mopped up my trousers and today you are preventing me from leaving a room. One can only wonder what you might do to my person next. Perhaps tomorrow I will find myself tied to a chair and at your mercies."

Don't miss
UNBUTTONING THE INNOCENT MISS
by Bronwyn Scott, available July 2016 wherever
Harlequin® Historical books and ebooks are sold.

www.Harlequin.com

Turn your love of reading into rewards you'll love with
Harlequin My Rewards

**Join for FREE today at
www.HarlequinMyRewards.com**

Earn **FREE BOOKS** of your choice.

Experience **EXCLUSIVE OFFERS** and contests.

Enjoy **BOOK RECOMMENDATIONS**
selected just for you.

PLUS! Sign up now
and get **500** points
right away!

Earn
**FREE
REWARDS**
HarlequinMyRewards.com
Join
Today!

MYR16R

Love the Harlequin book you just read?

Your opinion matters.

Review this book on your favorite book site, review site, blog or your own social media properties and share your opinion with other readers!

Be sure to connect with us at:
Harlequin.com/Newsletters
Facebook.com/HarlequinBooks
Twitter.com/HarlequinBooks

JUST CAN'T GET ENOUGH?

Join our social communities
and talk to us online.

You will have access to the latest
news on upcoming titles and special
promotions, but most importantly,
you can talk to other fans about your
favorite Harlequin reads.

Harlequin.com/Community

Facebook.com/HarlequinBooks

Twitter.com/HarlequinBooks

Pinterest.com/HarlequinBooks